'A Bluebeard retelling of profound beauty and wisdom, *Sour Cherry* shows us how abuse traps people in stories that help them excuse it – but also survive. Theodoridou is a novelist with a poet's ear and a playwright's nose for irony. His prose is lyric, yet exquisitely controlled: every word feels necessary and inevitable. Like Angela Carter, he uses fairy tale to trace the dark undercurrents of human desire. But *Sour Cherry* transcends the form of the fairy tale retelling. It moves like a dance, resonates like a chorus; you wake from it as from a dream. Read it and be changed.'
B. Pladek, author of *Dry Land*

'Captivating from the first page to the last, *Sour Cherry* is a haunting novel that weighs in with *Wuthering Heights, Jane Eyre, The Turn of the Screw* and the very best of Angela Carter – but Theodoridou writes with a magnetic strangeness that is all his own. Not many can pull off what he has, bringing new blood to folktale archetypes, blending mystery with a burgeoning, inevitable dread. Heartbreaking and tender, *Sour Cherry* is a dark delight. It›s so damn good I›m already looking forward to reading it again.'
Natasha Calder, author of *Whether Violent or Natural*

'*Sour Cherry* is a song you think you've heard before, but never in this voice. This story knows how dreadful longing is, and how cruel hope, how loving and being loved makes monsters. With bitter irony and utter, intoxicating sincerity in every sentence, Theodoridou opens the body of an old story with a knife, and makes of it a house for you to be haunted in. A magnificent novel and, unbelievably, a debut-you must read this as soon as you can.'
Vajra Chandrasekera, author of *The Saint of Bright Doors* and *Rakesfall*

'Gorgeously written and stunningly good.'
Allison Epstein, author of *Let the Dead Bury the Dead*

'Unputdownable and haunting . . . In his thrilling debut, Natalia Theodoridu asks: Why and how do bad men wield power over their victims, over bystanders, over the stories we tell ourselves? How is violence justified? I didn't want to put this book down, and now that I've turned the last page, I'll be haunted by it forever.'
Eman Quotah, author of *Bride of the Sea* and *The Night is Not For You*

SOUR CHERRY

Natalia Theodoridou

WILDFIRE

First published in hardback in 2025 by
WILDFIRE
an imprint of Headline Publishing Group Limited

I

Cataloguing in Publication Data is available from the British Library

Hardback ISBN 978 1 0354 1614 1
Trade Paperback ISBN 978 1 0354 1615 8

Typeset in Scala by CC Book Production

Printed and bound in Great Britain by Clays Ltd, Elcograf S.p.A.

MIX
Paper | Supporting
responsible forestry
FSC® C104740

Headline's policy is to use papers that are natural, renewable and
recyclable products and made from wood grown in well-managed forests
and other controlled sources. The logging and manufacturing processes
are expected to conform to the environmental regulations
of the country of origin.

HEADLINE PUBLISHING GROUP
an Hachette UK Company
Carmelite House
50 Victoria Embankment
London EC4Y 0DZ

The authorised representative in the EEA is Hachette Ireland,
8 Castlecourt Centre, Dublin 15, D15 XTP3, Ireland
(email: info@hbgi.ie)

www.headline.co.uk
www.hachette.co.uk

for all of us who got out
and for all of us who didn't

Urak, asszonyságok?
Ím szólal az ének.
Ti néztek, én nézlek.
Szemünk,
pillás függönye fent.
Hol a színpad:
kint-e vagy bent,
Urak, asszonyságok?

(Ladies and gentlemen?
Here comes the song.
You watched, I watched.
The curtain of our eyes is raised.
Where is the stage:
outside or inside,
Ladies and gentlemen?)

BÉLA BALÁZS, PROLOGUE TO THE LIBRETTO
FOR BÉLA BARTÓK'S *BLUEBEARD'S CASTLE*

(DAWN. THROUGH THE WINDOW, POOR LIGHT.)
This is a fairy tale.

The ghosts shift along the walls of our apartment. I correct myself: *his* apartment. Everything is in order, the way he wants it, the furniture luxurious but sparse, modernly eclectic: a sofa clad in green velour, the kind of wooden dining table you'd find in a monastery, a glass cabinet, this armchair. The walls are blue. For once, there is no wallpaper. The ghosts pull on the gauzy curtains instead, their mouths open and empty. This is a protest, I know. They don't like it when I imply our stories are not true. So I try again.

This is a fairy tale, I say, but everything I'm about to tell you is also something that happened. In another time, another place.

Better?

The women look at their dresses, which used to be white, before they were red. They run their palms across their own bodies. Beads fall soundlessly to the floor.

But I'm not talking to them now. I'm talking to you.

Here is the key, I'll give it to you: this is a fairy tale because I need the distance.

You fuss with my clothes, my hair, my skin. You worry over me, as if I'm not your mother and you're not my child, our roles upended, permanently disturbed.

I'm fine, I tell you. Listen.

The clock on the wall with no wallpaper ticks forwards, and I try to remember how to tell time. My mind lags numb, numberless. I turn to the window for answers – what is time, after all, but an encounter with the passing of light? There isn't much of it left. A day, perhaps: one dawn, one noon, one dusk. After our light runs out, people will come. They will open our doors. They will walk in, they will go looking, and they will find us. They will take you away, take me away, too. I glance at the closed bedroom door. The women in their frocks avert their eyes, palms before their spectral faces, *No, no, don't go there. Not yet.*

This morning, after he fled with you calling after him, terrified and confused, you asked if he's always been a monster. You ask it again, now. The light doesn't wait, so I must tell you while there's still time – while I can still speak, and you can still listen.

But how do I tell it? How do I talk about this?

The ghost women reach, arms outstretched, and I reach, too, for what I know, for what can grow, for things passed down skin to skin, mouth to mouth. Then the ghosts speak. *Start again,* they whisper. *This is how you do it, see? You start with milk.*

So I say: This is a fairy tale.

It begins with a wet nurse. With Agnes, at the beginning, or close enough. This is how I imagine it, and her, not-quite-mother and not-quite-wife, the first discarded woman.

2

The wet nurse

They hired Agnes to nurse the child without asking for references. It should have given her pause – in the village, you lived and died by the opinion of others; without your neighbours' good word, you were nothing. But she saw the mother from afar, when she came down to the village with a servant, looking for help: the shadowed eyes, clavicles knifing her dress. How could Agnes say no? Besides, she had milk; what was she supposed to do with it? Let it go to waste, let the child starve? She wasn't a monster. And is there anything more enjoyable in life than being needed?

She said yes.

She had thought she'd walk to the manor house; she didn't have much to carry, only a bundle of clothes and her good Sunday shoes, a golden necklace given to her by her mother before her passing a few months ago, the chain so thin it felt like thread, and a book she couldn't read, with a castle painted prettily on its cover. She had spent the entire night imagining her journey to the house: how she'd walk across the village carrying her bundle, her breasts heavy, her shoes muddy from the road, the villagers eyeing her silently and crossing themselves. How she'd go up the hill along the brambled road only carriages ever took, to haul things for the residents or ferry them to the town when the mistress felt lonely or the master had business to attend to. Agnes wasn't sure what kind of business it was, and she never asked.

'They say you don't see the mistress, but you hear her,' a woman had said to Agnes at the market, not long ago. 'They say there's something wrong about her, and the house is overrun with rats and worse things, and you'd do well to stay away from it.'

Still, Agnes had said yes. So she'd walk all the way up that hill despite the burn in her calves and the stitch in her side, and then she would pause by the black iron gates to catch her breath and take in the house, the exquisite sight of it, equal parts unnerving and breathtaking. She'd linger there a while. The high arched windows with their tinted panes would shine in the sunlight like a crown. There might be people behind those windows, looking at her, thinking about what a long way she'd come, waiting for her to walk up the path and rattle the bell to be let in.

But they sent a carriage. It was waiting for her when she stepped out of her father's house ready to face the village, the road, this new life. The driver flicked her an appraising gaze. It lingered a moment too long, making her shiver in her shawl. Then the horse snorted its impatience and the driver turned away. She climbed in, and off they went.

There was no need to pause at the gates, either. The carriage rolled through unceremoniously and delivered her to the front door. The road was cobblestone, flanked by statues of lions and stags and animals she didn't recognise, their paws gripping the ground, their faces mournful with mouths hanging open.

When the horse stopped, the driver didn't open the door for her, but the carriage remained still long enough for her to determine she should get out.

It was the cook who greeted her at the door. A short woman, too thin for a cook, with flushed cheeks and tight, grey curls that escaped from her cap. 'The mistress is not feeling well,' Cook said. 'She's sorry she couldn't welcome you herself.'

Agnes extended her free hand to grasp Cook's and also curtsied a little. 'I'm Agnes,' she said. Though the information seemed unnecessary, the meeting felt unfinished without it.

Cook gave her a lopsided smile. 'Sure you are,' she said. 'Come with me.'

The place smelled of dust. Few people worked for the couple, far fewer than were required to keep such a massive house clean, warm, and not falling apart. Later, she'd hear the stories about servants falling ill, waking with bruised knees they couldn't explain, and field hands quitting after nightmares no prayer would keep away.

Agnes would hear all the stories, she'd tell a few herself, and maybe she would even believe a couple were true. But, for the moment, she was taken with the high ceilings, the echoing rooms, the animals stuffed and mounted on every wall. Cook led her through the corridors, her shoes tapping on the dull marble of the floor. There were paintings too – strange ones, by Agnes's estimation, though she didn't have much experience in art, only the one painting that hung in her father's house. It'd been payment for the family's single horse, given to a stranger – a beautiful young man who'd passed through the village. He'd made a good case for himself, moved her father to tears over how much he needed that horse. But he had no money, and

5

instead had offered to paint a picture for Agnes's father – an original, he'd called it. Agnes's mother thought the idea was crazy, as did everyone else who heard about the offer; is it any wonder that people in the village thought her family was odd? But her father agreed to it, and so the stranger sat in the middle of their kitchen and created a painting just for them. Agnes watched the whole process from start to finish; for the two days it took to complete the painting, the stranger didn't sleep, and neither did Agnes. She saw the mountains take form, the trees come to life, the quiet stream running down the middle of the canvas, bisecting it – and the perspective was off enough for that stream to seem as if it were pouring from somewhere high up, perhaps even the sky. By the time the stranger was done, she could have described every detail of the painting with her eyes closed. Not that anyone ever asked her to.

The paintings in the manor house, though, were nothing like that. No quiet bucolic scenes, no faint blue mountains in the distance; they were dark, sinister, the creatures in them barely human. There was a woman with a rosebush for hair, holding an apple and gazing at the viewer with not a hint of emotion, and a curly-haired man with an enormous mouth and tiny hands, sitting on a sleeping horse, and a creature that sent chills down Agnes's spine not because of some such fantastical detail, but because its eyes were far too human, the face familiar.

Finally they reached her room. It was small and plain, cold like the rest of the house, but Agnes found it cosy. She immediately liked the tall window that overlooked the grounds and the woods beyond – there were fields on the other side of the house, but she couldn't see those – and the creaking of the floorboards reminded her of her father's house. There was even a dresser and a mirror, and her bed seemed not too soft but not too hard either. It was perfect.

After Cook left her alone, Agnes unpacked her things, hung up her dress, put the book on the dresser and hid the necklace in a handkerchief stuffed into her good shoes. Then she padded through the house on her own, marvelling at the strange paintings and the imposing columns that held up the ceilings. When she got tired, she went back to her room and opened the window to let in the breeze. It was a good view: the woods, the pretty garden that sprouted from the grounds. And then, out of the corner of her eye, a flash of something white, moving between the trees. She was leaning further out of the window to get a better look when she heard the baby cry. It was a terrible sound. A desperate, lonely sound.

Agnes would always remember the first time she saw the child. It was later that same night, hours after her arrival at the house – *the castle*, she'd already dubbed it in her mind. The mistress appeared only for a moment to greet her and hand her the swathed, squirming creature. The woman was in her nightgown, her eyes sunken, with bruised half-moons hanging underneath them. The baby screamed, inconsolable, so Agnes took it, and the mistress disappeared as soon as the bundle left her arms. Agnes wouldn't see her again for days, but thought of the mistress escaped her mind in that moment, because all her attention was on the baby now. His red face, his eyes so full of rage. If his tiny fists hadn't been tucked inside his swaddle, he'd have clawed her eyes out.

She sat in the nearest armchair with him in her lap. Cook was there, too, observing, overseeing – but Agnes barely registered

7

her presence. She freed her breast from her blouse and cradled the child's head, her arms sure, undisturbed by his squirming and his screams. She didn't think of her own baby then, his cold body, his blue face, the little lord's milk-sibling. Instead, she leaned back on the chair and stared at the room, the animals crawling on the walls, the dust on the windowsills, the strange paintings, the floor. And then, the baby was quiet. She fit his angry little mouth like they were made for each other.

'What was the child's name?' you ask, and I pause.

Does it matter? I wonder. Sometimes you become a character in someone else's story and so lose your name. Sometimes, you give it up willingly. Because a name can also be a burden, a legacy and a responsibility. A curse, even – and he, for now, is only a child. So I will not give him a name. For as long as I can help it.

They were inseparable after that. Agnes would feed the baby until he fell asleep, then take him to her room and place him on her bed. She'd cover him with a scratchy wool blanket she'd crocheted herself and sit by his side to watch him sleep. At night she'd often wake up with a start, certain the little lord would be blue in the face, that there'd be a night terror sitting on his chest, suffocating him, but she only ever found him fast asleep in the same position she'd left him in. Whenever he cried, she'd pick him up and soothe him, and, when that didn't work, she'd place him on her lap and tell him the stories her mother had told her when she herself was a child – some of which I've heard, too: stories of princes who did great violence to save their princesses, stories of women who suffered terrible trials to save their men. Sometimes, the men in them had wings, the women ursine ears. Often, the princes and queens had eyes the colour of the sea – but Agnes changed that, and made it so their eyes were the colour of the woods, because she had never seen the sea. What else were fairy tales for, after all, if not for showing you the world as it is and helping you survive it? And sometimes, Agnes made up her own stories, some of which she'd crafted in her mind months and months ago, thinking she'd get to tell them to her own baby. Others she concocted on the spot, inspired by the paintings in the house: about lambs that could speak, about mothers with urns for hearts, and about birds whose eggs, if eaten, would hatch inside your body and teach you the language of the winds.

Life for Agnes took on that watchful quality it tends to do around small children, the hours no longer narrated by roosters and mealtimes and clocks, but by the needs of the little lord.

She didn't call the child anything, and, when he learned to talk, he didn't call her anything either. Together they existed, a knowing between them that went beyond names.

Agnes went back to the village once a month to see her father. Her old home seemed smaller every time she visited, as if her stay at the house diminished everything else in her life, like a distorting mirror. And, each time, though it would be years before she admitted this to herself, she was glad to be back in the dusty halls of the castle, to be enveloped by its musty smell, stared down by its dark walls.

She only met Lord Malcolm weeks after she'd started working for him. She had just returned from her first visit home. The baby was asleep in her arms, and Agnes was heading upstairs to her room when she saw a tall, thin figure standing in front

9

of the great fireplace in the sitting room. He wore a set of keys around his waist. She took him for the groundskeeper or one of the servants, so plain were his clothes.

Agnes watched from the doorway. At first, she thought he was crying – it was the faltering way his back shook beneath the light fabric of his shirt. But as she stood there, she realised she'd been wrong: the man was laughing at the fire. It made the keys rattle.

'Why are you doing that?' she asked.

The man turned to face her. She recognised him from the painting with the sleeping horse, though both his mouth and his hands looked normal in person. This man was no grounds-keeper. His hair was curly and the same black as the child's; so dark that, when it caught the light just right, it took on the most beautiful blue tint. The lips, too, resembled his son's. Thick and perfectly shaped.

'Doing what?' he asked back, his voice too deep for his frame.

'Looking at the fire like that,' Agnes replied, now suddenly embarrassed by her own insolence.

But the man seemed intrigued by her directness. 'Because it's beautiful,' he said. 'Because I'm in awe that a thing this powerful can be contained so. It's man's greatest achievement. Don't you think?'

Agnes thought that was the most ridiculous thing she'd ever heard – besides, she'd lit the fire before leaving for the village, and she was no man.

She said so.

Instead of getting angry, the man burst out laughing. A full-throated laugh, coming from deep in the belly.

'Hush,' Agnes whispered, but it was too late. The baby had

already woken up and begun to cry. 'Look what you did,' she said.

The man looked at Agnes and smiled. He said, 'Look what you made me do.'

The child's nails grew too fast. Agnes cut them every morning but at night they dug again into her breasts, carved tiny crescents into the skin of her forearms. He was always hungry, his teeth sharp like needles. All babies have sharp teeth, she knew, but not like this. Once, the child bit her so hard she had to check her flesh in the mirror twice, certain he'd torn away a piece of her. But she didn't mind. When the baby nursed, Agnes's head emptied of everything else, of the world and everyone in it. There was only this child.

She understood that his need to be loved was great, and so Agnes loved him greatly. If anyone had asked whether she'd have changed anything, as I'm told people did, later, after everything – she'd have said no. She wouldn't change a thing.

The mother was a spectre. Agnes glimpsed her white night-gown turning a corner or fleeing up the stairs. The few times she had a chance to look at the woman's face, Agnes thought her beautiful, despite the wan skin, the downturned lips. Even on the occasions when the master invited Agnes to dine with him, claiming he enjoyed their conversations, the mother joined them only for a few minutes, and she didn't eat at all.

Tonight was one of those times. Outside, it was still light, a fresh spring evening, but in the dining room the air smelled stale, heavy with the scent of game cooked in red wine – venison, Agnes thought, shot and bled by the master himself. She'd just taken a sip of wine when the woman entered the room. The drink burned the roof of Agnes's mouth, made her gums grow numb, coated her teeth with a sour film.

The woman was still in her nightgown, her hair loose and greasy. 'I'm late,' she said, but her husband waved her words away.

'You can never be late, my love,' he said. 'Agnes was keeping me company.'

She turned to Agnes, alert for a moment, and Agnes felt as though she'd been caught stealing. Blood rushed to her cheeks. She couldn't meet the woman's gaze, so she looked down at her hands instead.

The moment was gone quickly, the alertness too. The mother sat down, elbows on the table, one hand supporting her head, lips sealed tight. She stared at her food, and she stared at the child, and at the woman who cared for it, and at her husband, who didn't speak another word.

When his wife left, the master leaned back in his chair and his shoulders fell; in disappointment, yes, but also, Agnes thought, in relief.

A few moments passed quietly, the little lord's calm breathing the only sound in the room.

'What's wrong with her?' Agnes asked, in the direct way she'd come to understand the master appreciated.

He remained silent for a long time. Agnes thought she'd been mistaken, that he was angry at the bluntness of her question. But, when the man stood and approached, it wasn't to punish her or send her back to her room. Instead, he touched her shoulder gently so she would stand, and led her to the window overlooking the garden, the stone fence, the cultivated land beyond.

The man's body felt large next to her. He smelled of wine and straw. She wanted to touch his beard but didn't.

'What do you see?' the man asked.

She looked; the garden was fierce and green, with tangled brambles and flowers that didn't keep to their beds. The stone fence sported moss – dead yellow and grey. The field was green too, dotted with red. So much red.

'Poppies,' she said.

The master nodded, smiled.

'This land turns corpses into flowers.'

When the child was weaned, he could already walk on two strong feet, pull at the weeds in the garden with two strong arms and pluck them from the earth's fist. Agnes imagined she'd be dismissed now that her milk was no longer needed, but nobody told her to leave. She could choose to leave herself. To go back to – what? What was there for her in the village? Not even a stranger who came, who loved her for a night, who painted, who left. Not even a blue-lipped baby to call her own.

So she stayed. Let her milk run dry. Gradually she understood she was to be the child's minder, though nobody told her as much. Besides, the mother seemed so helpless around the child, and he was so attached to Agnes by now – did she really have any choice in the matter? It seemed natural that she would stay.

They slept in the same bed often, the boy curled up against her, seeming both softer and more angular than Agnes expected his body to be, his fingers grasping her arm so tightly her flesh bruised. He smelled darkly of the forest; not the clean scent of trees, but the musky tang of their insides.

The child grew and his face remained as lovely as it had always been – though, sometimes, when she looked into his eyes, Agnes saw a shadow there, a hard thing her stories said might nestle in the eyes of a monster. But she was only a girl from a village. What did she know of monsters?

She oversaw the boy as he played in the field, whipping the tall yellow stalks with a birch stick she'd cut for him and watched him peel carefully with his short fingers. She loved to witness the boy in nature; he'd run to the pond and throw stones at the ducks, laugh first and then frown, as if surprised by his own violence. They spent hours in the fields and meadows. She would carry him on her back and he would point at the sky or an insect or the flowers, and she would tell him all their names – because it seemed important for him to know the names of things, even though the two of them needed no names for each other.

One day, she'd taken him to a nearby stream to wash his face, and he'd splashed too close to the jagged rocks. She yelled at him to come back at once. But he didn't listen to her, kept inching closer and closer to those murderous rocks, which could shred his tender flesh to ribbons. She got so angry, she wanted to make him obey, wanted to punish him. She waded into the water herself, grabbed him by the chin, and said, 'Stop!' She wanted to shake the little beast, to make that darkness in his eyes disappear. She squeezed his chin and shook him hard, once, twice. Three times.

He didn't fight. He simply stared at her with the calm of a man, the petulance of a little god, and, for the first time, Agnes grew afraid of him. But a breath later he was nothing but a boy again, hanging from his minder's arm, his clothes wet, his dark curls plastered to his skull. She let him go and they lay together on the riverbank to dry in the sun. He played as if nothing had happened between them, walked his fingers all over her bare arms, pretended they were dancers doing pirouettes and *grands jetés*.

Then it was lambing season, and the little lord made his first friend: a white thing that smelled of milk and wool. He loved the lamb. He could tell it apart from all the other lambs by its bleat, by the way it tilted its head slightly, which gave it an appearance of shyness unusual for a lamb. He held it in his arms tenderly, careful not to hurt it, burrowed his face in its soft wool, fed it milk from his palm. They ran and jumped together in the grass and, when they both tired, he placed it on top of him as he lay with his back to the ground and his face to the sky.

She would never forget the little lord's first friend. When, later, people would come to her and say he's evil, nothing but a well of pain and pestilence, she'd want to say, how could he be? And hold up that well-loved lamb as proof.

But it was clear to Agnes that the boy needed the company of children, too. He had lived almost a decade on this earth without another boy or girl to call his friend. His father chastised Agnes when she brought it up. Said that, for people like them, friends were a weakness, and the boy was needy enough as it was. But in the end he relented. He arranged for a group of children to come to the house once a week. They'd arrive in a carriage his father sent to the village and spill out like screaming demons dressed in their best. As soon as they set foot on the fabled land of the big house on the hill, they'd scatter in the garden and in the field as if their time on earth was running out and they needed to make the most of it, know all of it with the soles of their feet.

At first, they didn't include the little master in their games. When Agnes saw him standing in a corner, looking longingly at the other children playing games so foreign to him they may as well have been speaking their own private language, she nudged him and urged him to join them. But he retreated into the house, where the children were not allowed unless it rained, and then only in a corner of the great room. So she scolded the children and admonished them to include him, or else, she said, they would never be allowed back. That earned her nothing but a red-faced growl from him, but the threat worked. The children had simply been too shy of his wealth, she told herself, intimidated by his high breeding, the enormous walls that enclosed his life, all so unlike their own. But after a few scraped knees and copious amounts of dirt under their fingernails, they recognised him as one of their own.

By the time the children were sent back to their homes, the boy glowed with a wild joy, and, when he lay exhausted across Agnes's lap, he moaned – it was undeniably a moan, a thing he felt so deeply it pained him.

'I love the children,' he said. 'I love them all.'

(THE SUN IS COMING OUT.)

The ghosts interrupt. They object to the way I tell the story.

What do you want? I ask them. Am I being too kind to him? Too lenient with Agnes?

Do you need me to say he never loved anything?

These are not things the ghosts have answers to. Their words are rehearsed, their names borrowed like their costumes: an Ophelia, her hair still wet from the river. An Isolde. A Phaedra, thinking of bullish love. Even a Medea, heart-stricken, aphasiac, dreaming of a chariot eclipsing the sun. And yet, they question my choice to tell this like something that happened hundreds of years ago. Not now. Not in the twenty-first century.

I look down, at my own clothes. Sweatpants, a torn shirt. Slippers left by the bed, and I don't dare fetch them from behind that door. So: feet bare on the wooden floor. What costume is this? What role?

The ghosts talk all at once, trying again. But on this home-made stage of ours, I'm the one who must play composer, director, light designer, must speak all the roles myself.

Will you be quiet? I plead with them. Only for a minute, just so I can come up with the right words.

The first blight

A couple of summers later, the crops suffered with blight. Nobody thought much of it at first; such things had happened before, after all. They happened all the time. Except other ills followed, stranger things. The cattle stopped giving milk; ewes stopped birthing. Everywhere in the village, the fruit darkened and fell off the trees. The sight of them knotted a lump in Agnes's throat. The air stood still, and, when the wind blew, it was laced with a smell no one could quite place – something repugnant, something rotting and old. One night, the house shook and the ground split open. The earth exhaled a cloud of dust. The stone wall that circumscribed the property crumbled.

Men of knowledge from the city were summoned to provide the master with an explanation, but their remedies for the crops and the livestock offered no relief. While the village suffered, Lord Malcolm's household survived on their hoarded goods, their storage rich and bountiful beyond imagining. The mistress wept for the lost animals, the blighted land.

The children kept coming to play with the little lord, though in smaller numbers – some mothers clutched theirs close and refused to let them go to 'that wretched house'. But some still came, and this was all that mattered to Agnes. As she helped the last of the children into the carriage at the end of one day, the driver, Robert, held her gaze and touched her fingers, told her it would be all right. She pulled back her hand, gave him a cutting look. The little lord eyed the suffering crops with his jaw clenched, as if staring down an adversary.

And then, suddenly, before the end of summer, Robert's prediction came true and everything went back to how it had been before. The animals livened, the ewes' bellies swelled with new, healthy lambs, the trees bore fruit so big their branches bowed to the ground, and fresh grass carpeted the fields, green and thick. But the lump in Agnes's throat refused to budge, no matter how she coaxed it.

Most of the children came back, resumed their play. One time, Agnes saw them all gathered around a patch of tall grass. They were looking down at something, peering at it intently. Then, one by one, they took turns bowing to the ground. Agnes thought maybe they'd found a strange animal – something venomous that they shouldn't be touching but would surely, undoubtedly, touch. She ran to stop them; when she reached them, she saw they were all gathered around the boy, who was kneeling in the grass. One girl told Agnes to leave him be, in a tone that made her sound too grown-up, almost reverent, and the others fell into silent nods of assent. After a moment, the little lord stood and let them drape his shoulders with their arms. He smiled. He looked fine, only startled, as if he hadn't expected the other children to embrace him so, and also grateful, as if he hadn't thought he deserved it.

Agnes never did figure out exactly what had passed that day, but she placed this exhibition of affection towards her charge in the same category she put the fecund land, the green-again grass, the swollen bellies of the ewes.

Lord Malcolm thanked the scientists for their delayed miracle, and made a large donation to the church for good measure. He was not particularly religious, but he was a practical man, and Agnes liked that about him: he held on to what he thought was right but was not too proud to change his mind, or have it changed.

Then, the dogs.

The master had no special fondness for any of the animals he kept. They were tools, all of them – the cattle definitely, the horses, too, and even the three hounds he took hunting. These hounds were meek, obedient things that adored their master and the boy with a wide-eyed ferocity that could melt your heart. They never made a sound, except when their master needed them barking over a fallen bird or a stag shot through the neck.

But on the nights before the accident, the dogs howled. Agnes thought they felt that something was not right with the world – animals can sense that sort of thing, can't they? They screamed for hours. The master went out first to scold them, then whip them, and then, when he gave up, it was Agnes's turn to go out to their kennel and bribe them with treats and petting hands. She walked by the flickering light of an oil lamp. The wind brought with it the memory of snow, though the weather had not yet turned – it made her skin bloom into gooseflesh.

When she reached the door of the barn, she didn't understand what she saw. The dogs, yes, and in front of them something else, shadowy and unfamiliar. She blinked and held her lamp higher: it was the child. How had she not known him? He stood in front of the dogs, his hands on their heads, speaking to them. Agnes gasped. The boy was slick with something that looked like blood.

She ran. She knelt next to the boy, handled him all over to check for the bleeding wounds she'd glimpsed – his head, his back, his belly, his legs his arms his eyes his neck his neck—

There was no blood, no wounds. It had been nothing, nothing, just the uncanny workings of the night. The boy submitted himself to her furious inspection silently, staring at her with his forest eyes.

'Are you all right?' Agnes asked him, her words almost drowned by the whining of the dogs.

Again, he spoke no words, but turned his gaze to the beasts.

'What were you doing to the dogs?' she asked, and she'd meant to say *"with"*—*with* the dogs, not *to* them, because that sounded strange, didn't it? What could a boy have been doing to the dogs he so loved?

The boy lifted his long-nailed hand to her face and caressed her cheek carefully, while Agnes braced herself for pain that didn't come.

The next day the village children came again to play with the little lord. They spilled out of Robert's carriage as they did every time, and the boy joined them with a serious look on his face, which wasn't unusual – he always looked a little grim, and that had worried Agnes until she accepted that his joy was not incompatible with his seriousness. Together, the children ran to the back of the house. They liked to play on the boundary between the fields and the woods, where the two kinds of territory merged, that long strip which was neither cultivated land nor wilderness.

Agnes kept herself busy. She tried not to hover where the boy could see her, while also avoiding Robert's inappropriate stares. She did, however, note that the man's body was pleasantly compact, and that his face was puffy in a way that made him look always just-woken and kind.

Agnes swept the stone paths around the pond, then pruned the dead roses from the bushes that grew in the rock garden; the blight had robbed the house of its gardener, and she was the next best thing. As she scooped up the dried heads of the flowers and snipped, scooped and snipped, she lost herself for a while, following the thread of a memory: She'd been cutting the child's nails, back when he was small. He'd held out his hands to her, his fingers spread and his eyes perfectly trusting as she drove the clippers over the edges of his fingertips. She'd collected the precious little crescents in her palm – she remembered telling him they were treasures. Though he'd been far too young to understand, he'd given her the brightest laugh, as if he grasped both the hyperbole and the compliment in the words.

She always wondered how much he'd understood, how much he remembered. Of all the stories she told him, which ones would stay with him, and which would fade?

I pause while you give me a look.

I am transparent, aren't I? And you've always been smarter than I am.

Cries and barking and growling pulled Agnes out of her reverie. She dropped her shears and the basket of beheaded roses and ran. The children were standing close together, their bare arms around one another; some were hiding their faces in their hands, others were crying. The little lord stood alone, next to the dogs – of course the dogs were there; she'd heard barking. There was foam in the grey one's mouth; was it rabies? No, the dog was calm now, not mad with rage or fever. It was looking at something on the ground, something mangled and small. Another boy.

Agnes fell on the dry earth next to the child. He was hurt badly, his belly, his side, his head, his neck. He was bleeding but breathing. Agnes tore long strips from her skirt to tie around the boy's wounds and ordered the shirt off the little lord's back to bunch and push against the boy's bleeding head. She knew immediately that his head wound was probably a scratch – a sharp tooth, maybe, dragged along the skull's fine cocoon; but that's the head for you. The tiniest scrape gushes so much it looks like it can bleed the whole body dry.

Agnes started giving orders to the children: fetch this adult, put pressure here, hold his head, get those dogs out of my sight.

A little girl with yellow hair and skin as pale as a cloud whispered something at Agnes, too low for her to hear. Of all things, this was what made blood rush to her head and her throat swell. 'Speak up, girl!' she shouted.

The girl swallowed and tried again. She raised her arm and pointed at the little lord.

'He did something to the dogs,' the girl said.

'What?' Agnes asked, her hands still, the blood on them drying more quickly than felt possible.

'I did nothing!' the little lord protested, but the girl continued.

'He was saying something to the dogs.' Then, to him: 'I saw you. That's why they attacked.'

Agnes dismissed the girl. 'I have no time for this,' she said. 'Help me, both of you.'

The girl looked at Agnes for a moment as if not understanding what was being asked of her, but then she knelt next to the injured boy, and so did the little lord. The other children stood where they were, looking on in horror and fascination.

With the help of the children, who made sure no part of his body bent in ways it shouldn't, Agnes slowly turned the boy to the side to aid his breathing. Because the boy *was* breathing. He was still bleeding from his head and from the deep, long cuts on his belly and neck. His eyes were closed, his mouth half-open and full of dirt. His wounds would scar, but he was alive. That was what mattered, Agnes thought. The little lord hadn't killed anybody.

Her own thought made her shudder. It was the dogs, she chastised herself. The dogs.

Soon, Robert arrived and helped Agnes transfer the child onto the carriage to be taken back to the village. There, the boy would be seen to by a doctor and by his parents. Since Robert had taken off in a hurry with the wounded boy, the rest of the children were left behind until another carriage could come and collect them. Cook wrangled the rattled children to the kitchen, where she plied them with tea and biscuits. Agnes studied their ashen faces but didn't try to comfort them. She had nothing to say to them, and they had nothing to say to her; even the girl who'd tried to blame the little lord had fallen silent. She had a biscuit in her hand.

'Aren't you going to eat that?' Agnes asked gently.

The girl looked at the biscuit with something between wonder and surprise, as if she hadn't realised there was food in her hand, or she'd forgotten what she was supposed to do with it.

'Yes,' she said, 'thank you, yes.'

She set the biscuit down on the small table next to her. It remained there, uneaten.

After the children had gone, Agnes approached the little lord. He was studying the wall of the great room, his eyes unmoving. He did this often, stared at something that to the rest of the world might seem wholly unremarkable as if it were the most curious thing he'd ever seen. If he noticed Agnes watching, he'd turn his head the way a cat does when it knows it's time to be fed. What does it matter that it's not really hungry?

Now Agnes knelt next to the boy and put her arms around his waist. He stood, stiff and immobile, still looking at the secret happening on the wall.

'Are you all right?' she asked, and only then did he turn, a look of betrayal on his face.

'You believed her,' he said. 'The girl who said I did something to the dogs.'

Agnes's chest tightened, because yes, yes, she had.

'And you didn't?' she asked, leaning back and away from the boy so she could look him straight in the eyes, pluck the truth from those depths.

Instead of protesting or squirming free of her hold and yelling about his innocence, the little lord went back to staring at the wall and the private thing there, the corner of his lip quirking up, his face as satisfied as a cat's.

Agnes couldn't sleep that night. The child no longer shared her bed; he was old enough to have his own room, though from time to time he padded back to her bed in the night, seeking her. She missed his weight next to hers. She wasn't a slight woman, but there were times she felt so light, so impossibly light, that even a breeze could lift her and carry her away. She fought the urge to tether herself to the bed at night, or to fill her pockets with stones to keep her grounded when she walked. The little lord seemed like that kind of stone to her.

After hours of wrestling the bed covers, she finally got up. Her skin felt clammy, her mouth dry, with an aftertaste of marrow sucked from bone. The air stuck wetly to her face, and she was cold. She stood on the naked floorboards, tested the wood with her toes, and wrapped herself with her woven shawl. She didn't move; for a while, she stayed there, breathing in the cold. She shivered. The house was quiet, but it was not asleep.

She'd always known not to be curious. Her mother had told her a story, once, about a lord and his strange beard, and about his many wives, each succumbing to her curiosity, peeking where she shouldn't and so meeting her end.

And yet, Agnes wandered out of her room and down the long corridor. She passed the little lord's chamber; his door was halfway open, as always. Inside, the boy was asleep on his back, his breathing slow and heavy, his lips parted.

She continued down the hall and into the great room, where she sat on the sofa, facing the empty expanse of wall the boy had stared at the day before. It was still empty, didn't look like anything at all. She ran her hand over the silk covering of the seat. She never allowed herself to sit on that sofa, though nobody had forbidden it. Still, it was so soft and welcoming, so like an embrace. She gave herself up to it.

Just before she fell asleep, she thought she heard a voice call for Agnes. She wondered, briefly, whose name that was.

(SPOTLIGHT, NARROW BEAM.)

You stand up abruptly, knocking over the antique lamp that sits on the coffee table. Its ivory base is sculpted into the shape of a fish, now flopped on its side. You eye the closed bedroom door with suspicion.

'I heard something break,' you say and take a tentative step that makes me want to leap out of my armchair and grasp you, stop you, save you.

When? I ask, not moving, hands feigning calmness on my lap. Just now?

'No,' you say. 'This morning. Before he left.' Your eyes shine in the pale light. It's not yet noon.

I can't let you open that door, can't let you see. I need more time.

It was nothing, I tell you. I touch the back of my head without thinking, and a strange sensation goes through me. Something old, something new.

I stall, leave the armchair to right the toppled lamp, return. Finally, you sit down again, your legs crossed and your back against the sofa. You've always liked sitting on the floor, since you were little, staring up at the TV, every single one of your toys strewn around you, your action figures, your tiny swords. You ate on the floor, even slept on the floor. I used to tell you

27

off for that, but today it suits me fine. The bedroom door is behind you once more, safely out of sight.

You're still in your pyjamas. Blue, with tiny antlered deer.

It was nothing, I repeat.

You don't believe me, I can tell. But you humour me.

'And the boy?' you ask.

The red-haired girl

News of the injured boy arrived a few days later, and it was good: the boy was recovering. He was still too distraught to hold long conversations about the incident or anything else, but he was in health good enough for the whole thing to be forgotten. His mother sent his older sister to the house in his stead, a red-haired creature all eyes and limbs. It struck Agnes as an odd thing to do; as if there were a quota to be met, and one child could replace another so long as the total number remained the same, like a tribute sent from the village to the house on the hill, lest its monsters venture out of its labyrinthine grounds and demand more than the agreed price of peace.

Besides, the sister was too old to be playing with children – too old, even, for the little lord, who was no longer so little, already a shadow on his upper lip and even a few hard curly hairs breaking the skin of his jaw. But the girl didn't seem to mind. She sat in the children's circles and sang their songs, hiked up her skirts to play their games in the mud and chase them all around the garden.

The little lord didn't play. He stood apart, watching them, watching her. Agnes sat with him, listened to his breathing the way she liked to do. 'She must be sad about her brother,' she told him. 'Why don't you comfort her?'

The little lord turned to face her, part offended, part intrigued. Then he looked back at the girl playing in the mud. He stood, but instead of joining the children, he stormed off and disappeared into the house.

That night, the boy walked into Agnes's room and climbed onto the bed with her. 'How would I comfort her?' he asked.

Agnes brushed back his inky curls, tucked one behind his ear, ran her fingers over the hair on the soft skin above his lip. 'Tell her you're sorry.'

The boy stiffened. 'But it wasn't my fault!' he protested.

'No matter,' Agnes said. 'Say it anyway. You can be sorry for things that are out of your control.'

He mulled this over, surrendered to her touch, as if her hands on his head soothed something in him. 'What else?' he asked.

Agnes thought. 'Give her flowers,' she said.

'What kind of flowers?'

'Ones you pick yourself.' She had almost said 'kill', but didn't.

Later that night, Agnes dreamed she woke up and the boy was gone from her bed. She crossed the room to the window and spotted him in the garden – the little lord, digging up the ground with a spade. At first she thought he was pulling weeds, but then he turned around clutching a mess of things to his chest, and she saw them, his muddy bouquet. The flowers were a deep, muted purple, almost black. He brought them up to Agnes's room and offered them to her, soil still clinging to their petals and stems. She accepted the bouquet with a smile and pushed her nose against the flowers' dark heads, though the smell – like burnt hair mixed with fermented milk – made her sick.

She started awake, and the boy was breathing next to her. Agnes pondered his outline. She remembered the way he'd brought the flowers back in her sleep, like a trophy, like a hunter returning from the woods in the early morning with a deer draped over his shoulders, blood spilling out of it like a great swath of expensive cloth.

The boy was quiet that day, and she didn't say anything to him, didn't ask him whether dark flowers had haunted his sleep. She had him close; that was enough.

The next time the children came, the little lord did as Agnes had instructed. She watched. The little lord took the girl to the side, a serious look on his face, held her hand and told her he was sorry. The girl studied him for some time, then put one hand on his chest and the other on his eyes, and told him he was forgiven. Agnes thought the boy would protest his innocence again, but he stayed silent instead, his eyes covered by the girl's hand.

They spent the entire day together. Agnes had had enough of this watching – she left them for a few hours and helped Cook make a large pot of beet soup for the children. Agnes wondered about Cook sometimes, what she loved, whom she needed, what it felt like to be her. Who had she been, before this house and its masters? When had she lost her name?

When Agnes went back out to search for her charge and his new friend, she found them in the field. The girl sat on the grass, and the boy was braiding red poppies through her hair. He seemed transfixed by this task, his fingers exploring the girl's scalp, adding flower after flower to her crown.

Agnes was so taken with the scene she didn't notice Robert until he was standing so close his shoulder brushed hers. She spun around, something hot streaming from her eyes. Robert grew serious at once, and he cupped her face with both his hands. 'What's wrong?' he asked. 'Where does it hurt?'

She clasped her hands to her belly, thumbed her chest. Her cheeks were burning. 'Everywhere,' she said, sobbing. 'Everywhere.'

She started noticing Robert more after that. He was tall, broad-shouldered, sun-kissed, with quick hands and a wide smile. He'd been working for the boy's father since he was a boy himself.

'You've known the lord a long time,' Agnes said as they walked together in the idle time between unloading the children and loading them into the carriage again, limbs heavy with exhaustion and clothes caked with mud. 'What do you think of him?' she asked. 'Of his wife?'

The question took Robert aback. He stopped and stared at her, then started laughing. 'I don't think about them much,' he said. 'Do you?'

'So you simply serve them,' she said, with more spite than she had intended. 'You're here to do as you're told, then go back home at the end of the day and forget everything you saw.'

'That's one way to put it,' he said with a shrug. Then added, winking: 'But I don't forget every*one* I saw.'

Agnes laughed, because he had said this in a playful tone, as if it were a joke. But he didn't laugh again. On the way back, Robert took her hand and kept it in his until they were in sight of the house and the children. The little lord sat with the girl – her name escaped Agnes, or she'd never sought to find out what it was. They were on the steps in front of the big entrance, their knees touching, a kind of tiredness on their faces, but otherwise content. The boy saw Agnes with Robert, noticed something – the connected hands? Some new familiarity in their gait? – and stiffened, gave her a look she'd seen him wear before. It wasn't a pleasant look.

The girl soon went home in Robert's carriage and the little lord disappeared into the house. Agnes wondered if he would come to her that night, if he'd bring her flowers again – then remembered he'd never brought her flowers at all.

While the boy grew closer to the girl from the village, Agnes flirted with the driver. Robert fetched the children and Agnes made sure everyone was happy and safe, and then together they walked into the forest, all the way to the clearing where Agnes retreated when she wished to be alone. If she wondered what that meant, she'd realise it meant: away from the boy. Robert took her hand and ran his thumb over her knuckles, then kissed her palm, her neck. Later, more of her, on the ground among the moss and the ferns and the wild flowers.

The boy was jealous, though he never admitted it with words. He still slipped into her bed some nights, and she noted how different his body looked now, strong in places that had been soft and childish before.

One night, she caught him looking as she undressed. She'd never shied from his gaze before, but she did this time. 'Look away,' she snapped, and he jutted his chin at her, petulant.

'Why?' he demanded.

*   *   *

They lasted a whole year like this. Months of working and slip-ping away with Robert, a winter of clumsy hands under her clothes and then a mild spring, and a new summer of warm nights next to the boy's sweaty skin, lulled by the crickets' song. Every so often, Agnes dreamed that the house was a mouth, and her job was to lead the children into it, let them disappear, unsung, into its gullet.

On Saturdays, Robert stayed in one of the spare bedrooms so they could attend church together early on Sunday morning. He crept into her bed at night, when he found it empty of the child, and if anyone noticed, no one objected. Not even the little lord.

August brought rain with it, and the boy was quiet and moody, the girl nervous and erratic around him. Still, Agnes felt no need to approach her, to ask what was wrong. Only once, when she noticed her eating cherries, she told the girl to always spit out the stones. 'If you don't,' Agnes said, 'a cherry tree will sprout from your belly.' The girl smiled and thanked her, and swallowed the pits anyway.

(DIRECT LIGHT, WHITE.)

Agnes's warning makes you giggle. You think it silly, an old wives' superstition, the frivolous things women believe in. Perhaps that's for the best – though I do wish I'd taught you better.

The red-headed ghost plays along. She holds her long braid to the side as if someone's pulling her hair, the silent re-enactment of an unspoken scene. Her face is pale, blue like the wall, like an egret's egg. Her whole body heaves, and out come the cherry stones, one after another, more and more, countless.

I never knew if you could see the ghosts, though I wondered often, before. Now you say nothing and, for that, I'm grateful.

The heart is deceitful above all things

Robert fell ill. His skin grew pale, and his eyes looked as if they'd sunk deeper into his skull. He was late regularly, which was unlike him. His hands felt clammy against Agnes's skin. She implored him to go to the doctor, and he promised he would. By harvest, he seemed better, and Agnes took heart that he'd get over this, whatever it was.

One Sunday morning she woke alone in her bed. The fire was dead and she shivered in the freezing air. She went to the window. The summer was ended and, outside, the first snow of the year fell thick and fast. She put her hand on the glass pane and drew in a sharp breath when she saw the yard covered with it, completely white under the soft blue light. It filled her with such dread that she jumped when Robert walked in and put his hand on the small of her back.

His face was gaunt. She could see now that he was emaciated, given while she wasn't looking to whatever this wasting disease was that was ravaging his body, eating him little by little right out of her arms.

'Where were you?' she asked.

He shook his head. 'Nowhere,' he said, and she smelled acid on his breath. He sat her in her chair – the one she used to sit in when she nursed the little lord – and knelt at her feet. She stroked his head and he looked up at her.

'I have a confession,' he said. His voice was steady, his face flushed.

'We're not in church yet,' she said, but her little joke brought no mirth to his eyes.

'I never went to the doctor,' he said.

She kept stroking. She was silent. He needed to talk, and so she would let him talk.

'I thought I'd be fine,' he continued. 'So I didn't do anything. I went on as I was, because in my heart I knew I'd be fine.'

'"The heart is deceitful above all things",' she quoted, '"and desperately weak. Who can know it?"'

He looked up at her. 'You?' he asked. 'A Bible verse?'

She thought. 'Yes, well. Sometimes.'

'But I think it says the heart is wicked, not weak.'

Was that true? Perhaps. 'Still,' she said, 'who can know it?'

He rested his head on her knees and she stroked his hair, tried to memorise the feel of it on her skin. She knew the nights they had left were numbered. A dozen emotions could have rushed through her then, frustration and shame and so many more, but I think none did. She was simply numb before this thing, this manly thing she knew so well yet had no name for.

Robert wasted away faster than the snow melted.

Agnes rode to the funeral with the little lord and his father, but Lord Malcolm's wife stayed at home, hostage to her own secret grief.

Robert's father was there, with the coffin. Agnes had never met him before. Robert hadn't offered to introduce them, and she hadn't thought to suggest it. She would never have been Robert's wife. What would have been the point? She hadn't wondered about Robert's mother either; she'd accepted she had been absent, most likely taken by a fever or by the woods, as mothers so often tend to be. A distant figure, a woman-shaped blur.

Robert's father was old and stooped, and after his son was put in the ground he went home in the carriage Robert used to drive. He seemed so small in it, like a child, a boy who had no business in the driver's seat, no place holding the reins of horses, his fingers wrapped nervously around the braid of leather.

Lord Malcolm's face was ashen, and he seemed grief-stricken – so grief-stricken, in fact, that Agnes wondered: had he and Robert been close? Had she missed something?

The little lord remained impassive, scuffing the ground with his foot now and then, or looking up with narrowed eyes, as if he were sizing up the clouds, or the sky itself, against his grudge.

And Agnes, did she cry? Later, after everyone was gone and people asked her to recount this story, Agnes tried to recall how she'd felt that day. She told them she had wept, of course, that she'd bawled and some women from the village had held her up. But it was only a story – or probably one, because she couldn't remember at all.

The boy did come to her that night, bringing with him flowers that weren't diseased. He put them in a glass of water on her nightstand, then climbed on the bed and curled up beside her, his face against her back, breathing in her hair. 'I'm sorry,' he said, his voice thicker and deeper than she remembered.

She turned over, put her fingers on his face gently.

'For what?' she asked. 'For what are you sorry?'

She waited, though she didn't know what she was looking for. Perhaps she was curious to see his face when he told her, to find out why a boy of fourteen was sorry for something in which he'd had no part. Or maybe she wanted to see what the flowers looked like in the morning light, when everything was easier to understand. To see how long it would take for them to wither.

The boy's father was careful and mild around her after Robert's death. He called Agnes by her name often, and looked at her in a way she thought kind, which she felt was more than she deserved. Who was he to her, and she to him, after all? She was allowed time to herself, without the need to mind the little lord or his companions, but she found she had no use for such time. No use for herself either. She developed a bad habit of bringing up memories of Robert, from early in his illness, like that one time he had gotten up before dawn, the first in the whole house to rise, and cooked breakfast while she was still rubbing the sleep from her eyes. She remembered it so vividly, so clearly that she thought she could smell the greasy bacon, hear the pans clang together downstairs. But then she remembered Robert was dead, and she felt such a stabbing, such searing pain in her chest that she became sick. And when she was back to herself, she wondered: whatever is the point of grief?

So Agnes returned to her chores. Took on more, in fact, because one of the servants had left while she was plunged in the blue of her loss and she'd hardly noticed. She spent her days working on the land: clearing the overgrowth and the brush, digging new beds and pathways and planting azaleas – but wait, no; they don't grow in this country.

It's important to get these details right, isn't it?

I try again: Agnes planted fragrant herbs and roses in the garden. The boy joined her, sometimes. He liked flowers. He would kneel, brush his fingertips over the petals and take in their scent. It pleased her to see him like this, though the feeling was fleeting. Was that happiness, Agnes wondered, that thing she felt? What kind of person would that make her? She burned deadwood and collected seeds. She did so mechanically, all muscle and no heart, but nobody minded, and only the little lord commented, in his muted way of sneaking up on her when she wasn't looking and whistling in her ear, his breath tickling her skin.

The mistress of the house remained as absent and unseen as ever, but did call Agnes aside one day, asked if she was feeling unwell. Was it her heart? The mistress put her hand to Agnes's chest and felt her pulse, checked for pins and needles in her limbs, for irritation in her eyes and ears. But then, instead of asking Agnes if she'd eaten something that disagreed with her, or if she'd been sleeping badly, the mistress told her she knew what it was, that it had happened to her too, and that there was no cure except the river or the long road that led away from this house. The woman's voice trembled and her face seemed much older than she was, or more weathered, like a thing shattered and put back together again hastily and with no skill. Agnes was repulsed, and yet she reached out and touched the woman's face. The gesture wasn't meant tenderly, and the woman didn't take it so.

'What did he do?' Agnes asked. 'Tell me.'

The woman's face twisted. 'But that's just it, isn't it?' she said. She showed Agnes her empty palm. Then she touched Agnes's breast, traced something there that only Agnes could remember – the memory of a mouth, the echo of a bruise, the smell of milk soured too soon. 'Nothing. Nothing that fits a mouth, a tongue. You simply carry it with you, wherever you go, in the river or on the road. It stays.'

When the boy's mother abandoned them, the master of the house didn't leave his room for days. Food was delivered to him on a tray left outside his door, but it was usually retrieved untouched hours later. He only took tea sweetened with honey. Cook made Agnes go inside after a week, to coax some soup into the man, to force him if she had to.

The room smelled dank. The curtains were drawn shut and at first she could see nothing at all. Agnes stood by the door, holding a tray of soup and bread, while her eyes adjusted. Finally, she saw him: he was sitting on the edge of his bed in his nightshirt, its fabric hanging off him like the cerements of a ghost.

I glance at the ghost women, despite myself. They scowl. They don't appreciate being used as metaphors. But how can you tell a story without them?

Agnes put down the tray – this man didn't need soup. She went to the window, opened the curtain – only one side; too much light would be cruel, and she didn't want to be cruel. He didn't complain. He stared at his feet. What did you do, she wanted to ask, to deserve this? But she didn't ask anything. She sat by the man on the bed, studied his greasy hair, forbade herself to recoil from the smell of unwashed skin. 'My lord,' she said, and then, 'Malcolm.'

He turned slowly to face her, his eyes suddenly alive, as if he had just realised she was there in the room with him. Her. Not a ghost, and not someone else.

'Come on,' she told him.

She took him by the hand like she'd done with the boy count-less times before, and he followed, more obedient than his child had ever been. She stripped him and deposited him in the bath, which she filled with hot water she'd ordered brought up from the kitchen. She washed him with a sponge, every inch of him. She lathered his long hair with soap, rinsed it, then lathered it again until it shone and sang under her fingers like string.

By the time she had the man back in his bed in clean clothes, the soup cold on his nightstand, some life seemed to have been restored in him. She turned to leave, but he held hard on to her wrist. 'Agnes,' he told her.

'Yes, my lord?'

He stared at her for a few moments, not speaking, his breathing strained, his lips a knot.

He untied it, tied it again into something other than what he'd meant to say. 'You're good to my son,' he said.

The boy tried to hide how much he missed his mother, and he managed it, with everyone but Agnes. He didn't ask to see the girl from the village for a while, and sent the children away when they visited in Robert's father's carriage. He took to walking in the woods alone, pacing the fields. Agnes watched the little lord from afar and sometimes saw him fall to his knees and beat the earth with his fists. She could tell where he'd done it because, in the days that followed, anything that grew on that patch of earth would be diseased, and no animals would go near. Briefly, she thought of her own child, the boy's milk-sibling, dead for as many years as the little lord had been alive; she wondered what he would have looked like, who he'd have grown into, had he lived.

She chased the thought away. Her own child? Who was this, then, if not her own child?

She tried to make him laugh, to keep him in the house and get him to eat, but he was so like his father, and it was hard work to keep them both alive.

Malcolm called her to his room often, invited her to the dinner table nightly, until Agnes imagined that, to anyone peering in through the large dining-room windows, they would resemble a little family. The intimacy between them didn't escape the boy's attention, which tightened something in Agnes's throat. She thought of Robert, and wondered what might happen to Malcolm, but the boy seemed content to let his father escape the path of his jealousy.

Slowly, foolishly, she eased into a life that did not belong to her.

It was during that time that they first talked about the boy's nature. Agnes was in Malcolm's bed, naked, staring at his bare back as he stood by the window and gazed at his crops, his animals, his land. He was the one who brought up the subject of his son: how the land seemed to render itself barren and unyielding around him. The effect he had on animals and on people. How his body seemed so natural, so gifted and so wrong at the same time.

43

The boy's earthy smell was in Agnes's nostrils still, always.

'His mother was ill with him,' Malcolm said, facing Agnes. 'During the pregnancy. She had lost so much weight, it was as if the baby was eating her up from within. But she held on to him, and her own body fought her. When he was born . . .' He trailed off. 'Well, you know how she was. We needed help. She couldn't bear to be around him at all.' Malcolm looked out the window again, at what was his. 'Sometimes I was afraid she would kill him.' Then, in a lower voice, he added: 'Once or twice, I wished she had.'

Agnes did not let herself react to the words. She reached out and picked up Malcolm's set of keys from where they rested on the nightstand. She ran her fingers over each one without saying anything. She knew when men wanted to talk with little interest in being heard, so she waited for him to go on.

'We found a man in the village who knew about such things,' Malcolm said. 'He came, he saw. He said my wife was doomed. That the boy was cursed. Didn't say by whom.' Malcolm shrugged, shut his eyes for a few moments. 'I believed him. Even wondered if I had played my part in this curse.' He paused. 'Despite everything I ever stood for, I believed him.'

'And yet, you hired me to nurse the child.' She didn't mean it to sound like an accusation, but how could it not?

He shrugged again. 'I thought, maybe, tenderness would change him. Make him into something soft and innocent, like a baby.'

She nodded. She'd felt that, too. It was all she felt, sometimes. If she loved him enough, maybe the curse would be lifted. Maybe, if she loved him well enough, this one could be saved.

*   *   *

The boy spent most of his time with the horses, but he also started seeking again the red-haired girl from the village, the one Agnes had once told him he should comfort. She wondered, now, what that coaxing had birthed.

The little lord had started filing down his own nails. All the animals were nervous around him, except for the horses. They were gentle with him, and he was gentle with them, too – the gentlest she'd ever seen him. He put his hand on their muzzles and touched his forehead to the side of their strong necks. Before long, he could ride bareback, control the animals with the tiniest twitch of the muscles in his legs. When he could get away with it, he slept in the stables, keeping warm with the horses' breath. One time, Agnes asked him why he did that; he said the horses had once been his mother's, so being close to them made him feel like he was close to her.

'She loved you, you know,' Agnes told him, even though she didn't know if it was true. Had she really loved him?

Did Agnes? And, if she did – would it ever be enough?

The boy took a long time to answer, and when he did, he didn't look at Agnes. Only at the horses. 'Do you think everyone is worthy of love?' he asked. 'No matter what?'

The question broke something open inside her. She realised how guarded she'd been with him, though she'd never meant to be. She reached for him and caressed the side of his face, the way she used to do when he was small. She'd watched his body grow firm and long, his shoulders broad. The shadow under his chin was now proper stubble. He's still a boy, though, Agnes thought. It was his body that lied. 'I don't know,' she said. 'But you are.'

'Worthy?' he asked. 'Or loved?'

That night, she dreamed of her own mother. The woman in Agnes's sleep was old and hunched over, as she'd never been in real life. Her hair fell out in clumps. She sat at the dinner table with Agnes and Malcolm and the boy, an empty chair on her right. Agnes dreamed of a wet winter, of rainstorms that flooded the rooms, the stables, the fields outside. The animals drowned; bloated corpses floated down the river, the flesh peeling off them. The boy stood on a balcony, watching the river grow and grow into a sea, rise up and reach him, until he, too, floated away, with the rest of the animals.

Whose idea was it for them to go on the hunting trip? The boy, when she asked him later, said it was hers, and maybe he was right, though she couldn't remember for sure. But it was Malcolm who grabbed with both hands that vision of becoming closer with his child, of a chance for father and son to bond over cold forest nights and the carcasses of fallen game.

They would be gone for three nights. Agnes and Cook packed the food and candles, the water and wine. The horses' eyes were ringed with red. Agnes thought it a sign but didn't say a word about it. So yes, perhaps it'd been her own idea.

She watched man and boy disappear into the woods on their horses, carrying blankets and dried fruits and meat and bread wrapped in cloth, their weapons bundled on the third horse's back. First, the trees shielded them from her sight, but she kept watching until the sound of them faded away, too, and then they were truly gone. In the quiet, she heard the rustling of leaves, and the echoing silence of the house behind her. She felt the earth move beneath her feet and she grabbed on to the balustrade to steady herself. It might have been her idea, but

Malcolm had made his own fate so very long ago. And she knew, somehow, what was coming. She knew she couldn't save him. She could save no one at all.

She spent most of the next day in bed, the rest wandering through the empty rooms. She dismissed Cook until the men were back. The sound of rain reached her through the window, a steady patter on the glass, and, when night came, the crickets, the hoot of an owl. Agnes thought of her mother, those stories she'd told about the forest that surrounded the village, how it always tried to claim you, no matter who you were or why you dared venture into it. She imagined a forest a thousand miles wide, and she kept walking and walking, following the boy and his father through the fog and the trees. No matter how fast Agnes went, she couldn't catch up.

The second day was dry, so she walked through the garden and the fields beyond, breathing in the loamy wet smell of them. Every now and then, she placed her hand on a different part of her body, pressed the palm there, to see what it felt like to be on her own, her body unseen and unheard and untouched by another. It had been years, she realised.

All night, the dogs whined and the remaining horses snorted their distress. At dawn, Agnes grabbed a musket and walked outside.

(BEAT.)

I pause to wonder at Agnes's musket. Is that detail right? Is this the kind of weapon one would carry in a fairy tale? This story is true, yes, but like all stories it has its quirks, its moments of mutating and slipping from my grasp. And I know how careful I must be, amateur historian that I am. I can be wholly accurate when narrating murderous hands and the rages of men, but you will catch me out on the slightest thing, the colour of a curtain, the potato in a meal, an ill-timed musket.

So, then: Agnes grabbed a weapon and walked outside.

A wolf, a lonely wolf

Agnes was wearing a man's coat, and on her feet she wore a pair of boots Robert had given her the day before he died. The coat was too big for her, the sleeves almost covering her hands, and the boots were loose on her too. Robert had taken the laces out, saying they were a nuisance, and somehow it had felt wrong to replace them.

When she reached the stables, she saw the boy pacing next to his horse, back from hunting a full day early. Even from this distance she could see the sweat on his face, the way his hands kept clenching into fists, the tendons in his neck straining.

Then she noticed it, the second horse, the awful bulk draped sideways over the saddle. The third horse was gone.

The earth rumbled underneath her again. She felt its moan in her knees, so loud it almost brought her down. The weapon slipped from her hands. Agnes swallowed the thin air, searched for words, failed to find any.

The boy looked at her. His eyes were clear, his lips thick and wet, the hair on his chin coarser, longer, curlier. He put a hand on the horse's neck and spoke softly. 'Something attacked us,' he said. 'In the woods. It was dark. I couldn't see.'

Agnes felt the coat slip from her shoulders before she realised she was heading for the ground too, falling with it. She took a few lurching steps towards the horse before her knees gave. Her hands wanted to reach for that shape on the horse, and at the same time she wanted to touch the boy, bare his skin and look for wounds to tend to, search for scratches to kiss better, ask where does it hurt. 'Have you been injured?' she asked, and he almost laughed at her, his lips quirking up before he could take hold of himself and furrow his brow like he'd seen people do when distressed. 'I'm fine.' A pat on the horse's neck again, a glance at the awful shape. 'It's Father.'

Malcolm was draped over the horse's saddle on his chest, arms dangling. The boy or maybe the rain had washed his face clean of blood and grime – Agnes had not known the boy to be so merciful.

You flinch, now, and I can already see the dark look in your eye, the seed of an idea there, that old boyish thing.

I carry on.

Malcolm's hair was wet. Agnes touched it, brought a tuft to her lips, kissed it.

'Agnes,' the boy started, and this time his voice sounded heavy to her, some lump obstructing his throat – was it guilt? Shame? Grief? He'd even used her name.

She held up her hand to hush him. She didn't want to hear from him. Not now. Not this time.

There was no way she could carry the man to his bed, and she had no intention of leaving him out in the cold or in the barn with the beasts until the men came the following day. She took the horse's reins from the boy's hand and led the animal to the front door, then up the great steps and right into the house.

The horse followed her reluctantly, its large body out of place on the stairs, its heavy breath a challenge to the house's silence.

A little more coaxing and they were at the threshold of the lord's bedroom – her bedroom. Malcolm's head hung off the side of the horse. A small panic gripped her; would the horse fit through the door? She ran her palm over its velvety snout and pulled on the reins. It stepped over the threshold. Agnes breathed out.

As gently as she could, she slid Malcolm off the animal and onto the bed, then rolled him onto his back and slowly stripped him of his clothes.

It was only then that she could see the full extent of the damage his body had sustained – his torso was a mess of bruises and cuts. One arm was shredded from the elbow down, hanging by a few threads of tendon and sinew. A sweet, putrid scent like fermented apples rose from him.

Distantly, she noticed that the horse was no longer in the room. Instead, the boy stood in the doorframe, his head tilted, arms at his sides, his father's keys already hanging around his waist. When had he taken them?

The boy observed her. This grief. She hadn't expected it, or not so soon – hadn't felt it the day Robert died, or when her mother died before him. She had felt it with the baby, yes. But she wouldn't think of him now.

'Wolves,' the boy said, and then corrected himself. 'A lone wolf. Set his sights on our prey.'

What prey? Agnes thought. The boy had brought back no kill; no felled deer, no bundle of birds, not even a rabbit. Only his father.

The worst wound was on Malcolm's neck. The flesh there was torn open, as if something had taken a bite out of him. Agnes touched his neck with a trembling hand, felt the cold skin and the gaping hole. She hauled herself up on the bed and lay next to the man, his chin grasped in her hand. She teased his face towards her own. His eyes were closed – whose mercy was this? Not the rain's – and his face was serene, as if he had simply slunk into a black and bottomless sleep. She leaned closer and kissed him. His lips parted slightly at her touch, and a forest smell spilled out. Something moved inside her – a gag, a sob – and yet she reached for his mouth, pried it open with her fingers. It was full of leaves. She started pulling them out, handful after handful of wet leaves coming up from deep inside his throat, more and more, as if the forest itself had passed through him.

When people asked her what had happened, she repeated the boy's story about the lone wolf that mauled a man, drunk on the scent of prey.

She never said anything about the leaves, that autumn in his mouth.

At night, she dreamed of the river again. She was drowning, along with all the dead animals, the water soaking her skin and hair. Together they floated, a dead overflow tumbling towards the sea.

And then Agnes was awake, her body still above the covers, her lungs pulling in air, despite everything.

The boy lay next to her, fast asleep. His breathing was slow and deep. She watched him for a long time, her chest crushed with something warm and vast.

She did find bruises on the boy's body that couldn't have been caused by any wolf. His hair was long now, touching his shoulders. When had it gotten that long?

The boy let Agnes tend to him, clean his body the way she'd cleaned his father's, run her fingers over the little veins that spider-webbed outwards from his black and blue. He didn't speak another word about what had happened, and neither did Agnes.

The morning of the funeral, her whole body ached as if she were the one who'd wrestled the wolf. She could hear the creaking of steps, the repeated thud of the front door, the whisper of voices in the house as people got everything ready. The wind was coming in from the south; she could smell it in the air, that warm marshy scent. The whole house was laced with it. The taste of salt and mud filled her mouth and she sat up, reached for the glass of water on her nightstand to wash it out, but something startled her. The glass slipped from her hand and fell to the floor. Impossibly, it didn't shatter.

At first Agnes thought she saw Malcolm, his body wrapped in sheets, his face a bloody lump. But it was a woman who stood at the door of Agnes's bedroom. She wore a white coat and a veil over her face. Her feet were bare, which surprised Agnes even more than the woman's uninvited presence in her room.

Then the woman lifted her veil. It was the boy's mother. Was she still mistress of the house? This room had been hers long before it was Agnes's. Had she come to claim her place now that the lord was gone?

As if reading her mind, the woman lifted her hand. 'I'm not staying,' she said.

Agnes swallowed. 'The funeral is today.'

The woman didn't show any emotion. 'I'm sure you have arranged everything.'

'I have.'

The woman's eyes flicked to the right, as if she'd seen something there. Agnes followed her gaze but saw nothing. 'And the boy?' the woman asked.

The boy. Nobody called him that. He was the boy only to Agnes.

'Your son?' Agnes replied. Something sharp slipped into her voice without her noticing. 'You should talk to him. Comfort him. It's what mothers do.'

The woman's mouth twisted briefly – a moment of emotion, too light-footed for Agnes to catch and inspect it. 'I'm sure you'll do a better job of that than I ever could.'

A compliment wrapped in thorns. 'Then why are you here? If not for the funeral and not for your son?' Agnes asked.

The woman took some time before replying. She ran her hand over the doorframe, cast her gaze around the room with something like fondness. 'Leave, Agnes,' she said. 'If you still can, leave.'

Everybody leaves him, Agnes thought. Could I? And then: How could I?

'Never,' she replied, putting the unbroken glass back on the nightstand. 'Not ever.'

The funeral was a quick and muted affair. The boy's mother slipped away before anyone knew she had returned, but everyone else came to see Lord Malcolm off. The whole village, dressed in black. Agnes stared at their faces, these people she used to know. Their names escaped her. Nobody spoke, though she was aware of their eyes on her. They must have had opinions about her. She didn't care.

Agnes walked with the procession and then she bent next to the casket and kissed Malcolm's lips one last time – they were cold and felt like dirt to her now. She thought of the leaves. Something moved in the distance – she could feel it there, watching her. The forest, perhaps. The animals.

Slowly, Malcolm's body was lowered into the empty hole in the ground. It had turned out there was a will, and it stipulated he wanted no priest at his funeral. If this scandalised the villagers, no one said anything; and, after all, they still came. Some threw flowers onto the casket, white hyacinths and common bluebells.

Cook cried. The boy looked on, his face impenetrable. He stood next to Agnes, and she could hear his calm breathing. When the first shovelful of soil hit the casket, he reached for her hand.

(NOON LIGHT, HARSH.)

Do you think she made it, I ask them, in the end? Agnes. The woman who raised him.

The ghosts pretend they don't understand me. I sense they're mad at me.

Is it my accent? I tease.

They don't respond. They fuss with their costumes or braid each other's hair instead, fix their exaggerated make-up, meant to be seen from the last row of a big theatre. The lighting in the apartment does them no favours. They crave something more flattering: a bastard amber or a flesh pink.

They say, *Talk about something else*, or so I think.

Cook, or What's in a name?

The solicitor came the very next day to oversee the transfer of Malcolm's estate. The little lord got everything: the many houses his father owned across the country, the land, the horses, the title. Agnes didn't have any official relationship to the lord. She had merely been his child's minder, now redundant in more ways than one. Yet she was offered a small allowance and the right to continue living on the property for as long as she desired. The solicitor also gave the little lord a ring that had belonged to his father, though Agnes herself had never seen it before. The ring was engraved with Malcolm's initials, flanked by two tiny rubies. The boy slipped it onto his finger. He would never take it off again.

The little lord took on his new role the same way he'd taken the ring – slipped it on with natural ease, surprising no one. He was sixteen.

Cook left a few weeks later. When Agnes asked her why, she said she couldn't bear it, this house, the silence. The boy. Agnes didn't argue, though she pretended not to understand what the old woman meant. She paid Cook an extra month, and wished her well.

The boy insisted Agnes continue sleeping in Malcolm's room. She objected, but not for long, and not hard enough. He watched her sleep – gradually, she became convinced he was always awake, that he never slept at all, though his face remained forever untroubled and calm. She would talk to him sometimes, to hear another living voice, but he rarely responded, and when he did it was with one word and no more. He never left the house.

The boy was the forest, she thought. He was the river and the land.

The house filled with his smell, and strange things occurred: the food in the pantry went bad too fast; the chickens laid eggs that contained nothing but blood; the dogs turned feral and ran away.

Dead birds fell on their doorstep every day, as if they were pulled to the house, compelled to crush themselves on its bulk. Agnes scooped them up, tenderly at first – she even buried some in the garden under the roses – but eventually she got so used to their dead eyes and stiff little wings she simply swept them aside and let them crumble on the ground next to the steps. She began to think of the house as a mouth again, meant to lure the birds in. Other things, too. She thought of Robert, how he'd bent over her in the hallway, his hands tangled in her hair, their bodies pressed together. Had he been lured in? Had she?

In the end, Agnes forced the boy out of the house. She rarely touched him these days, but when she did, his skin felt brittle, as if he might fall apart under her fingers. Outside, he walked the gardens, reluctantly at first, and then he ran in circles through the fields and the tall grass, whirling his arms and shouting at the sky. He seemed so childish to her, then. The red-haired girl joined him, sometimes.

Agnes found herself fleeing to the kitchen, walking barefoot on the stone slabs, the cold soothing her. She could almost feel

Cook sitting at the table next to her, speaking harsh, comforting words to her about perseverance and doing nothing but one's work. She tried to recreate the old woman's recipes, to get the smell just right. She dreamed often that the boy was hers.

When new staff came on to help with the estate and the harvest in the busy summer months, they asked Agnes her name, that name which had been of so little use to her since she came to this house. What good was a name to her? All she was now was the role she played in this boy's life, and she accepted that role whole-heartedly. Except the boy had long stopped needing a wet nurse. So who was she to be?

She told them to call her Cook. She spent most of her time in the kitchen anyway. Yet the boy often called her Mother these days, and she didn't object to that either. She simply said yes.

I've heard that later, much later – after the boy and the girl had left and come back, but before they left again – when someone asked Agnes if she'd known what he was all along, and why she hadn't done anything about it, she said: We love the children we are given.

(KITCHEN WINDOW, BRIGHT.)

Without a word, you shuffle to the kitchen. You loot the fridge and make yourself a sandwich, because of course you're hungry, and of course you need to eat. There's still so much living to do here, in this body of yours, and isn't that always the problem with grief? You put your beloved in the ground and you still have to fill your stomach eventually. Your bones are broken, your neck in pieces, your heart bruised blue, but every day the sun shines audacious outside.

The window casts a cross along your face as you handle the sharp kitchen knife, and I trail behind you, anxious, useless. Should you be handling knives? I don't ask it, cower from your big-boy protests. You are almost ten years old, you'd say – which is to say nine, not even ten. Your hair has gotten so long, blue-black curls down to your shoulders. When did it get so long? How did I not notice? Does it grow unnaturally fast? I need to take you for a haircut soon, I think, and almost laugh at myself.

And so, after we settle back in the living room, me in my armchair, you on the floor with your back to the sofa and your sandwich on your lap, the ghosts pacing quietly in our orbit, I continue:

When he told me the story of himself, he said that as a boy he liked horses the best. They were eager and fast, their eyes

60

fearless and bright, their skin strong and thin and covered with a sleek layer of sweat. His father's steed was the fastest of all. He remembered its smooth muscles under his hand, the way it heaved beneath him with every sprint. Horses were so easy to be around – people say they spook easily, but they didn't, not with him. They were one of the few animals that accepted him for what he was – whatever he was. They didn't mind his smell, either.

He'd always lived in the house, so the house was his. The fields felt like home, too, and he told me he was born there, on the cold clay ground, to a wet nurse called Agnes. He was a baby, a boy, a man, a lord. He was the forest and the river.

'I don't understand,' you say. You chew slowly, thoughtfully, with your mouth closed, like I taught you, like the good boy you are. 'How can a boy be a forest? How can a man be a river?'

The boy, the man, the lord

The stories Agnes told him were the only ones he ever knew: stories of warm milk, earth, late-summer grass. Of curses broken, if only one were loved enough. When he was small, Agnes cradled him, and he watched the way she chewed her lip as she thought up her tales. There was the story of the prince who could leap over the highest castle walls and ride dragons he had tamed himself; the princess who sang the birds down from the trees, who could kill with a single look, who found her true love in the depths of the sea, in the belly of a fish; the man with wings so strong he could fly to the moon; the woman with ears so sharp she could hear the voices of the trees. The stories changed the more she told them. The prince slew the dragon; the princess's song turned birds to stone. The wings were gifts, given to the boy by his father. He did fly to the moon, but the moon had a taste for flesh; it ate the boy alive. The sea was a liar.

His father felt like such a man to him, conjured up by a fairy tale: a face like an old gauntlet, like a horse's hoof, like bark. By the time he told me this story, all he remembered of his mother was the pain in her voice when she said his name, her throat sculpted into a small, blind tunnel. People said that the little lord was a dark thing, a cursed thing that only brought misery and plague. It was better she left. Left him.

His own body felt like a pitch-black room with no door, no window. His skin was cold and hard. He could always smell a storm on the horizon, and his sinews tightened like ropes when danger was near, his blood foaming like a frightened horse's mouth. He hunted at night, alone, his eyes as keen as those of nocturnal beasts.

The little lord knew everyone in the house and all the children by their smells. With time, he trained himself to remember their names, too, because Agnes insisted he should. 'It's what people do,' she said. It's not what we do, he wanted to tell her, is it? We need no names. Aren't we people? Names felt to him like skins, containers that could themselves be removed, repurposed, replaced. He learned this girl's, though, the girl that would become his wife. It was Eunice.

He rolled that name around in his mouth sometimes, like sour candy: Eunice. Eunice.

But he had enjoyed the company of children. He thought of them, now that he was fatherless, motherless, friendless. He sat in his father's study, his hands flat on the table. They'd almost accepted him, hadn't they? At one point. For a time.

The day Eunice's brother was hurt, the children were playing a game they'd devised themselves, and they let the little lord be part of it, at which he rejoiced, surprising himself. It was a simple game, as games that involve only a single piece of rope tend to be. The children tied him up with the rope and threw stones at him. It was simple, truly, the simplest game there is. The sun shone hot, but the ground was cold – it was not yet fall. The children ran around him, and then they knelt by his feet. They asked him if he could feel the grass, ordered him to run barefoot to prove he could. They told him they would take him to the river and make him walk in, still tied with the rope, and stay under the water so they could see if he would live or drown, if his forest mother would come claim him, save him. They smiled, and he wanted to smile, too, but he couldn't. He looked at the trees, at their branches, the leaves, the bark, at the wind on the leaves, the sun. His eyes hurt, but he knew he couldn't close them, not now, not ever. All would be lost if he did. If he closed his eyes, the world would disappear.

Then that boy grabbed him. Didn't he?

He couldn't remember what happened next, and whether the dogs were already there or whether he called them somehow. But a little girl said he'd done something to them, provoked them, made them do his bidding. They had been there when it mattered, in any case. There was no barking, was there? No snarling, either – only that boy's head in their mouths. And screaming.

He wondered: was his mother there for this or had she already left him by then?

The little lord – not so little any more, a man almost – tapped his knee, slid his father's ring off his finger and then back on, moved his father's ink bottle to one side of the desk, then the other. He was glad he couldn't remember. Memory doesn't always offer the best counsel.

Through the window, he saw Eunice step into the garden, dressed in black for his father. He asked her once why she wouldn't take off the black – it'd been months. 'He was kind to me,' she had said. Was he? When? He hadn't seen it. Had his father been kind to him, too? When?

There it was, now, her knock on the front door. He left the

study and headed downstairs to find Agnes letting in the girl, then going back to her kitchen without another glance.

Eunice embraced him. Her hands were cold, her cheeks, too. They went out into the garden together, into a nook where they knew Agnes couldn't see them. She didn't watch them the way she used to any more, and they no longer needed to hide, but the habit stuck. They sat on the cold stone, their bodies huddled together. He had understood early that he was supposed to act a certain way around the girl. So much hung in that balance, so many unspoken things, such truces. She smelled of mint and soap, of milk and blood. Sometimes he thought he wanted to eat her, to suck on her flesh and drink the marrow from her bones. But he was afraid he'd scare her, if he ever spoke of such things. So he simply stayed close, breathing in her scent.

Eunice took his hands in hers and looked him in the eyes. She smelled of blackberries, too, he thought, and the village's fires. 'How are you feeling?' she asked, and, when he didn't reply, prompted him again: 'Do you miss him?'

She meant his father. It felt odd and significant at the same time: this was a moment that should teach him something. The question meant: a boy should miss his dead father. A good son.

He breathed in, a shuddering in his chest.

'You say he was kind,' he told her. 'But he was not kind.' His voice was bass, it was gravel. It was the river and its banks.

A breeze passed between them, rustling the dead leaves on the ground. Eunice leaned back, studying his face. Her eyes were wide-set, her mouth small. He reached for her stunned face with his hand, and she flinched. His long, sharp nails nicked her cheek. He drew blood.

The girl's hand covered her cheek. He pulled back, heat

rising in him. Without a moment's thought, he tore his clean shirt and dabbed her blood with it.

'I'm sorry,' he said, 'I'm so sorry. Does it hurt?' and she kept shaking her head, denying her own pain as her eyes streamed.

He filed down his nails more diligently after that.

Later, he sat with Agnes in the great room and they ate together. He watched the fire, he watched the door, the wall. Agnes, as always, watched him. He pushed the food around on his plate, like he used to when he was a child and acted difficult so she would feed him.

'You're not hungry,' she said.

'No.' It was true, he wasn't.

Her eyes were small and deep. They saw everything. 'You didn't mean to hurt her,' she said, and his hand flew to his lap immediately, as if burned by the fork.

Of course she'd noticed his filed nails. Of course, of course.

'You're trying your best,' she said.

It rang hollow in his ears. False.

I pause because I see something happening behind your face. You open your mouth, close it, then try again. You ask me if you did something wrong this morning, to make him angry, to make him leave. You think it was your fault.

I remember his face, after the blow, after the crack. Look what you made me do, he said. Like he'd said before.

Not your fault, I tell you. Again and again. Not your fault, never your fault. You did nothing wrong.

Now listen:

The little lord left Agnes in the great room and returned to his father's study. He took out the ledger his father had kept, which he'd discovered after his death – that day in the woods, he would not think of it, that head hanging over the saddle, swinging, he would not – and which he had been studying since, trying to decode its contents. He flipped through pages and pages of entries, dated and numbered in his father's neat cursive. The entries rarely included names – just, 'the child', and 'the girl', and, occasionally, 'A' – but it was not difficult to surmise whom his father was writing about. There were no great conclusions drawn, no pronouncements about anything, only observations of the most mundane things: their comings and goings, what they wore, what they smelled like, what they ate.

There were descriptions of the boy's mother, too, and those he cherished the most. They were both more elaborate and more dispassionate than the rest, almost clinical. They detailed her moods, her comportment, the number of hours she sat alone by the window, how many glasses of water she drank, what her complexion looked like in a given day's weather conditions. He wondered if such things could truly capture his mother. Milky, sallow, transparent – did such words contain anything of hers? He thought not. It was madness, surely, for a man to watch his wife grow old and desperate with a child beside her, to write about her in such detail and still not know her at all. There were snippets of dialogue, too, things she said, like: 'I shall not look at you,' and 'Where does a mother's heart grow, then? Does it grow with the child in her belly? Does it grow in the river, in the fields?' and 'Malcolm, I am scared of our son.'

The boy had always known that last one, of course.

'Your mother is not well,' Agnes had told him, once. 'You cannot hate her for it. You can blame her, and you should know none of it is your fault, but you cannot hate her. You hear me? You cannot do that.'

He'd nodded then. He remembered that.

Eunice came back the next day, and the day after, and the day after. The world slowly warmed and bloomed around them, the grass turned green and the birds sang in the trees. The girl still wore black, so out of place on their walks through the woods, this solemn figure amidst the mad flowers. On one of their walks, they found a meadow and settled on the soft grass, his back to the trunk of a tree, the girl in his arms, her delicate shoulders pressing against his chest. Eunice had brought a small book and read to him, about a prince and a woman with no voice. They lived in a palace, his mother and father were dead, and the prince was sometimes a bear.

Her voice was like honey, so sweet he barely noticed the words.

'Why do you wear black, still?' he asked her. Suddenly he wanted the black off her. Wanted it more than anything.

She lowered the book, laid it flat on the grass and turned to face him. She thought about her answer for a few moments. 'I don't know,' she said. 'Out of respect.' Then, thinking better of it, corrected: 'For you.'

'For me?'

She touched the fabric of her dress. Felt its texture.

'I think you are upset by your father's death, but, for whatever reason, you cannot show it. And so, I can share this grief with you. Wear black for you.'

'On my behalf?'

She nodded.

He palmed her shoulder. It felt so small in his large hand. When did his hands get so large? 'I don't want you to,' he said. 'I want you to wear the colours you like, and no others. Not for me.'

She stared at him, her eyes big, her lips red, so red. He leaned in; wanted his mouth on those lips.

They parted for him, and she breathed deeply.

He moved back. 'Do you want me to stop?' he asked.

She shook her head. His hand pushed the black of her dress off her shoulders, off her body. Rid her of it.

Later, he asked the girl, 'How did you know what to do? With your mouth, with your body?'

Eunice hesitated before answering, sensing, perhaps, the trap buried in the question. 'I've done such things before,' she said.

'With whom?' he asked.

'With Anne, of course,' she replied. She meant one of the girls who came from the village. Did Eunice have such close friends? Had he been told that name before? Maybe. Soon, it slipped his mind again.

The crops died again after that. This time, the boy told himself, I shall stop this blight. He put his hands on the soil and thought he felt something surge through him and seep into the land. But the blight didn't stop. Later, he told himself he hadn't tried hard enough. Later still, he told himself he hadn't really wanted to.

How young he was back then, how in awe of it all.

You inspect your own hands, now. You wonder, perhaps, if they look like his, and I want to tell you, no, don't worry, they don't. They don't.

The ghosts accuse me of lying. They say: *He never felt bad for anything. Never apologised for anything. Why are you making excuses? Still, after everything?*

Soon, Eunice moved in to live with him and Agnes. It didn't please Agnes, but she didn't object. These days, she kept her thoughts to herself.

The crops continued to wither, the world warping around them. Horses died in their stalls, which pained the boy greatly, but he survived. The dogs gave birth to litters of wolf pups. The pestilence spread again to the surrounding area, the village, the villagers. Strange things occurred: A young girl's skin started peeling off her bones and no one could do a thing about it; a man was strangled by his own hair. The wells gushed with bile, and the flowers smelled of nothing at all.

The villagers came to him, begged him to fix it. Fix what, he wanted to ask; this is the way of the world. He told them he would try. He would do his best.

The crops kept dying, the soil hard as rock. 'How will we eat?' the villagers returned to ask him, as if he should know. It didn't occur to him to show them to his storage rooms.

Somehow, they all grew older. The house grew with them, the rooms sprouting like new branches, the breath of the forest pushing its way inside, down the long corridors, into the kitchen, where Agnes cooked unrecognisable things that tasted of sour cherries. The boy ate them in silence; the girl didn't eat at all.

The river swelled. The wild lands beyond the estate drew closer, until the manor was surrounded by a dense forest, and the river had become as vast as the sea. He should have been able to do something. He should have known what to do. His father would have. Did.

In his despair, the boy visited the graveyard where his father lay buried. He walked numbly among the gravestones, the flowers wilted and curled to brown, the air thick with the smell of rot, the silence of the dead as loud as ever.

His father's tombstone was half-covered in moss and soil. He stared at the name on the stone for a long time, marvelling at the concept of it, the idea of marking the earth with something of such inconsequence. His father was not here – and yet, all the boy wanted was to stay here, where his father remained.

'Did you curse me?' the boy asked his father.

He touched the stone. It was icy beneath his fingers. He fell to the ground and sobbed and begged for guidance. He received none; the grave was mute, the soil too. His eyes dried quickly.

The next time the villagers came, they did not come seeking advice or charity. They came with pitchforks, with torches and knives; they came for someone to blame. At first, they didn't storm the house but simply gathered in the yard like a flock of crows. They waited. They carried cages and pitched tents on wooden poles to sleep in. Eunice peeked through the windows at them. She knew all of them, but they no longer knew her.

In the end, of course, they broke in. They dragged the boy outside and threw him on the ground. They beat him with sticks and stones while Eunice screamed and Agnes watched, tears streaming quietly from her eyes. He felt so little. Didn't even defend himself; he just let them do what they willed. They tired faster than he had expected. They left him there in the mud, and he remained motionless as the crowd dispersed, taking their cages and pitchforks with them. Agnes and Eunice came to fetch him after. He never found out what the cages were for.

The next day, he left his bed and went down to the village. The dead littered the streets, the stench of decay so strong it nearly took his breath away. No one came out to attack him this time, and from behind the closed doors he heard the low-pitched songs of mourning.

Another attack would come, he knew, sooner or later. When people have nothing, hurt is all they have.

'We need to leave,' Eunice told him. Begged him.

He said yes.

It makes him sound like a victim, doesn't it, this telling? Almost makes me feel sorry for him. Almost.

He implored Agnes to come with them in turn. He fell to his knees and grasped her hands. Eunice looked away, as if to shield her eyes from his begging. But Agnes shook her head. She disentangled her hands from the boy's and cast her eyes over the great room. She said she'd stay with the house. As if the house were not a thing – not even a mouth or a wound – but a person.

And he? He let her go. Told himself he'd never needed her at all.

The carriage moved through groves and forests and towns. Eunice read to him. Sometimes she cried. She wore red, blue, pink. No black any more, not ever. Is this love? he wondered. He thought it might be a mercy if he threw himself out of the carriage and moved on alone. He could go north, as far north as possible, leave Eunice behind. Save her from himself, and from whom she would become with him.

They got married on the way, in a chapel on the side of the road, their whole household packed and waiting outside, the one horse he had allowed himself – the most beautiful brown steed – grazing on the frost-bitten grass. The priest was a short man with a long beard. He eyed them, asked if they had anyone to witness for them, and they told him they did not. But the girl was wearing white, and the boy-man was in black. The priest left them in the chapel to breathe in the frankincense and be weighed up by the golden saints and their angels armed with flaming swords. When the priest came back, he was with a stooped woman, her head covered with a brown cloth.

'She'll be your witness,' the priest said. 'When you leave here, you will be man and wife.'

The man couldn't explain how he chose the place they'd settle down in, what it was that made him look at the sleepy town and say, Here, this is where we'll make our life. Perhaps it was how little it reminded him of the landscapes of his childhood: no dense forest to court the town, no river nearby. The house he picked was not a cold mansion made of slabs of ancient stone; its walls were not decorated with strange paintings of beasts devouring their own heads and silk-clad ladies worshipping at their feet. It was a small, simple thing, between two other similar houses. It was owned by an old widow who lived two streets away. From the top floor, he could see the fields: golden wheat and red poppies and nothing else. A land untouched by rot.

Eunice wept as their things were carried into the house. The man didn't know why she cried, and it didn't occur to him to ask. He took her shoulders in his hands and kissed her forehead, told her, 'Don't cry, don't cry.' He wiped her tears with his manicured fingers and she bunched his hair in her fist until it hurt. 'My love,' he said.

She promised she would never leave him.

Life was strange without Agnes, but he grew accustomed to it quickly enough. Together, he and his wife built a household of their own: they hired a cook, a housekeeper, someone to tend to the horse. They took long walks through town, dressed in their finery, things they found in his father's dusty boxes and chests: lace collars and coats hemmed with gold-twined thread, alabaster pins, buttons made of mother-of-pearl. The towns-people eyed them when they stepped into their shops. There was always a moment of silence before the chatter resumed, and it was that moment of silence that set them so clearly apart from everyone else. He relished it, though he couldn't say why.

The town itself was quiet, peaceful. The fields spread over the plains that surrounded it as far as the eye could see, and, when the wind blew, it was the only sound. He liked to lose himself in the town's streets, to discover new corners hidden between its narrow cobblestone alleys, then emerge again to watch the slow sinking of the sun among that sea of wheat.

On one of these walks, he found a curious shop, its window lined with shelves and each shelf filled with the most exquisite things: urns made of crystal and filled with an unidentifiable blue powder, candles shaped like a man's hand, chalices holding colourful feathers so bright they made his eyes water, and other objects the likes of which he'd never seen before and which he could not possibly name. He was charmed by the shop, the strange and pointless beauty. He stood in the open doorway and watched a tall, soft-jawed man with eyes that glittered place the tiny figurine of a woman on a shelf. The woman was nude and posed as if she were about to jump into a pond.

It took a while for the Shopkeeper to notice him. When he did, he smiled widely and openly. The Shopkeeper was young. Perhaps, the man thought, not much older than himself.

'See anything you like?' the Shopkeeper asked, and it felt like an invitation, so he allowed himself to look around freely, to be enchanted by this much fragile beauty: a bird with a key on its back; a vase of white porcelain so delicate it seemed to have been carved from a cloud; a comb made from the spine of a fish.

He bought the comb. As he left the shop, the man smiled his warm-eyed smile once more. He said, 'Come again.'

When the man returned home that night, he presented his wife with the comb but didn't mention the Shopkeeper. Eunice studied the fine, strange thing for a while. She had delicate hands, but the comb seemed too delicate to be handled even by fingers as fine as hers. 'What is it for?' she asked.

He took the comb gently, as Eunice stood, watching him, holding her breath. He brushed back her red hair and pushed the comb's teeth through it, then caressed her cheek, carefully, with the backs of his fingers.

Eunice grasped his hand and kissed the palm. She didn't seek a mirror to look at herself. 'It's beautiful,' she whispered.

They lay together on the sofa of their new living room. Wondered at this new life of theirs and everything it could hold.

(AFTERNOON, SOFTLY.)

I recall the first time I entered his living room. It was after a show, something Victorian with twenty-first century sensibilities. I had changed out of my costume, but he asked me to keep my make-up on. I said yes.

The first thing I noticed when I walked in was the cabinet of curiosities in the corner, filled with the strangest, most delicate things. It was a different apartment, then, but the cabinet was the same, except now there are more things in it. He told me to come closer, opened it for me to appreciate the beautiful things he collected. Perhaps that should have been a clue. He has always been a collector.

I walk over to that cabinet now, unlock the glass door and pick up a small rabbit made of clear crystal. It feels like nothing on my palm, but the gesture makes you gasp – we're not supposed to touch. Only to look.

I return to my armchair.

It's all right, see? Nothing bad happened.

The rabbit is still in my hand. It refracts the soft light, and a knot gathers around my navel, because the day has slipped into afternoon. Was I supposed to meet someone today? Yes. My friend, Nadya, your godmother. This is our little system, my failsafe. If I miss our weekly date after her morning show with no word, it means something is wrong. If I miss it, she must come.

I think of the first time Nadya and I worked together, back before you were born, back when I still worked. Our dresses were white, the stage bare. There were many doors. What a private foreboding, I thought later, after I met him, after the ghosts. An oracle so cryptic – who could have deciphered it?

I imagine leaving here. Getting into a car, meeting Nadya downtown, embracing in the street, then a drink near the sea, the breeze in our hair, this place forgotten, this morning forgotten. What was it? Just a story.

The things we collect

The next day, he ordered a cabinet made of the sturdiest glass to hold the precious things he was meant to possess. He returned to the shop daily and bought all kinds of objects: a crystal vase, a small box filled with dried flowers, a candle that smelled like oranges and looked like a dog, a figurine of a young man with his hands on his hips, and a bird that, when wound up, sang a complicated and sad song about a young woman who fell in love with a wolf and whose father, to protect her from the beast's jaws, built her into a wall. The process of selecting the objects felt to him like a kind of education, each choice containing a lesson in surprise, a knowing of the self through the objects one wished to possess: and today, he thought to himself, what will I take?

The Shopkeeper was pleased with the man's choices. 'You have interesting taste,' he told the man one day while wrapping up the curious things in thin white paper.

The man didn't know how to respond to that, so he simply handed the Shopkeeper his money. Their fingers brushed as the Shopkeeper accepted the coins. The man couldn't tell why, but the Shopkeeper's skin made his own shudder with pleasure, and the little hairs on the back of his neck stand on end, the way they did in the presence of unseen predators in the wooded night.

*　*　*

He didn't go back to the shop for a few days after that. At night, he lay staring at the play of moonlight on the walls, his wife's warm body curled against his back. When sleep finally claimed him, he dreamed of nothing.

One afternoon there was a knock on the door and, when the man opened it, the Shopkeeper was standing at the threshold, holding something wrapped in fine paper. He seemed so out of place there – is a shopkeeper still a shopkeeper when not at his shop?

The Shopkeeper held the wrapped object out to him. 'It's been a few days since you last stopped by the shop, and this came in,' he said, his voice full of nervous snags. 'I thought you should see it before someone else claims it. I thought you'd like it.'

He blinked. 'How did you know where I live?' he asked, and then, as if remembering his wife, corrected himself. 'Where we live?'

The Shopkeeper crinkled his nose and the corner of his lip lifted up into a smile that implied he was surely being teased. 'My lord,' he said. 'Everyone knows where you live.'

It felt odd to be called 'lord' by this man, though that's what most people called him in those days. He invited the Shopkeeper in.

The Shopkeeper examined the living room openly, without the reservation one might expect from a stranger stepping into a rich man's house for the first time. The Shopkeeper let his gaze roam over the wallpaper – green leaves on red – and the furniture, the tables, the chairs. He spotted the cabinet and walked excitedly to it. Most of its treasures came from his shop, and that seemed to fill him with not a small amount of pleasure.

The man motioned for the Shopkeeper to sit and meet his

wife, who joined them. She served them tea and biscuits sweetened with honey.

'You're not from here,' the Shopkeeper said, accepting the tea. 'Where are you from?'

The lord shifted where he sat, but Eunice rested her hand on her husband's knee.

'We travelled from far away,' she answered.

'How come?' the Shopkeeper asked.

Instead of replying, she nodded towards the wrapped object. 'I believe you brought us something for my husband's collection? How thoughtful of you.'

The Shopkeeper chewed a bit of biscuit and wiped his hands on his trousers before handling the item. 'Yes, of course,' he said. 'How silly I am.' Carefully, he handed her the parcel. 'Please.'

Eunice unwrapped the offering slowly. It was a wooden box, simple and unadorned. Inside, there was an assortment of clay figures: one holding a basket, another holding a flower. Smaller ones, too – children, the man assumed. One that looked like a dog or a cat. A little lamb.

You eye me as I describe the box. You have one just like it, don't you? It was a gift from your father. This was a slip. I didn't mean to get so close. But it's too late now, and you let me go on, saying nothing.

Eunice passed the box to her husband. He ran his fingers over the lid, feeling the smoothness of the wood. It smelled faintly of cedar. The figures themselves were rather crude, but he found that made them even more attractive to him. 'You have a good eye,' he said to the Shopkeeper. 'And a good sense of what I might like.' His own voice sounded strange to him, inflected by something he could not name.

The Shopkeeper brightened. 'You do like it, then?' he asked.

'Yes,' the man said, closing the box. 'Very much.'

He paid the Shopkeeper as he showed him to the door. Before he left, the Shopkeeper touched the man's arm lightly.

'Come again by the shop,' the Shopkeeper said. 'There's more, my lord. There's always so much more.'

Afterwards, the man went back to sit on the sofa where the Shopkeeper had sat. Some of his body's warmth still lingered on the cushions. The man felt peculiar in his chest, not quite empty but not quite full. For a while, he could not speak.

Eunice studied his face. She let some time pass, sipping her tea.

'He's an interesting young man,' she said then.

'What do you think is interesting about him?'

She folded her hands on her lap while she thought about it. She said, 'He's not afraid of you.'

He looked down at his own hands. He was still holding the small box with the clay figures.

He opened it, then closed it again.

Over the following week, Eunice spent much of her time setting out the clay figurines and observing them; he caught her doing it when she thought he wasn't looking. She was smiling, content. It all brought him an unfamiliar joy, and he loved watching her arrange the people and animals and children, then rearrange them, then rearrange them once again. Sometimes she spoke to them, as if they were alive.

Eventually, he did go back to the shop. The Shopkeeper greeted him warmly, even though his words were formal.

'Welcome, my lord,' he said. 'Did you enjoy the box?'

'My wife is taking great pleasure in it. Thank you.'

The Shopkeeper nodded gracefully, and the lord had the distinct feeling they were playing some kind of game. A game of pretend, each of them assigned his special role. But to what end? Who wins in this game, he wondered, and who loses?

He realised his hand had been balled into a fist so tight his nails had dug into the skin of his own palm. No matter how scrupulously he tended to them, his nails kept growing faster than he could file them down.

He studied the store's wares. The shelves on the left were lined with ceramic vases and small figurines performing simple gestures that, rendered in clay with such passion, were made to seem like great feats: a boy about to set a bird free, a goose chasing after a fox, a woman cutting down a tree.

There was a marked smell in the air: wood shavings and wax. On the right, silk scarves and a little glass cabinet filled with painted wooden boxes. None were like the one the Shopkeeper had brought to the house.

'See anything you like?' the Shopkeeper asked; the exact words he'd used when the man had first set foot in the shop.

'Anything you'd suggest?' he countered. He found he was more interested in what the Shopkeeper thought he might like, than in what he actually did.

The Shopkeeper tapped a finger on his lips, thinking, or pretending to think. Then, he disappeared to the back of the shop for a few minutes and returned with a small wooden horse sitting on his palm, its ears perked up, its saddle painted a cheerful, bright red.

'How did you know I like horses?' the lord asked.

The Shopkeeper smiled, his teeth white against the light brown of his lips. 'I didn't,' he said.

The lord started to open his purse to pay, but the Shopkeeper waved the purse away. 'No, no,' he said. 'Please. This one's a gift.'

The lord shook his head, unable to understand – offended, almost. 'But I can afford it,' he protested. He barely stopped himself from jingling his purse in the Shopkeeper's face, to prove how much he could afford it.

The Shopkeeper laughed beautifully, his dark eyes narrowed with pleasure. 'Of course you can,' he said. He took the lord's hand and placed the horse on his palm, then curled his fingers around it – carefully, so as not to cut himself. 'Have it anyway.'

The man didn't show the horse to his wife, and he didn't know why. It was the only object he didn't proudly display in his cabinet, the one possession he never felt like boasting about; this he tucked away in the inner pocket of his thickest coat in the wardrobe, one he rarely wore. Every now and then, he made his way between the furs and slipped a hand inside the coat to thumb the wooden horse. He ran his fingers along its flank quickly, his heart fluttering as if he was doing something illicit.

He kept going back to the shop. The Shopkeeper showed him his new bounty of strange items: a small bear, a soldier made of obsidian, a piece of broken pottery on which a butterfly was painted in chalk. The Shopkeeper also started telling him stories, either about the objects themselves, or about the way he had procured them. Of the bear, he said: 'This one I found in the river when I was a boy. My father was very angry with me for keeping it. He threw it into the sea. But by some twist of fate, I found it again decades later, when I went fishing.' Of the soldier, he said: 'This one was a gift from my best friend. He's dead now; I miss him.' And of a locket that was not for sale: 'This one was given to me by a former lover when we parted ways.'

'Why did she leave you?' the lord asked the Shopkeeper, who raised his eyes to him and smiled.

'I left him,' the Shopkeeper said, 'because I wanted to come to this town and open this shop.'

The lord heard the words, understood.

Over the next few months, he came to know a few things about the Shopkeeper: he was proud of his shop and each item in it. He was not wealthy. He cared more about the objects finding 'good homes' than he did about making a fortune, or even a living.

Whenever the man returned home after his time at the shop, Eunice greeted him without asking where he'd been, and he never told her. He knew she had a life of her own, too. There were hidden rooms in both of them that the other would never see. He was fine with that.

One day, the Shopkeeper showed him a tiny boat made of porcelain, its sail a transparent, fragile-looking piece of paper that curled dangerously in the moisture of his palm. It had belonged to a boy who loved the sea and its secrets more than anything, the Shopkeeper said. It was given to the boy by a girl who adored him, but never understood him.

The lord couldn't help but feel as if he'd heard these stories before, or versions of them; and something queer twisted his gut. A kind of nostalgia for a world he could never truly know, for people lost and unknowable.

The Shopkeeper was bemused when the lord refused to purchase the boat. 'Are you certain?' he asked.

'I can't,' the lord said. 'It's too sad.'

The Shopkeeper smiled. 'But isn't life, too, sad?' he asked. 'Isn't that what life is, all sad things, marvellous things?'

Their exchange was cut short by a man who walked into the shop. He was clearly wealthy, with a servant in tow. The servant's eyes never left the ground, neither to admire the wares on the shelves, nor to acknowledge the other men's presence.

The Shopkeeper touched the lord's hand in a way that meant they would continue their conversation later, and greeted his new customer with a deep bow and a tight-lipped 'My lord.'

The wealthy man surveyed the objects that lined the shelves with a look of disdain. 'Are these expensive?' he asked loudly. 'Are they rare?'

'Which ones, my lord?' the Shopkeeper asked, barely managing to conceal his irritation. 'There are items for every purse, and each one carries its own value, which is not always tied to its price tag.'

The customer sneered. 'I want the most expensive things in your shop,' he said. He turned to his servant, whose eyes remained on his toes. 'That should impress her, eh? Don't you think?'

The Shopkeeper proceeded to take down a large crystal globe from the top shelf – the crystal so fine he needed to wear gloves to handle it, and could not breathe directly onto the glass for fear that it might shatter. 'This is from the low countries,' he started saying, 'fashioned by—'

'I don't care,' the customer said, cutting him off. 'Just wrap it up. I'll take it.' He considered the shelves once more, then added: 'In fact, I'll take them all.'

The Shopkeeper looked confused. 'All the globes, my lord?' he asked. 'I'm afraid I only have the one.'

'No,' the customer said, amused. 'Everything in the shop.'

The Shopkeeper swallowed audibly. 'That would be a generous purchase, my lord,' he said, 'but I like to think each item in the shop is precious and unique. A bulk purchase like the one you're proposing would diminish their true value.'

The customer glowered at the Shopkeeper. 'The purchase I am proposing?' he echoed. 'Are you refusing to serve me, good man?' The threat in the customer's voice was as palpable as it was unspoken.

The Shopkeeper took a step backwards. 'Of course not,' he said. 'I'll start wrapping everything up for you.' He paused, then added: 'It may take a while. I am going to need assistance.'

The customer shrugged and moved towards the exit. 'Not a concern. You can deliver the wares as soon as possible. My man will give you the address and settle the bill.' The customer glanced at the little boat, still in the lord's long-nailed hands, where the Shopkeeper had put it. He realised his palms were cupped protectively around that fragile sail. 'I want that, too,' the wealthy man said. 'Unless you've already purchased it, sir?'

He wanted to curl his fingers around the boat, crush it to nothing, if only to shield it from that man's gaze. 'Yes,' he said. 'I have.'

The customer raised his hand. 'Apologies, then.' He nodded at the only person in the shop he considered his peer and left.

It took three days and two extra pairs of hands to pack up the entire shop, and the Shopkeeper was in a foul mood for all of it. The lord lent the Shopkeeper a carriage, and, though the

Shopkeeper refused at first, in the end he used it to deliver the items to the customer's mansion. Then, he closed up the shop and bolted the door, though there was nothing inside to protect any more except that tiny porcelain boat.

'It will take a while to fill again,' the Shopkeeper said mournfully.

The lord put his hand on the Shopkeeper's shoulder. Something came over him; some feeling for this young man, new, untainted. He wanted to share something with him. 'Let's go away for a few days,' he said. 'To the wilderness, where no people live.'

The Shopkeeper laughed, thinking it all a joke. But the lord squeezed the Shopkeeper's shoulder and said it again, until he was sure he had been heard.

They went on horseback. The Shopkeeper held on to the lord, hands gripping his waist pleasantly. The wind was behind them, and he could smell the Shopkeeper's scent, a mix of sweat, of rosewater and of something indefinably human. The leather of the reins was warmed in his hand, and the horse's powerful beat beneath his legs lulled him into a looser grasp on time. The plains stretched around them for miles, studded by small copses of trees. A herd of deer ran before them briefly, then disappeared into the tall grass.

At last, they found themselves in a forest, near a river, a place the man knew in his bones. They were far from any town, any village, any noise. They ate persimmons and drank blackberry wine they had carried in great flasks made of sheep skin.

'They had persimmons?' you interrupt, incredulous. They are rare, in this country. When we find them in the supermarket, we stuff our bags with them. Pile them on the kitchen counter until they ripen. Have a feast.

Yes, I tell you. Why not?

In honesty, I don't know what they had. He didn't tell me such details, but, when he recounted this part of the story, he sounded so happy I cannot help but imagine it as something fantastical. A night tinted with magic.

So yes, they had persimmons. The Shopkeeper told him some people think this is the fruit the ancient Greeks called lotus. Eat it and you will forget.

They ate. Unripe, the persimmons numbed their gums.

They bathed in the river and lay together under the stars. They built a fire and talked late into the night. The Shopkeeper told his tales: of a young girl who followed the boy she loved to the end of the world, only to realise she never truly loved him. Of a woman who collected broken things and tried to mend them, all to no avail, her items always beyond repair. Of a king whose arrogance was his undoing. Of the serene life of a shepherd, who never wished to be king. Of the heir to a kingdom's throne who became an outcast. Of a fearsome beast whose heart was made of gold, and of a man whose heart was made of bone.

'These are all other people's stories,' the lord said to the Shopkeeper. 'I want to hear a story of your own.'

The Shopkeeper remained silent for a long time. Then, he spoke of how he came to this region as a young man, after a spell at a monastery in the far north; how he liked it so much he stayed. Found work on the docks of another town, learned to mend nets and sell fish. How he left that job because he started finding objects among the nets so beautiful he wanted to save them, share them.

'Is this why you decided to open the shop?' the lord asked. 'Why you decided to collect things?'

The Shopkeeper gave him a strange look. 'It was never about collecting for me,' he said. 'It was about everything the objects stood for. What, when offered, each one of them could mean.' The Shopkeeper breathed in. Then, he continued. 'My father was a shopkeeper,' he said. 'On the day he died, I was in his shop, playing at being a shopkeeper like him. He was cleaning and sorting his wares, and I was imitating him, being extra careful not to break anything. I thought I was doing a good job, but then my father turned to me abruptly and ordered me to go play outside. I didn't want to, but he insisted. I ran out of the shop but turned around every few steps to watch him. He put the bauble he was cleaning back on its shelf and sat at his bench behind the counter. Now I think he must have felt something coming. Did he know he was about to die? I watched him for a long time, or so I thought. I was young, and to the young even the smallest fractions of time tend to feel like centuries. His face was grey and his smile had disappeared. His mouth was open, his gaze distant. Then he fell. The bench collapsed behind him, and he was dead.'

The lord thought of his own father's death, then, and something made his skin crawl: the familiarity of the trip, the darkness of the night, the horse's breath. The wolf. He shuddered, shook the memory from his shoulders.

Then the Shopkeeper told him another tale, one of pestilence and grief. A tale of stone-birthing ewes, trees that sprouted mouldy fruit, ground that bled.

'Where was this?' the lord asked. 'When did it happen?' He

tried to keep his voice level, his hands calm, but the Shopkeeper noticed his agitation.

'It's just a story,' the Shopkeeper said as if apologising. 'I don't know that it's true.'

The ghosts revolt. They slap their arms, bend themselves to the floor. They huddle around the cabinet in the corner, then slip inside it and crowd behind the glass, their hair brushing all the curious little things. You don't pay them any mind, absorbed as you are in the tale, so I continue with the man's words:

'Why do you tell stories if you don't know that they're true?'

The Shopkeeper looked away. The two men were silent for a long time, listening to the sounds of the night, the whisperings of the forest, the river.

'Truth is a dangerous thing,' the Shopkeeper said eventually. 'It has teeth, which it uses to eat uncertainty, to eat possibilities. I like my stories to be just stories, and, in their telling, to leave the world with more possibility than it had before.' The Shopkeeper reached for the lord's hand.

The lord, too, thought of possibilities then, of the many different ways to tell stories, and of the monsters they can breed. He imagined that this man had seen him as he truly was. And then, he wondered: what have I showed him?

In the morning, they rode back.

Eunice greeted them with a kiss on her husband's mouth and one on the Shopkeeper's temple, a light and tender thing. The man saw something pass between them, something secret, unspoken, that he was not privy to. It surprised him, but he quickly realised it didn't trouble him. He was sure their relationship was not one of flesh – but, even if it were, he thought, what of it? He was the thing they had in common, and he understood by then that he had no knowledge of how the people in his life viewed him, no way to change their minds, and, perhaps, no reason to.

Eunice invited the Shopkeeper to their house often after that, and the three of them developed a sweet and quiet friendship, the details of which I never quite got to know, and which, even if I had, I don't have time to tell.

Almost a year passed this way and, for a while, life went on without grief. The Shopkeeper stocked his shop again, slowly, with fewer and even rarer things than before, and found solace in the fragility of his wares. The lord connected with old friends and associates of his father's. They helped him invest; his fortune grew and grew. His wife was quiet, but she did not seem unhappy. The Shopkeeper was a frequent guest at their house, and morning often found the three of them still around the dinner table, deep in laughter and conversation, clutching wine glasses, their heads light, their hearts full. And the man almost allowed himself to believe this was it: that he'd been saved, rid of the gloomy infections of his childhood, or even that he had never been to blame at all. It was the house, he told himself. It was the forest, the land itself.

But one morning he was woken by the shriek of his wife. He rushed down the stairs and out of the house to find Eunice kneeling on the dirt. His horse was on the ground next to her. She caressed its flank and cried into its mane. Foam and blood leaked from the animal's mouth. Its eyes were blank.

'Get inside,' he told her. His voice was low. It smelled of rain, of fallen leaves, of wet soil.

She did as she was told.

Something quivered inside him. Something old, rising from a slumber he had mistaken for death.

He lowered himself next to the horse and put his hand on its side, kept it there until the skin went cold beneath his fingers. His stomach churned, and he understood he wanted something broken. And what was there to break except the things closest to him?

He went to the shop and started taking things down from the shelves, ordering the Shopkeeper to wrap them for him.

The Shopkeeper put his hands on the back of the lord's broad neck and made the kind of sound you'd make to calm an animal, something wild and feral.

Was that what he was? he wondered. Was he wild? Was he feral?

He had let this man see him, the truth of him. And so, he thought: let him see this, too.

'It's all right,' the Shopkeeper said, his hands still warm on the lord's skin. 'Tell me what's wrong.'

'I want it all,' the lord said coldly. 'Everything in this shop. Whatever it costs, I'll pay it.'

The Shopkeeper thought he was joking at first: a crude joke, for sure. But then he saw something in the lord's eye that made him go silent. He started wrapping, one fragile item after another.

The lord watched him do it. The Shopkeeper's lips were pressed into a thin line, his jaw tight, eyes severe. He didn't ask for assistance this time; he wrapped the entire shop himself and even hauled the treasure to the carriage on his own.

When the job was done, the Shopkeeper stood inside his empty shop and opened his palms before the lord.

'Why?' the Shopkeeper asked.

Somebody – maybe it was Agnes, or maybe it was someone else – once said of the boy, the man, the lord: he couldn't help it. This destruction was in his nature.

At his most arrogant, he thought he knew otherwise. He imagined leaving, taking himself somewhere far away, where there was very little he could hurt. He could live alone there, seen by no one, everything around him a wasteland. Surely, he wouldn't rot the entire world. So, he could help it, he told himself, in a way. Of course he could. He just chose not to.

At his weakest, he reasoned: and wasn't that choosing in his nature, too?

(WINDOW LIGHT, ALL MANNERS OF NATURAL.)

'So he did have a choice,' you say. For the first time, you sound angry, and that scares me. 'Didn't anybody try to stop him?'

The ghosts have taken their seats at the dining table, as if preparing for a feast they know is coming. *Join us,* they whistle. They worry the scuff marks in the wood with their nails, their fingers worn raw. A single lily is wilting in the vase, orange dust underneath it and everywhere the smell of standing water.

Join us, join us.

The phone rings. It's Nadya calling, I'm sure – because I'm late, so late. The ghosts cover their ears against the intrusion of the sound.

But don't you see? I ask them. I'm not like you. Someone cares for me. I am not yet forgotten.

'Should I answer it?' you ask, but I tell you no, please, don't.

Nadya will come looking.

The ghosts laugh, not unkindly, despite my own cruelty. *Bad things happen when women go looking in this story,* they say, *like in every other story. Don't you know this?*

I turn to you.

We don't have much time. I need to tell you what comes next.

Strange weather

The man never saw the Shopkeeper again, and his wife rarely mentioned him. Sometimes he thought he spotted the Shopkeeper in a crowd, a glimpse here and there, but, when the crowd parted, it was never him. His cabinet of curiosities overflowed with items he found in other shops, other towns and villages, and in the fields themselves, offered up by the land.

The weather turned strange; it was the talk of the town. The sun set early, and the rains, when they came, carried with them the scent of decay. The fishmonger complained he couldn't get fish for his shop any more; fishermen's nets came up empty, or, worse, full of stones. The plains around the town grew soft, then muddy, then bubbled with green sludge that teemed with tiny red worms.

The townspeople whispered about it, muttering under their breath, afraid to meet each other's eyes, afraid of the answers they might find there. But at night, they talked among themselves, in the tavern and under the tree in the square. It's a contagion, they said. A plague. A pestilence. It's the punishment for our sins. It's God's will, they said. It's the end of the world.

When Eunice took the man's hand and told him they had to move, he simply nodded. For a while, he'd thought this day wouldn't come. Now he knew it was always coming, and everything else had been a tale he told himself, like a child. People are who they are, what they are, he thought. Who was he to change it? Who was he to be saved?

The new place they moved to was on the edge of a town where they knew no one, and no one knew them. He bought a big house by the river with a garden and enough room for several horses. He placed his cabinet in the corner of the living room. He'd had everything wrapped in tissue, which he now unfolded himself, tenderly, carefully, as if each object were a tiny creature, something sleeping that he didn't wish to wake. He filled the cabinet again with his curious possessions, rows upon rows of them until the shelves were overfull. What he couldn't fit into the cabinet, he kept in big wooden chests.

In the evenings, he stood on the balcony of the house, waiting for the sun to set, for the moon to rise, for the darkness to spread across the land like a stain.

My voice hitches. I look at your upturned face, and a memory strikes me of telling stories on a stage, an audience captive in the cave-like belly of a theatre. I listen for the sound of the elevator, for steps coming back, but no – here, for now, we are alone. Alone enough.

I grip my own hand, steadying it.

In this new place, I continue, his wife asked for a child. The child was born. The child was a son.

(DIRECT SUNLIGHT, REMEMBERED.)

I found a photograph of a child, once, tucked inside a shoebox at the back of the closet. There were other things, too: a fishbone comb, actress headshots, locks of hair, rhinestones, pieces of fabric torn from a dress, or a costume. I didn't understand what these things were, what they meant. Not at first.

The boy in the photograph was posing in front of the ruins of a castle I didn't recognise. He was wearing a T-shirt and holding a cap. The sun was in his eyes. He looked a little like you – a few years older, in his early teens. I don't know when the photograph was taken.

Your father never talked about it. When I asked him, he got mad. We argued outside the theatre where I worked at the time. He squeezed my arm so hard it bruised for days. Didn't care that people stared.

Something feels heavy in my belly, now, in my chest. I don't want to tell this part of the story. I look to the ghosts for help. They stand behind you, mute, staring. There is soil on their bare feet, as if they went treading through the gardens of my fairy tale, where they don't belong.

I say it again: I don't want to speak of this.

I played a man one time, years ago. A young prince who dressed as a girl to court the maiden he loved. I imagine myself

97

going out in drag, now, a king of my own making, with my deceitful heart, broad shoulders and a thin moustache and no child to call my own.

The red-haired ghost walks over to me. Eunice, I whisper, using the name I gave her, because I never knew her real one. I remember the first time we met, I a living woman, she already gone. It was shortly after I found the box, those sleepless nights. You were a baby. She simply appeared and stood over your crib in her transparency, her fingers on her lips, her hair a red cascade. I wasn't scared. She said, *You have a beautiful son. Now listen.*

I did. Listened to her fragments and half-sentences. Pieced them together, as best I could.

After her, the others started coming, one by one at first and then all together, in their multitudes.

Who are you? I asked them.

They pointed at the things in the box, the fading headshots, the fake jewels, the locks of hair. *Listen,* they said with their mouths, *listen* with their fingers, *listen* with their broken skulls, *listen, listen, listen.*

I turn to Eunice now, my voice a plea, a prayer, a lament. I don't want to tell it, Eunice, I don't.

She bends and whispers into my ear. She says, *It's okay,* or so I think. *I'll tell this one.*

And so I lend her my mouth, my throat, my tongue. The softest of possessions.

Tristan

The first thing Tristan knew was pestilence. The smell of rot. The sound of mourning. He learned to speak early. His first word was 'Father'.

They moved from village to city to town to village; from small rooms they all shared together, to large, sprawling mansions with countless chambers and pieces of furniture covered with white sheets. They reminded Tristan of the hulking shapes of ships he'd seen shrouded in fog once, when they'd stayed, briefly, at a seaport whose name he had never learned to pronounce.

Tristan's father was large, his voice booming and all-encompassing, the curls of his beard so dark that, when the light was just right, they seemed blue. A castle of a man. On Tristan's fifth birthday, his father gave him a small wooden horse. It didn't look new; its chipped ears scratched his hands, and the paint had long ago rubbed off its saddle. But Tristan loved it and cherished it more than any other toy he'd been given.

His father never touched him, rarely spoke to him, and he wondered often if what he saw on his father's face was fear. But occasionally his father looked at him with such tenderness that Tristan's heart lurched in his chest and all he wanted was to run away, to hide from that look he didn't know what to do with.

The boy played outside often. Nature appealed to him; it seemed dangerous and inevitable, with its shadows, its quiet corners, its sudden, snapping teeth. He could trust in its cruelty. It reminded him of his father.

His mother floated around the house, her clothes never black, her hair always red. He saw on her the traces of his father's moods: a torn lip, a bruised cheekbone, a broken pot that she quickly put away, out of sight. Sometimes Tristan caught her gazing at him and his father with a far-off look, as though she stood behind fogged glass. She hardly ever laughed. His mother would cradle him, caress his hair, tuck him into bed, kiss him on the forehead, whisper stories in his ear. Stories of young boys whose fathers were bears or kings or bears who were themselves kings, who lived in castles and forests. Stories of heroes who killed their fathers and saved their mothers. Stories of men who were transformed into rams, who grew and bred and were killed and eaten by beasts and humans and then resurrected, again and again until everything they knew crumbled around them, and they buried themselves and were reborn as new things. Stories about young men who were beasts waiting to be turned back into men. She kissed his father on the mouth every morning and every night. The women in her stories died often, and badly, and beautifully.

Sometimes she stopped narrating and stared at her son, her hand caressing his cheek. She told Tristan he had his father's eyes.

When he was still very young, they moved to a house that overlooked the ocean. His mother said she liked looking at the sea. Tristan went to the beach with her and they ambled together along the surf. He liked to walk backwards and see the footsteps they'd left behind: one set coming, one going. He loved the briny air that drifted inland, mingled with the scent of roses and jasmine that grew in his mother's garden. It was the happiest he'd ever been.

They didn't stay in that place for long. One day his mother took him from his bed and hastily bundled him and his clothes into a carriage, saying they were moving to another town nearby. She had trouble opening the door of the house because the front porch was covered in what looked at first like skeins of white wool – but then Tristan saw them for what they were. The dead bodies of seagulls: hundreds of them. The birds were piled on top of one another the way he'd seen his father pile his prey after a day of hunting. Tristan ran back to the porch while his parents loaded everything they could onto the carriage. He needed to touch them; he couldn't help himself. The birds were soft against his fingers, their downy feathers slick, their eyes open and staring. They smelled of death. Not rotting flesh but something else, thick and with an underlying sweetness.

One day, the boy fell ill. He could not sleep, but neither could he stay awake. His mother held and rocked him, singing softly in his ear. A beast had lodged itself inside his body – had he swallowed it without knowing? – and it was clawing its way out. He screamed in pain. In his fever, he glimpsed his father looking in from the door of Tristan's bedroom, his face half-obscured. He did not come in.

Why doesn't Father love me? The question echoed in the chamber of his skull. His mother put her hand on his forehead, as if she'd heard.

'Don't mind him. He's only scared. You just get better for me, all right? That's all you have to do.'

Tristan did recover, but the sensation of that beast inside his body never went away. He could feel it there all the time, a gnawing in his gut, a stone hidden underneath his skin.

If he kept quiet, he could hear the beast breathe.

This house was always cold, and so he'd leave it often to wander the town, his own face reflected back at him from windows, from ponds' surfaces, from the water in the fountain of the town's square. Tristan carried a small knife he'd sharpened himself, the blade honed until it could shave the peach fuzz on his chin. Once, he sat on the fountain's steps and tried to cut his hair, holding the knife in front of his face, a drop of his blood falling into the water below.

He may have been open-hearted and kind-faced – that's what his mother says, anyway – but people kept their distance, and he never made a friend. His father called him 'the boy', or 'my son', but his mother called him always by his name.

One day when his father was away, Tristan and his mother sat in the garden. Her skin was pallid and cool. Something had happened between Tristan's parents the night before, but he didn't know what it was. He'd heard his mother cry through the night, seen his father storm out early in the morning, opening the door with great force, as if he meant to tear the house down. Surely, Tristan thought, he could.

In the garden, he asked his mother what had happened.

'You know your father,' she said, and pressed her lips into a smile. Her eyes were wet.

He knew his father. He wondered: Will I be like him when I grow up?

'When he comes back,' he said, the muscles in his jaw so tight he thought his teeth would break, and yet he could do nothing to loosen them, 'I'll have words with him.' He'd heard the phrase recently and it had imprinted itself on his tongue. It had been said by a man in the tavern when another questioned his honour. He'd said to the other man: 'If you weren't so drunk, I'd take you out back and have words with you.' It seemed to Tristan a powerful thing to say, a thing men said: something full of threat, both sharper and less lethal than a knife.

'No,' his mother said, 'you won't,' and he didn't know if she was telling him not to, or if she didn't believe he would.

She turned away from him, and for a while he thought she'd forgotten he was there. Then she spoke again.

'Listen to me, my Tristan,' she said, still looking away. 'You are my dear, sweet boy. Your father is nothing like you. Things lie inside him that we cannot know; things that can snap and hurt him and us. That has always been true about him. I've known it since the very first time I met him. I accepted it. But you, you're something else.' She put her arms around him and pressed him to her. 'You're not him, and you will be the best man you can be. Like the young men in my stories. Remember the stories?'

He did remember them, and the young men, but he wasn't sure which ones he was like – or supposed to be like. The ones whose fathers were bears? The ones who sprouted wings and flew away? The ones who turned into forests?

When the carriage pulled up to the house, his mother straightened and Tristan's nails dug into his skin. But then his father came up the pathway and his face was open and bright, so open and so bright Tristan forgot what words he'd been meaning to have with him. The man brought flowers, a bright yellow that he pressed into his wife's arms before scooping her up and covering her face in quick, tender kisses.

He took her inside, and she let him. The flowers fell to the floor. Tristan was left alone to contemplate the fireflies that were just coming out, smelling the approaching dusk. The flowers flooded the air with the scent of honey and soil.

When his parents came down to dinner that night, his mother was changed. Her face seemed serene, her posture relaxed, her hair loose. His father was in a sunny mood as well, and he even tried to make small talk with Tristan, asking the boy about his day and his time in the garden and the things he'd learned. Tristan caught himself easing into the conversation, and, when his father asked for wine, he was up and rushing to the cellar before he even knew what he was doing. He lugged a jug filled to the brim up the stairs without complaint, though it was almost too heavy for him. His father held up his glass, eyeing Tristan, and the boy, smiling, filled it.

A month later, along with the first heat of summer, a man came to visit. The man was a merchant, travelling with his own caravan. The man invited Tristan's father to visit the caravan where it had settled for the time being, on the outskirts of town. His father asked Tristan if he wanted to tag along. He said yes.

The caravan was big, with many wagons and many people aboard. Tristan liked the feverish colours of their clothes, the shapes of their faces and the drowning smoke of their cooking fires. The man wanted his father to buy something, anything:

he tried to entice him with silks and spices, rare oils and sweet, ancient wines. Tristan's father kept declining, until he came across a small thing that looked like a fantastic animal made from amber-coloured glass, so thin and so delicate it might break at the slightest pressure. 'I'll buy that one,' his father said of the small thing. His face was dark, closed around something Tristan couldn't unlock. The man bowed and took his father's coins and wrapped the unusual animal in gold-threaded cloth.

While this transaction was taking place, Tristan had time to observe the man's family, who sat peacefully in the background, pretending not to see them. Tristan felt invisible, or transparent, made of glass. The merchant had a small, pretty wife who laughed often, and a daughter, and a little boy. They were beautiful children, the boy not unlike the girl. They had big eyes and soft hair and long, slender limbs. Tristan imagined what it would be like to travel with them, to have a brother and a sister to love. To have a small pretty mother who laughed.

Back home, his father unwrapped the glass animal he'd bought and placed it in the cabinet with his other treasures. He ran his fingers over them so lightly, so tenderly. When Tristan tried to bring up the caravan, the merchant and his little wife, how wonderful they were, like something out of a fairy tale, his father looked at him blankly, distracted for a moment, his mind on something that Tristan could never know. Then he ruffled his son's hair. 'What a vivid imagination you have, boy,' he said. 'You take after your mother. Sometimes I wonder if you're my own son at all.'

And yet, his father started spending more time with Tristan that summer. He gave the boy work to do, told him that, though they had others labouring for them always, people less fortunate than them, a man had to know how to work his own land. He showed Tristan how to hold a scythe, how to harvest the ripe crops, how to bundle and thresh.

It was hot, hard work, but Tristan loved all of it: the sun on his back, the pain in his muscles, the golden wheat.

You listen to all this mesmerised, your eyes half-closed. Imagining, perhaps, yourself in those fields, under that sun.

Afterwards, when everything was said and done, neither of them could remember what the disagreement had been about. It may have been an argument about the mysterious ailments that had started plaguing this town, just as they had done the town before, or maybe something about the weather turning and the men who claimed they could predict the whims of the winds. In the end, did it matter? Outside, the dark was falling while father and son stood facing each other in the kitchen with the low fire in the hearth next to them painting their faces something biblical, a pall of smoke hanging in the air. They breathed hard, and neither knew what he was meant to do.

It was Tristan who suggested they sort it out by competition. He wasn't quite sure where he'd gotten that idea – whether it'd been from his mother's stories or from something said at the tavern about the honourable way to solve differences between men when having words had already failed. His mother protested, told them they were fools, with no more sense than a pair of stags locking horns. But neither of them cared.

The boy was twelve. His father said yes.

And so it was decided they would walk to the old well in the field behind the house. They would both go in, one after the other, and see who could climb out the fastest.

Tristan's mother begged him not to go, not to be so stupid. She grabbed his father by the shoulders and shook him, stared pleadingly into his eyes. Tristan didn't know what she saw there, but she let her arms drop and only implored them to be careful.

They went as they were, in their thin clothes, in the falling night, when the moon above was just a curve and it seemed the world was gathering itself up, preparing for the darkness that would come.

The well waited, open as a mouth. His father went in first, using a length of rope that he tied to the well's spindle. Tristan touched the dark lips of the well and his mother stood by him, and they both held their breath as the man splashed into the depths. When the rope went taut again, Tristan's mother turned to him, her eyes frantic, her breath so shallow it hardly clouded the air before her.

'Please, Tristan,' she said. 'Don't do it. There's still time. Say you are afraid. Just let him win.'

The wind shook the trees around them, and Tristan heard a dog howl in the distance. He thought that had to be a sign, but a sign of what? A cheer of victory, or an augury of defeat?

He counted the minutes on an old pocket watch with hands shaped like keys. Not ten minutes had passed when his father pulled himself out, his wet hair and beard sticking to his face, his nails broken and his fingers all bloody. He staggered onto the grass. He grabbed the boy with those bloody hands and hugged him tight. Tristan felt his father's heart beat fast against his chest, and the weight of his arms around him, and all the while his mother cried quietly behind them.

Tristan didn't say he was afraid. He went in next, using the rope in the same fashion as his father.

When he was halfway down, he wondered at the utter blackness that surrounded him. He'd imagined he might be able to see the stone gullet of the well, or even get a glimpse of moon reflected in the water below, but there was only the rope, his hands clutching it, his feet scraping against the stones.

Down he went.

As Tristan reached the water at the bottom, a memory struck him. He was a child again – four, maybe five years old – and his mother played a game with him where she would tie his hands together behind his back, cover his eyes with a blindfold, and lead him around the house, asking him to identify each room by its sound, its smell, the subtle differences in the way the air moved within it. He was never very good at it, but he liked the feeling of her hand, trusting her to take him where he needed to go. Sometimes she left him in a small space enclosed on all sides. He could touch wall or wood in every direction. He would spend hours there, trying to guess where he was, failing to find his way out.

The water was shockingly cold. His feet didn't touch the bottom. Tristan thrashed, fighting to stay afloat as he palmed the rough walls. He gave himself a moment to breathe, though he knew time was slipping away – he could almost visualise those key-shaped hands ticking forwards. Then that moment passed, and he started climbing. His hands slipped on the moss-covered stone, and his nails broke, then broke again, until the pain in his fingers was so sharp it radiated all the way up his arms and into the sockets of his shoulders.

He was not sure how long he went on like that, but the faint outline of the well's mouth did not seem to come any closer.

All it took was a moment of distraction – a foot placed in the wrong groove, a loose stone – and he fell into the freezing water.

The impact knocked his breath out of him. His mother cried out his name again and again, until he found the rope and wrapped it around each hand and tried once more. But his arms shook, his legs trembled, and the rope rubbed painfully against his skin.

'Stop a moment,' he heard his father say from above, something like worry in his voice. 'Stop, and I'll pull you up.'

'No,' Tristan shouted back. 'I'm not done yet. I'm not giving up.'

He tried harder, his hands so cold they felt as if they belonged to someone else, his legs so scratched from scraping against the stone he could feel the blood soaking through his clothes. But he held on. He held on until he could hold on no more and everything went dark.

The first thing he felt was his father's strong arms under his body, cradling him. He was pulling him out of the well, the effort nothing to this man. His father didn't even grunt, didn't pant. When, at last, they crested the stone lip of the well, his father deposited Tristan gently on the ground, where his mother covered him with her hair, her hands, her tears. She was still saying his name.

They carried him back to the house, the boy's body secure against his father's chest. It was the closest they'd ever been.

When he looked up at his father's face, at his furrowed brow and his eyes sunk with concern, he saw something cold, the glint of a smirk, something satisfied.

Tristan stayed in bed for days. His mother brought him soup and cold compresses for the fever and cared for his wounded hands and feet. The fever went down eventually, but Tristan remained in bed even after his wounds were mere echoes of that night in the well.

His mother didn't rush him. Every day, she came into his room and parted the heavy curtains to let in the pallid morning light, and every night she came back to close them again. Tristan's body felt sluggish and foreign, as if it were no longer his own, but belonged to someone else, something else, larger than him, older, without a name.

One morning, as his mother was opening the window to the early sun and cold air, Tristan studied the back of her head, her arms, the way she held herself, and he could finally put a word to the way she moved: guarded. Not the movements of a caged thing, but something that knows danger lurks nearby, always and for ever.

Tristan hadn't spoken to his mother since that night, but now he found he had something to say.

'I didn't let him win.' His voice sounded as foreign to him as his body. 'But it didn't matter,' he continued. 'I lost, regardless.'

She held her breath, the rich fabric of the curtain still bunched in her hand. 'Yes,' she said. 'This time. Yes.'

In the end, Tristan left his bed and his room for the crisp morning air and the silence of the world outside. He decided to train himself. He would be strong. He would become a rival worthy of his father.

He began by climbing trees. The tallest, oldest trees he could find, the ones that grew deep in the forest's heart. He slipped many times, and once fell so hard he lost the world for a few moments. But then he climbed right back up and did it all again.

He worked on his stamina, too, taking long walks into the woods, for hours and hours. He began to see the forest around him differently, to recognise its spaces and patterns, which he recalled and navigated like landmarks. Months passed this way. Then a year.

Finally, Tristan decided he had to teach himself to swim, because he didn't know what the next competition would demand of him, but he knew that drowning was not a death he wished.

He took to the shore, where water met land, and stood there for a half-hour, maybe more. He could still feel the frozen sting of the well water on his skin. The sea was darker than the sky, the water wrinkled with foam. Near the bottom lurked large shapes, which filled him with a dread like a stone in his belly that could drag him down. He breathed the salty air, let it burn the back of his throat, then opened his mouth and stuck out his tongue, as if to declare to the ocean: I am like you. I inhale you. We are the same.

He waded in. The cold seized his limbs, and his flesh quickly grew numb. But he didn't resist it. He kept walking until the water was up to his shoulders, his feet tangled in the soft and slimy plant life of the sea. He opened his arms and let the waves almost knock him over. The gesture meant: I'll come back.

On his way out of the water, he saw another boy standing a

short distance down the beach. The boy was looking at him, but Tristan was too far to see the expression on his face, to know whether he was a friend or foe.

Tristan carried on towards the shore. By the time his feet touched dry sand, the other boy was gone.

This part of the story excites you, I can tell. Your heart beats faster in your chest, the muscles in your arms tense slightly in anticipation. It's because you recognise this story from other stories you've been told since you were born, by me and by others, by films, by your teachers, by your phone. By him – the only story he ever told you, isn't it? It's the tale of a boy born to be a hero. You know his shape. You know his path, his trans-formations. You know his trials and his journey in every detail, down to the trusted sidekick. You know, even, his adversary.

You think you know how this story ends.

Tristan did go back the next day, and the next. He walked into the water every day, and, every day, the other boy was there, watching Tristan as he ventured a little deeper and a little deeper still. He walked far out, until the water was just beneath his nose and each wave threatened to swallow him whole.

And just like that, he was ready. His feet let go of the kelp and his body fell backwards. The water buoyed him, and he floated on the surface of the sea, lifted up, accepted. He allowed himself to be held this way for a long time, the sun sliding across the sky.

An angry exhale shook his body, and water covered his face. Before he knew what was happening, Tristan was submerged, blinded by salt, his mouth full of water and seaweed. He fought, his arms on fire, his legs nowhere, his lungs ashes. He would drown after all. The well had caught up to him, as he'd always known it would – until an arm grabbed him around the chest. It was the boy from the beach. Neither friend nor foe, after all, but saviour.

He pulled Tristan all the way to the shore and laid him on the sand. Tristan coughed until the metal taste of blood filled his throat. Then he fell back and stared at the sky. He thought he was breathing for the first time; air had never before filled his body.

The boy sat beside him and didn't speak for some time. He had strong limbs, a soft stubbled chin, a long nose. He scooped up a handful of sand and let it dribble from his palm back onto the beach.

'What were you doing?' the boy asked. 'Trying to drown yourself?'

Tristan kept his eyes on a patch of sky framed by his wet eyelashes. 'No,' he said. 'I was teaching myself to swim.' He paused, looked at the boy. 'I'm training.'

The boy curled his lip, revealing his long, straight teeth. His smile made him look like a horse. 'For what?'

'To defeat my father,' Tristan said, though he didn't quite know what defeating his father meant. He imagined it now: the two of them facing each other in the clearing of a thick forest. A lone wolf crying in the distance, the moon slipping free of the clouds. The brief struggle, his father repentant but unsaved – no, not just unsaved but unsaveable, as all monsters are. Tristan walking away no longer a boy but a man, victorious, going back to his joyful mother and her lush, unrotten garden.

'I'm training, too,' the boy said.

Tristan pushed himself up on his elbows and stared at his saviour as the waves broke and receded. 'What are you training for?' he asked.

The boy looked at the sand and shook his head. 'Come again tomorrow,' he said. 'Maybe, if you learn how to swim, I'll tell you.'

The next time Tristan went to the beach, the boy was there, waiting. They didn't speak. The boy nodded at Tristan, and then waded into the water with him.

'Who are you, anyway?' Tristan asked over the wind.

'Halt,' the boy replied and, for a moment, Tristan thought he was telling him to stop – but no, it was just his name. He held it in his mouth, the lonely syllable of it. Halt.

They walked as far out as they could without losing purchase and then they threw themselves forwards, Tristan's arms and legs working the same way they did when he was climbing trees. He swallowed mouthful after mouthful of salt water, but he was swimming. Halt was ahead of him, so Tristan kicked as hard as he could until he caught up. Halt turned. The sun was shining on his wet face, and he stopped swimming so he could put his hand on Tristan's shoulder.

'You did it,' Halt told him. 'I'm proud of you!' He smiled his horse-like smile.

Tristan put his own hand on Halt's shoulder and they stayed there for a while, proud of each other, their legs kicking at the depth below.

They trained together after that. A year, maybe more. Halt lived with his mother, and he insisted on meeting Tristan on the shore or in the woods, never anywhere near the town. Every time, Halt was already at the meeting place by the time Tristan got there. Tristan never saw from which direction the other boy came; for all he knew, Halt lived in the woods. A boy raised by wolves, his father a tree, his mother a fiction. It didn't matter. All that mattered to Tristan was that, for the first time, he had a friend, someone who existed outside his father's realm. If Halt knew him, then Tristan could know himself. He could be someone separate; a whole other person.

The boys climbed trees together and swam often, in the sea or in a river that made Tristan feel like he was nothing but mud, a body held together by so little, easily washed away.

Tristan grew into young manhood effortlessly, as you will soon, like a blade slipping into water. And, eventually, Halt declared that, if Tristan wanted to defeat his father, he'd have to learn how to fight.

Tristan was fifteen.

The boys started with sticks, then rocks, then their bare hands. They whittled branches into points. The rocks, they took from the shore. Their hands were the last weapons; too animal, and it made them feel queasy, the way flesh slapped against flesh. They practised all day, on the beach, in the woods, in the fields. They swung at each other, and, almost every time, Halt would block Tristan's blows before they connected. Fighting didn't come naturally to Tristan, though he knew this was what boys were supposed to do. The few times he'd gotten into fights with other boys, he was always the one beaten. Tristan hated fighting those other boys, the way his body moved despite him, the way the air closed in around him like a mouth. But, with Halt, it was different. This was training; Halt wasn't truly his opponent. The world was, and they were together against it.

At first, it was hard to strike without recoiling as his skin cracked and split, but he kept at it, and, gradually, got used to the pain. He learned how to hold his hands in fists to protect his thumbs, how to bend his elbows into sharpness that could break ribs, how to make his own body a shield for his weak spots. He learned not to be gentle.

Losing to Halt filled him with a rage he'd never known before. Once, after Halt had thrown him to the ground and Tristan had admitted defeat, he took a rock and threw it at Halt's leg as the boy was walking away. The rock broke the skin, and blood ran down his friend's victorious calf. Halt looked at Tristan blankly. Without a word, Halt turned around and left.

Tristan punched the mud. He slammed his fists against the ground again and again, and with each strike, the earth shook beneath him, and the sky above him faded into darkness.

It took a few days, but Halt came back. They didn't speak about forgiveness.

'You become what you behold,' Halt said instead. 'So behold the sharp rocks. The swift birds. The hard ground.'

Eventually, Tristan beat Halt in a fight.

The boy considered Tristan for a long time, thumbing his swollen lip. Then he said, 'Maybe you stand a chance after all. Maybe we both do.'

After each training session, Tristan went home. Some nights he was so exhausted he couldn't eat or speak; all he could do was crawl to his bed and let his body collapse into a dreamless sleep until a new day started.

On such a night, as he was peeling his muddy clothes from his body, his mother walked into his room. She stood next to him. Caressed his hair.

'What do you want?' he asked her. His voice sounded harsh even to his own ears. He forced himself to blunt it. 'I'm tired, Mother.'

'Why are your clothes so dirty?' she asked.

He shrugged. 'I play in the woods with a friend.'

She picked up his shirt from the floor. The fabric was torn in places, the cuff stained red – he'd used it to wipe his bloodied nose.

'This is no play,' she said. She was looking straight into his eyes.

'Let me be,' he said, tearing his shirt from her hands and bundling it with the rest of his clothes. He tossed the lot into the corner, knowing full well it would be his mother who picked it up again. He softened. 'I'm sorry,' he said. 'I'm tired.'

Tristan let her caress his hair again, inspect his face, his bruised cheekbone.

'Do you want to hear a story, Tristan?' she asked. 'It's about a boy who tries to prove himself better than the gods, until the gods strike him down.'

He was in no mood. 'What gods?' he asked.

She pressed her lips together. Said nothing.

Tristan took her hand in his, gently, and brought it to his swollen lips. 'Maybe I'm strong enough to beat him,' he said. He thought of Halt's pride, Halt's hope. 'Maybe not yet, but one day.'

His mother gave him a smile and ran her fingers through his hair one more time. 'Yes,' she said quietly. 'Maybe.' Her hand lingered there for a few moments, as if she were trying to commit something to memory. 'My Tristan.'

Eunice pauses, still bent next to me. I turn to look at her. Her cold lips are almost blue. I put my hand on her cheek, and we continue. You hardly notice.

The next time the boys met up, a storm was blowing in from the sea, and the air was filled with the smell of rain. Tristan found Halt on the shore, but his friend held neither sticks nor rocks this time. He was simply standing on the sand, barefoot, staring at the brewing sky.

Tristan put a hand on the boy's shoulder. He knew this body so well, had fought with it, embraced it, bled by it. Sometimes he thought they were one, Halt and he. Was such a thing possible? For two bodies to hold the same person? For one person to be split across flesh and bones, names, circumstances?

Surely not. But he wanted it to be.

'Aren't we fighting today?' Tristan asked.

Halt took a moment before replying. 'No,' he said. 'Not today.' Finally, he looked at Tristan. His face seemed different; tense, somehow, older, the skin taut over his bones. 'Come on,' he said. 'I want to show you something.'

Halt led him along the beach. Tristan had walked this shore's length many times before. He knew the feel of its sand and pebbles under his feet, knew the texture of the dried kelp and dead seashells, and where the ground was treacherous, the rocks too slippery, the tide likely to be upon you when you least expected it. But this time Halt took him further than they'd ever gone before. They reached a cliff, and the boy led Tristan up a path between the boulders, until they came to a cave of black rocks smoothed to a shine by the wind and the rain and the briny breath of the sea.

Tristan hesitated at the mouth of the cave. But Halt tugged him along.

Inside, the cavern's wall was lined with lanterns, and the faint sound of voices came from deeper in the cave.

'Who's there? Where are you taking me?' Tristan asked, but again the boy only urged him forwards. He kept close to Tristan, their bodies touching, moving as one.

'This is what I'm training for,' Halt whispered in Tristan's ear. He stressed the last syllable. Halt had a peculiar way of speaking, sometimes: his words stilted and over-enunciated, as if he'd learned the language only recently.

As they walked further in, the cave narrowed – like a throat, Tristan thought – and the voices grew louder. Still, he could make out no words, only guttural sounds and a repetitive beat. Tristan rolled his shoulders, and he felt Halt do the same. He was on edge, aware, every little thing impressing itself on him: the roughness of the cave's walls; the distinct lack of any smell other than the ever-present scent of smoke. There was no damp, no mould; it was too dark for life to thrive here.

The light of the lanterns cast sharp shadows on the cavernous ceiling above. It reminded Tristan of a shadow-puppet show he'd seen once – perhaps it was when the man with the caravan came to town, perhaps some other time; he couldn't remember. But he remembered the deep sadness the puppets had made him feel. He had thought, what if those flat leather figures think they truly are alive? What if they feel their faces pressed against that paper screen and believe that is the real world? What an unhappy existence that would be, he'd told himself. How trapped they must feel.

At last, Halt and Tristan arrived at an opening – a stomach – deep inside the rock. A number of people were gathered there. Tristan counted twenty, though he was certain there were more, many more, lurking in the shadows. A fire blazed in the middle, fed constantly by an old man, naked but for a loin-cloth, his wiry arms and legs glistening with sweat. Next to the fire, a shallow and long rectangular pit had been dug and filled with red-hot coals. The people stood around it, chanting, rocking side to side.

No one acknowledged them. Tristan reached for Halt's hand, found it, grasped it. Halt shot him a look and nodded. 'I have you,' he whispered, and in that moment Tristan felt he could do anything. Defeat his father? That was nothing. He could eat mountains. He could break the world.

Halt squeezed his hand and said: 'Watch.'

He did. One of the chanting women broke away from the group. She wore a thin, grey dress. Her hair hung limply down her back. Her face was slack, her feet bare. And with those bare feet, she stepped onto the hot coals.

Tristan held himself back from crying out and rushing forwards to help her. The expression on the woman's face did not change, as if she felt no pain. She took another step, then threw back her head to face the darkness above. Like that, slowly, she walked all the way to the other side of the pit.

The air in the cave had grown warm. Tristan felt it on his skin, through his clothes. Smoke was in his mouth, down his throat. He wouldn't last in there for long, he thought. He would burn soon. Burn and burn until he died.

Halt must have seen something in his face, because he wrapped his arm around Tristan's shoulders and gently pulled him away as the chanting swelled and a man took his first steps into the pit.

Outside, Tristan knelt and emptied his stomach, then swallowed the fresh, cold air in hungry gulps. Halt squatted by his side and gathered Tristan's hair behind his head. Tristan pushed the boy away and placed his palms on the cold ground. He looked out at the ocean, the sleety grey of it. Finally, he stood and started to walk back the way they'd come.

Halt followed him in silence. After a while, he put his arm on Tristan's shoulder and made him stop. 'I thought you were ready,' he said.

Tristan looked at the sea again. His throat was scratched raw, as if he'd been yelling. 'Are these your people?' he asked.

Halt took a moment, but then he nodded. 'My people.'

Tristan wiped his mouth. 'Why do your people do that?'

'It's for protection,' Halt replied. He paused and licked his lips, trying to decide, perhaps, how much to say. How much Tristan was ready to hear. 'Faith allows us to walk on the coals without getting burned,' he continued. 'We feel no pain because the body is negligible; it doesn't matter. It's this faith and the fortitude it builds that will protect us, protect the world.'

Such strange words. Did Halt really believe this? Was the body truly nothing? Tristan should turn away now, he thought, go back to the well, jump in, fight those stone walls instead. Something he could see and touch.

'Protect the world from what?' he asked.

Halt's shoulders drooped, and it was his turn to look away. 'We won't know until it's time.'

Tristan was on his way to the beach at first light, still drowsy with sleep. He trudged along the sand and staggered up the sharp incline that led to the cave, not entirely certain what he was hoping to find. But there was no one there, only the bracing ocean air, the scent of dead seaweed.

He came back again every morning of the week and waited, but no one ever went in or out of that mouth, and only the faint echoes of smoke lingered to remind him of that night.

At the end of that week, a stranger came to their house. She claimed to be an old friend of his mother's from the village where they both grew up. A good friend, though Tristan had never seen or heard of her before. She was to stay with them for a few days. She was a teacher, she said. She'd moved away when she was young, and now she had come all the way from the capital to see how her good friend was doing.

'I wish I could have been at your wedding, my darling Eunice,' she said. Tristan had never heard anyone call his mother by her name before; his parents used no names between them, and the townspeople always called her Lady or Mistress or some such. It created a strange feeling within him, hearing that name, as if it made her more real than before but also, somehow, diminished her. In his mind, she'd been like the people that populated the fables she nurtured him on. They, too, had no names: they were Princes and Kings and Knights and Birds and Bears and Lakes. Mother and Father. Not Eunice or Anne, as the woman introduced herself to him. Not even Tristan.

'The wedding was such a private affair,' his mother said, caressing the woman's fair hair with the back of her hand. 'It happened so quickly,' she added. As though she were speaking of an accident.

Tristan's father stood by the door with his brow furrowed, as if contemplating a bad omen, some great impending doom.

With Eunice's encouragement, Anne quickly made herself at home. She lounged on the woven quilts and fixed dinner in the kitchen as if she'd lived with them for years. When they were together, the women entered a separate world, a sphere of their own entirely inaccessible to Tristan. It occurred to him, then, that maybe Anne was important to his mother for the same reasons Halt was important to him. Someone to define her as an entity distinct from her husband, his father. Someone to show her that life could be different.

I pause here and turn to look at Eunice. I tell her, I'm so glad you had Anne. She was your Nadya, wasn't she? We were both lucky in that way.

Eunice smiles bitterly but says nothing of our luck. Then, barely audible, she continues, and so do I:

Tristan's father grew distant, and some of his awkwardness slipped into Tristan as well, like an infection. Every day, Tristan walked to the woods in the cool spring air, let the sunlight fill him up so that no thoughts of his mother or of that strange woman could fit in his head. One day, he walked all the way to the river. He stared at the trees above, let the crisp air chill his skin, and then he walked into the water and let it take him where it may. The river carried him downstream like a leaf, and he watched the branches of the trees above, the slivers of sky in between.

After some time, the river deposited him into a nest of dead reeds. He crawled onto the riverbank, cold to the marrow of his bones. There he lay, and, for a while, he felt that he belonged. That he ought to stay there for ever, let his body be taken by the woods.

He hardly remembered how he got home. The women sat together in the garden, under the cherry tree. His mother's hand was in her friend's. The woman was studying her palm, running her finger over the lines. She pointed at his mother's hand and spoke softly.

Tristan went over. He couldn't help himself. The sight had filled him with a kind of urgency, something acidic pooling in the pit of his stomach. The women looked up at him, a little surprised and, the boy was sure, a little inconvenienced. Even his mother's face flashed a moment of annoyance before she managed to conceal it with a smile.

'What are you doing?' he asked them.

Anne had the same long hair as his mother, the same nose. He wasn't sure whether he found that comforting or upsetting. 'I'm reading your mother's hand,' the woman said jovially.

'How can you read a hand?'

She took Tristan's, pulled it close, palm up. He was too startled to resist. She traced the lines of his hand the way she'd done with his mother's. 'The palm's lines are the story of a person's life,' Anne explained. 'If you read them right, they tell you who you are and what you're meant to be.'

Tristan looked down at his hand. The lines there were close together, tight and deep, the pads of his fingers callused and hard.

'Would you like me to read yours?' the woman asked.

Tristan looked at his mother, hoping she would tell him what to do, but she simply watched, her breath held.

He retrieved his hand and closed it into a fist.

Tristan studied his hand often after that. He considered the idea of fate and marvelled at his inability to know his own body. His hand held a story, he thought, but one not meant for him to read.

Eventually, Tristan found Halt again in their usual spot, and that eased his heart a bit. It was morning. They sat on the beach together, their feet in the water.

Tristan talked about fate, what it is, how to know it.

Halt took Tristan's hand and pretended to read it. 'It's obvious,' he said. 'See this line here? It means you're going to die.'

Halt's lips were already curling into a smile when Tristan threw sand in his face. They both laughed.

As the laughter faded, Halt smoothed the sand with his hand. He drew a line in it. Then, he kicked the sand, and the line was gone. 'There you go,' he said. 'Fate.'

They returned to the cave a few weeks later. They heard the chanting before they even stepped into its great big body, before they entered its mouth, walked down its throat. Halt seemed stiff, taller than usual. He removed his shirt a few feet into the cave, even though the air was still cool. Tristan could see the tension in his spine, pulling at his shoulder blades. The air smelled of stale smoke. Tristan touched his own face, found his brow sweating prematurely.

They walked nimbly. This time, it felt like coming home.

When they reached the cave's stomach, the people were already humming their guttural beat around the blaze, the pit furiously red. A man walked on the coals, his head thrown back, his mouth open around a silent howl. He held his arms outstretched, palms up, as if expecting something to descend from that cavernous sky and land on his pleading hands. Tristan inched closer to Halt. His friend's breath came quick and shallow. A low moan escaped his lips now and then in rhythm with the chanting of his people. The smoke was in Tristan's throat, but this time it didn't bother him. Instead, a calmness descended on him and he thought, with no surprise, that he could live all his days inside this cave. It felt natural to be in it, and for a moment he had the sense that nothing beyond it was real; there was only this cave, only the shadows on its walls.

Then the man reached the end of his firewalk and Halt was no longer next to Tristan but approaching the pit. The people parted to let him pass. Tristan couldn't move. He didn't leap forwards, didn't reach for Halt's hand, didn't try to stop him. All he could do was watch.

Halt stepped onto the coals. His face was rigid and pale, lit by the orange glow of the coals, his eyes a million miles away. The chanting grew louder. Halt's torso leaned back as his legs pulled him forwards. The body is nothing, Tristan thought, it is nothing. On the wall, Halt's shadow flickered. It resembled a strange, antlered beast, walking backwards.

Tristan held his breath, not daring to exhale until Halt made it to the other side of the pit and resumed his place next to Tristan. His skin reeked of smoke, and his hair was plastered to his skull. He turned to Tristan. The faraway look was gone; now, his eyes were bright, alert, alive. His face glistened.

After the ceremony ended and the people dispersed, the two boys sat on the beach under the glimmering stars, the sand cool and soothing beneath their hands and feet. Neither of them had spoken a word since Halt walked on fire.

'I'd like to do what you did, one day,' Tristan said now.

Halt looked at him without judgement. 'Why?' he asked.

Tristan focused on the darkening sea, that great, writhing mass. 'I'd like to live like that.'

'Like what?' Halt asked.

'To be so alive I could die,' Tristan replied.

That night, back in his father's house, Tristan thought he could still hear the chanting, smell the smoke on Halt's skin.

He wanted to see Halt again the next day, but the boy was in none of their usual meeting places. Not in the woods nor at the shore nor at the mouth of the cave, neither that day nor in any of the days that followed. Tristan constantly scanned the world around him for any sign of Halt. A few times he thought he saw Halt between the trees, or he caught a glimpse of footprints on the sand, but when he drew closer to inspect them, they were only his own footprints, or the ocean's, or the birds'.

Tristan tried to tell his mother about his missing friend, the cave, the coals, but she didn't seem to hear him. Her mind was on other things.

Anne left. She kissed his mother on both cheeks and promised to be back before long. After her carriage disappeared in the distance, his mother stood there, her arms limp at her sides, her hair unbraided. Tristan hugged her waist, the way he used to do when he was smaller. She caressed his head.

'She'll come again, Mother,' he said, 'don't cry,' though she wasn't.

'No, darling boy. She won't,' his mother replied. 'Not to this house. Not to this place.' She glanced at the crops, the grass, the forest beyond.

By then, rumours had started circulating in the village: the crops were dying, the sky was turning dim, the animals gave birth to stones and two-headed beasts. People took to boiling water before drinking it, claiming the wells had all gone bad; Tristan's mother did the same, as if they were victims of this strange calamity just like everyone else. Perhaps she really did believe it, or badly wanted to.

This time, they didn't leave. It was a kind of optimism, or something daring. Something that said: maybe this time will be different. Maybe, in this place, by the time the summer is ended, we will be saved.

It was Halt who found Tristan on the beach, sitting on the sand, hugging his knees to his chest. Halt joined him, sat close enough that Tristan could feel the warmth of his friend's body.

'I've been looking everywhere for you,' Tristan said.

From the side, Halt's face seemed more angular to Tristan, like a chiselled statue, or a knife.

'I know,' Halt replied. The little muscle on the side of his jaw trembled slightly.

'Where have you been?' Tristan asked.

A shrug. 'Away.'

'Away where?'

Halt wouldn't respond.

Tristan leaned back on his elbows and stared at the sea. It

was teal today, the sky a bruised blue. His pulse pounded in his ears so loud he could barely hear the waves, the cries of seabirds above.

'People are saying the crops are cursed, the water poisoned,' Tristan said. 'Isn't that crazy?' He tried to sound brave, though he remembered when these things had happened before, in another place. He felt uncertain and small.

'It's not safe for you here any more,' Halt said.

Tristan sat up. He laughed, though Halt's face was serious.

When Halt spoke again, his voice was warm. 'You should leave,' he said. 'All three of you.'

An emptying out of the limbs.

'Where would we go?' Tristan asked. And then: 'Will you come, too?'

Halt stood, rubbed his hands together to get rid of the sand that had stuck to his palms.

'Was this what you meant?' Tristan asked. 'The thing you're supposed to protect the world from?'

Halt shifted his weight onto one leg and tilted his head as if the sun were in his eyes, though the day was thoroughly clouded. 'I have to go,' he said. 'It might be a while before we see each other again.'

He turned to leave, but Tristan grabbed his shirt and forced the boy to face him. 'I want to do what you do.' He spoke the words again, thinking them a spell like the ones in the stories his mother told, a magical phrase that would at last deliver him to his fate. 'I want to walk on fire. I want to protect the world.'

This time, Halt smiled. He put both hands on Tristan's shoulders.

'Tristan,' he said, 'you've been walking on coals your whole life. Don't you see? It's how you've always lived.'

The rumours turned out to be true, and the crops did die. The fields failed, the stalks became bent and ragged, the leaves eaten by locusts and birds. The ground turned black, writhing with long white worms. The valley echoed with the desperate bleating of livestock giving birth to monsters.

Tristan fled to the woods often, but it was no longer the refuge it had once been; the landmarks he knew so well were crumbling before him. Even the oldest trees, so thick and tall they used to kiss the sky, were little more than husks slowly sinking into the ground. Eagles fell out of the air, dead mid-flight.

At first, his father got angry at any mention of the town rumours, at the boiling water on the stove.

'It's only natural,' he'd say. 'What comes from the earth is always weak. Only by fighting the world can one become stronger.'

Tristan's father went out to the fields every dawn. He worked all day, as hard as he could, and the muscles on his arms bulged. His breath turned into puffs of mist, but he didn't shiver, and he didn't stop. He said that all a man could do was work harder and harder, and maybe his determination would be enough to stop the fields from dying. And when the plants fell apart in front of him, he'd shout and stomp his feet among the withering stalks, curse the earth and the sky.

Eventually, the man, too, became quiet. Mutely, he carried the dead lambs in his arms and buried them in the cold ground. He spent his afternoons on a chair in the yellowing garden, his hands idle, his eyes glazed over. At dinner, he sat with his head in his hands, not a word on his lips.

SOUR CHERRY

Tristan tried to talk to him once. He put his hand on his father's fist and spoke softly to him, the way he'd seen him speak to his horse when it got spooked. His father raised his gaze to meet his son's, but it was glassy and full of shards.

The days grew shorter, the nights longer. The world itself frayed in front of Tristan's eyes. He lay in the field, among the dying crops. He grabbed the coarse stalks and rubbed them between his fingers. They felt as slight and fragile as birds' bones. He didn't care that they broke under his touch: all he wanted was to feel them, to caress their pain, embrace it. Now, he thought, everything was as pained as him.

Rain would fall suddenly. The sun would be shining, and then, the clouds would gather from all directions, as if they had been there all along, hiding in the sky like a secret kept in blue.

When the people came for them with pitchforks and torches, Tristan remained transfixed in front of the window. He couldn't take his eyes off their faces, so angry in the orange light of sunset, so dense with rage, their fists raised, their eyes wide. He recognised many of them: The woman who had first walked on the coals. The man with his head tilted back and his mouth open to swallow the sky.

And Halt, among them. He was holding a long, thin branch, the bark peeled away, one end sharpened into a point, as they had done back in the first days of their sparring. What was he planning to do with it?

Tristan's father grabbed his son's shoulders and shook him, tearing him away from the window moments before a stone shattered it.

'The world isn't what you think it is, boy,' he said. 'Sometimes, it gets cold. Sometimes it dies. And sometimes, it is cruel like this.'

Are these people the cruelty, Tristan wondered, or are we? Are we the darkness Halt needs to protect the world against?

'I don't want to leave,' Tristan whispered.

'Then stay,' his father said, his voice deep and cold, a well and its stone walls and its standing water.

Tristan looked around. He realised that their household had already been packed – even his father's cabinet with all its curious, precious things.

His mother heaved a chest down the stairs. Her hair was loose and red around her neck, her features drawn. Sweat glistened on her forehead.

'What's in there?' Tristan asked, pointing at the chest.

'Dresses, my love,' his mother said. 'It's only dresses. Now hurry up.'

A carriage was waiting for them at the back of the house, the driver holding on to the reins, the horses stomping the ground, eager to go. By the time their belongings had been piled in, the garden was on fire.

The carriage turned onto the dirt road, bringing the crowd into view again. Darkness had fallen, and Tristan could only see the people by the light of the fire. Halt's arm was in the air. He still held on to his branch, but he no longer looked like he was brandishing it, only waving it. Not a menace, but a farewell.

As the carriage drew further and further away, the flames lapped at the porch, and the curtains in the front room caught. Tristan watched them dance aflame, wisps of fire flying up into the night sky.

* * *

They travelled for days. For weeks, it seemed to Tristan. And who am I to say they didn't? Some nights, they took up lodgings in rooms above taverns or guest houses by the side of the road; other nights, they slept crammed in the carriage, their heads on fur coats, their hands touching one another, grasping, as if to let go now would be the same as letting go for ever, as if this grasping was needed to keep one another tethered to this life, this lessening, this dying ground.

They forded a river that bisected the valley like a scar, and Tristan remembered a story his mother had told him when he was very little, about a river that once cut through the land where a woman and her child lived. One day, mother and child got lost in the forest. They walked and walked until they found the river, and then they followed it downstream until they came to a village that looked exactly like their own, except in reverse. The people walked backwards, spoke from the end of a sentence to the beginning, started all their stories with happily ever afters and ended them with wolves, cursed children, monsters birthed. Even the birds flew backwards.

Tristan stared out of the carriage window as the horses struggled forth. The water looked so thick, so dark and unforgiving, it seemed impossible to cross. He could almost feel it in his pores, enveloping him, making him heavier. Or maybe that was Halt, his memory and his loss.

They headed towards a snow-capped mountain range. His mother cried from the cold. His father wrapped Tristan in a big grey fur he said had once belonged to a wolf. He was warmed by his father's long, rough fingers on his back.

They passed through vast flatlands and dense forests; they passed through cities and tiny villages. It was in one of these tiny villages they finally settled. The place – hardly more than a cluster of houses – was built on flat land, bordered on one side by a forest and on the other by wide, barren plains. Little grew in this place, and the sea was miles and miles away.

The weather was milder here. The leaves on the trees were orange, yellow, red, and a gentle breeze came from the south, carrying the scent of flowers. Tristan found those flowers in the footpaths leading away from the village and into the woods. He'd never seen flowers like them before. They were delicate, with fine, long stalks. But their petals were jagged and sharp like improbable, pretty teeth.

The new house was much less imposing than the last, made of grey stones stacked one on top of the other, with small windows that let in so little light that lamps had to be used all day long. But, his mother said, this one would be harder to burn to the ground.

Tristan couldn't sleep in this house. He spent nights lying on his bed with his eyes open, listening to the low moan of the wind on stone, the slow settling of the house on itself, the muffled voices of his mother and father downstairs. They argued a lot. She cried often.

During the day, Tristan would find a flat, green spot in the garden to lie on. The sky above was too big, the clouds too white, the sun too bright. His mind travelled back across the rivers and cities and plains, all the way to the shore where he'd sat with Halt for the first time. He saw Halt there again, watching as Tristan fought with the waves. Halt's gaze was cold. A sharp branch in his hand.

Did this ever really happen?

When his father noticed his sulking, he scolded him.

'Friendship is a childish thing,' he said. 'A thing for no son of mine.'

You interrupt. 'Is friendship so bad?' you ask.

That's what this man thought, I say. That's what his pain taught him.

You nod as if you understand, wise beyond your years. Eunice's cold lips brush my ear. She continues.

A few days later, Tristan's father decided Tristan should have his own horse.

'But I don't know how to ride,' Tristan said. He hadn't been taught.

His father led him to the stables and showed him the horse that would be his: a white mare with a mane so red it seemed to bleed. His father caressed the horse's neck with such gentleness, such patient care, it made Tristan's spine tense and the little hairs on the back of his neck stand on end. It was an uncanny thing, startling, like a human form divined inside the torso of a tree, or a face formed by the inky shapes outside a window at night.

The man handed Tristan the horse's reins and smiled for the first time in weeks. They trained for hours every day. His father taught Tristan how to mount, how to hold the reins in a firm grip. He taught Tristan how to sit, how to stay on the saddle, how to guide the horse with his legs and core, how to read the ground ahead. How to win the horse's trust, and when to trust the horse to find its own way.

Soon, Tristan was good enough to ride the horse unsupervised. He rode it to the fields and to the woods, where he talked to the trees and the stones. He sat atop his horse for hours, watching the eagles soar overhead. The forest smelled green and earthy. It felt comforting, yet Tristan always sensed he was trespassing into someone else's territory. He would often listen out for birdsong, but there was none. There was, instead, the sound of the wind, a whisper through the leaves, a moan. The forest reminded him of his father: vast, overgrown, impenetrable. It had eyes. It was hungry. It had a dark heart, full of intention.

Still, Tristan tried to make a place for himself in the woods: he cleared the low vegetation under a spruce, marked his territory with rocks and sticks, carved a hole into the tree where he kept a knife and a few branches sharpened to points. He even built a structure out of long reeds, where he could sit if the rain caught him, or where he could sleep whenever he forgot himself until it was too late to find his way home.

In that structure, just large enough for him to lie on the moss-covered ground, Tristan contemplated his life before. His mind conjured visions of Halt: His face when they sat together on the sand, his back and the way the small muscles rippled under his skin when he walked ahead, leading the way into that stomach of a cave. His hair, shiny with sweat as he walked on the red-hot coals.

Tristan realised, then, that everything he did, everything he saw, everyone he met, he would always compare to Halt. And everything would always be found wanting.

He spent days alone in his forest refuge. But at times something descended upon his head and chest, and Tristan grew so sad he didn't want to live. The woods couldn't console him, nor could the sky, nor the earth. Even the birds he so longed to hear meant nothing to him. He always went back to his mother then. He let her cradle his head and breathed in her smell as the sun moved over their house and cast shadows on the walls.

It was on one such day that he went home and noticed the trees in the garden were dead. His mother's hair hung lacklustre, and her skin seemed bloodless, her frame thinner than ever before. She welcomed her son as she always did, but her movements were slow, as if she, too, possessed a great stone that weighed her down.

She made him sit at the table and set a bowl of broth in front of him.

'You've been spending all your time out there with the trees and the birds and the beasts of the forest,' she said. 'What good are they to you?' And then: 'What are you hiding from?'

He sipped the broth. 'What happened to the trees?' he asked.

She glanced in the direction of the garden, though she couldn't see it through the thick stone wall. She waved her hand. 'Nothing,' she said. 'Nothing that hasn't happened before.'

'And the animals?' he asked, even though he already knew.

She tightened her shawl around her shoulders, as if a sudden breeze had chilled her skin. 'Not yet,' she said. 'But soon.'

He placed the spoon on the table and stared at it for a few moments. It was silver, though no one had polished it in a long time. The bowl was fine porcelain. Where did his father's wealth come from? he wondered. So much wealth. So much death.

'Sooner than last time,' he said.

She nodded.

'Mustn't we warn them?'

She looked him in the eyes, something urgent in the corner of her mouth. 'Warn whom?' She shook her head. 'No. What would we say?'

'That he's a disease. That he's pestilence.' Tristan paused. Only his father? Not only him, surely. Maybe Halt and his people were right to come for them. 'That nothing but monsters will come of us.'

His mother turned her back to Tristan. She placed her forehead on the cold grey of the wall. 'We can't,' she said. 'They won't believe us. Not at first.' Another pause. 'And when they do, it will be too late. It will be the pitchforks and the torches again.' Her fingers felt for the grooves of the stone.

Tristan approached her, put his hands around her shoulders. She fit into his embrace whole, left room for more.

'Does that mean we shouldn't try?' he asked.

He had to tell them. He devised an excuse to have the whole village come together at the square while his father was away on a hunt, said he knew how to spare their animals, heal their crops, safeguard their wells. The crowd gathered. His mother was there, too. She shook her head, but she didn't stop him.

Tristan stood under a great plane tree and waited until everyone fell quiet. He hadn't planned exactly what words he would use to convince them, or what, exactly, he wanted them to do. All he knew was that he had to warn them, to save them, or at least give them whatever chance he could to save themselves.

So he spoke. He told them his father would destroy them and everything they ever cared for. That the world would soon be a dungeon, that their meagre crops would fail. Their trees would rot, their animals would give birth to snakes.

When Tristan was done, the square was quiet. It seemed everyone was holding their breath. Tristan imagined his mother coming forwards, saying his name, telling everyone that what he said was the truth. That he wasn't a prophet, but the son of a monster.

But she didn't.

First, it was just an old woman laughing. A jeer, a taunt. Then, others laughed with her. One person, two, a dozen. More. 'Go home, boy, you're drunk!' one of the men shouted.

The crowd scattered as people waved their hands dismissively at Tristan, not angry he'd wasted their time, not amused by the strange ramblings of the outsider, but eager to go home nonetheless. Only one young man didn't join in the mocking. He caught Tristan's eye and held his gaze. He had brown curly hair, a thick, protruding brow, and lips too full for his gaunt face, his hollow cheeks. What's your name? Tristan wanted to ask him. Do you believe me?

The man turned and left before Tristan had a chance to speak a word.

Eunice pauses here, and I can sense her shame. I hold her hand. We go on.

Tristan's mother stood still. She was looking at him, ignoring the jeering of the people around her. Then one of the women touched her shoulder and asked if what her son had said was true.

There was only a moment's hesitation before his mother shook her head.

'He's ill, you see,' she said with a sad, apologetic smile. 'He's always been a sickly boy.'

Tristan returned to the woods, to live there permanently, among the trees and the leaves and the silent birds. If his father heard of his conduct at the village gathering, Tristan never knew about it, and his father never came looking to confront him.

With only his horse for company, Tristan wandered deeper into the woods, further than he'd gone before, deeper, perhaps, than anyone had ever been. Here, the forest smelled old. Tristan marvelled at the tall oaks, their bark ancient and rough. He lived on foraged fruit and animals he hunted or trapped, then killed and skinned with his own hands.

After a while, his heart quieted. Tristan spent long hours lying on the dark leaves and staring at the canopy above. He felt the animals watching him, the forest itself holding its breath when he walked. But they let him be, and he them. Here, there was no grief, no shame, no sorrow. The animals knew death, but they did not know torment.

When his father's disease reached the heart of the woods, it was already too late. The forest started to wither around him. The ground grew soft in places, treacherous, ready to swallow him whole if he wasn't careful, and the trees twisted into themselves. The animals followed soon after: he came upon a snake with a single eye in the middle of its head, a toad with a gaping mouth on its stomach. Everywhere, the air carried the scent of decay. The conifers turned yellow, then brown, then black, and they oozed with a thick white substance, like pus.

Tristan knew he had to go back to the house, and so that's what he did, his mare's steps heavy and careful, his own chest a snare for his heart.

When he came up the road and caught a first glimpse of the house, he thought he'd been mistaken; that all the doom and misery he'd anticipated was just a reflection of his own sick mind. But the signs became clear soon enough. The green he saw was lichen, was rot; the roses reeked of blood. All around him, the garden stood dead, the trees naked and petrified.

He walked up to the front door and pushed his way in. The entranceway was filled with leaves, as if a great shedding had taken place inside. He wondered what had caused it this time. A young horse, dead in the stable? Something she'd said? A turning of the weather that had brought on one of his moods?

He found his mother next to the fireplace, its flame long extinguished, the ashes cold for days. Her skin was sallow, her hair dry and brittle.

'Where is my father?' he asked.

'Out. Riding his horse.'

Tristan glanced at the space around them: the disintegrating furniture, the bare walls, the broken crockery. Then he knelt before her. 'Let's go away from this place,' he said, grasping her shoulders gently. 'Let's leave it all behind, go somewhere else, start anew, without him.'

She looked at Tristan for the first time. Her eyes were dim, but her gaze was as loving as ever. She caressed the side of his face, rubbed her fingers on the stubble on his cheeks. Five years had passed since that night at the well. 'My boy,' she said. 'How beautiful you are. And how like your father.'

He recoiled. 'I'm nothing like him,' he said, sitting back on his haunches.

His mother smiled but didn't reply.

He crawled closer and put his head on her lap, like he used to do when he was small. She ran her fingers through his hair and scratched his scalp lightly in the way she knew calmed him. He closed his eyes and lost himself in her comfort. He imagined the fire burning beside them until everything went dark and quiet. He slept.

When Tristan woke, his mother was gone. He was still lying on the floor, a bundled shawl placed lovingly under his head. He searched for her in every room. Dust covered every surface. All the windows were shut. The house was empty, but, he thought, not inert. The doors creaked in some secret shifting of weight, some unknown draught.

He never found her. When night fell, he was still in the quiet of the house. He slept in her bed, under her covers, next to her pillow. In the morning, he left the house and walked through the village. The people were few, the dogs fewer, emaciated and limping. Some of the houses stood empty, the doors hanging open like the mouths of the desperate.

He found his way to the tavern where a few men sat, hunched, staring into cups of clear liquid or bowls of soup. They glanced at him when he walked in, and already he could see the smirk lurking around their lips, the disbelief still in their tired eyes, despite all that had befallen them.

He tried to talk to them again. To explain what his father was, what he did to the land, the animals, the crops. All he wanted was for someone to say: I believe you. But the men laughed at him once more, called him a fool, a mad boy. It was just a bad year and it would pass, they said. They had more important things to worry about – mundane things, material things – no need for fairy tales and cursed men. When he was gone, they would go back to their houses, light candles and pray.

He saw why his parents had chosen this village. The people were too meek in the face of disaster, too gentle to withstand what was in store for them. Otherwise they would be beating down his father's door by then, torches lit and pitchforks ready for the ones who had come and brought with them their strange plagues, their unhappy diseases that infected the earth, the water, the sky.

Tristan told them so.

In the end, they threw rocks at him to make him stop; even the ones who found him funny spat in his face, chased him through the streets, cursing his words and the bad luck they would bring.

Tristan ran through the village, not knowing where to go. He could hardly see in front of himself, and his breath scorched his chest. Finally, he stopped, steadied himself against a white-washed wall. There was no point. His father would stay here until this place was no more than a hole in the ground, the entire village nothing but a bog where things sank and festered for ever. And then he would move to a new place, take root there, let the tendrils of his malady coil into new lands, new lives, new skies.

It would go on like this, for ever, because his father fit every-where.

Someone touched Tristan's shoulder. He turned around, his hand balled into a fist, ready to defend himself against more ridicule and abuse.

But it was only the curly-haired youth he had seen at the square, back before the days of the forest. He was looking at Tristan kindly, eyes narrowed not with disbelief but with concern. 'Tristan,' he said. His voice was smooth and deeper than he had expected. 'Tristan.'

'You know my name?'

The man smiled shyly. He rubbed the back of his head. 'Everyone knows your name,' he said. 'Ever since that rambling speech.'

Tristan started walking away. 'I've had enough mockery for one day,' he said. 'I don't need another round.'

The young man ran to catch up with him, his hand on Tristan's shoulder again. 'No, I apologise. I don't mean to mock you,' he said. 'I know you're telling the truth.'

Tristan stopped in his tracks. He turned to face the man. 'How?' he asked.

They went to the woods. The man's name was Marius. Tristan took him to his makeshift hut in the heart of the dying forest. 'Watch your step,' he told the youth, and Marius stepped lightly, following Tristan so closely he could feel the warmth of his breath on the back of his neck. He wondered if, seen from behind the way Marius saw him now, he looked anything like Halt. Did this man feel at all the way Tristan had once felt when he followed his friend into the stomach of a cave?

They foraged for the few surviving berries together, then built a weak fire and sat on the ground to eat them. Marius's eyes shone in the light, and that only made them seem even darker.

'So?' Tristan asked. 'Why would you listen to me? What makes you different?'

Marius passed his hand over the fire, cutting a flame across the middle. Too quickly to burn himself. Tristan tried hard not to think of Halt. 'I . . .' Marius started, hesitated. 'I can see things most people can't.'

'What things?'

'The first time I saw your father, he seemed covered in a thick, wet shroud. I told my mother, then my grandfather. They laughed at me the way these men now laugh at you. I insisted, though. I knew what I saw. So they took me to a priest who read over my head, and to a doctor who ordered cold baths. I didn't speak of it again for months, but I could see right away that your father would bring disease and pain to this place.' He paused again. 'To any place.'

What did it feel like, to hear his truth spoken by another? To be understood that well by a stranger? Tristan had no word for it, because he'd never felt like that before. Even his mother, witness to his father's violence well before Tristan was born, didn't quite understand his father's nature.

Tristan told Marius as much, with clumsy words that said so little.

The young man seized Tristan's hand as he spoke those words that I know can break a heart apart and put it back together again: 'I believe you,' he said. 'I believe you.'

They became fast friends in this belief. They spent many days and nights in the woods, and yet nobody came looking for them.

Marius worked hard to keep Tristan healthy and fed well, his horse watered and happy. They both knew what had to happen, what had to come next.

The night before the day Tristan would finally face his father, he asked Marius to leave. 'Go back to the village,' he said. 'Be with your family now, with the ones you love.'

Marius shook his head. 'I won't leave you alone tonight,' he said.

'Aren't heroes supposed to be alone?' Tristan asked with a half-smile and a foolish heart that beat too fast.

'Says who?' Marius replied. His white teeth reflected the light of the fire.

All the stories, Tristan wanted to say. All of them.

But he remained silent. He tried not to compare this silence with those he'd shared with Halt.

Marius cradled Tristan's head and lay on the ground. They were on their backs, above them only the vast flatness of the sky. Tristan imagined it was Halt cradling him, though he knew the comparison was unfair, that no person could be a substitute for another. He imagined, also, everything that could happen still: the games they could play, the fires they could light, the life they could spend in each other's company.

'I don't think you should do it,' his friend said after a while.

Tristan pushed himself up. 'But you believed me,' he protested. 'You know why I have to do this.'

Marius refused to look at him. He picked up a dry leaf from the ground and crushed it between his fingers. 'I know. But I don't want you to.'

'You think I'll lose, is that it?'

This time his friend looked him straight in the eyes. 'I'm thinking of myself, Tristan,' he said. 'I'm the one who doesn't want to lose.'

It was Tristan's turn to look away. Isn't it better to have an effect on the world, he thought, any effect, than to pass through this life as if you never existed at all?

He kissed his friend's forehead. Said nothing.

*　　*　　*

This time, his father stood in front of the house, as if he'd been expecting it: his son, his challenger. Tristan waited at the entrance of the garden until his father joined him.

Eunice pauses, touches her mouth. She says, and I repeat:

Tristan didn't go inside the house, because he knew his mother would be there. If he saw her, he wouldn't be able to go through with what he had to do.

For this, he knew, they had to go to the forest.

As they rode their horses along the streets on their way out of the village, Tristan saw his father smile. It was a wild, toothy smile, a grin almost. Tristan felt that thing in the middle of his chest, that snared thing. He felt like laughing and like crying. As they passed the town's tavern, Tristan saw one of the men sitting on the porch, drinking. It was a friend of his father's — he'd been among the ones who'd spat at him before. Tristan waved; his father waved. The man lifted his cup and drank to their health.

When they left the village behind, Tristan's father whipped his horse and rode ahead at full speed. This was it, then. This was how the story would end: Once upon a time, Tristan chased his father into the woods, looking to drive a knife through his heart.

They faced each other at night, in a clearing by the river, with nothing to shelter them from the dimming sky that yawned above.

'I always knew it would come to this,' his father said. 'Ever since your mother asked for you.' He sounded tired. His hand opened and closed. This hand that would do such atrocious things.

Tristan pulled the knife from his belt and held it.

147

'Then let us be quick about it,' his father said.

Tristan dismounted. They were so close now, closer than they'd been in a long time. Tristan could feel the heat of his father's body. He could smell the night on him, and something else that came from his skin.

They circled each other. Tristan looked at his father's shadow, and, for a moment, all he could see was a black silhouette too big for a man, a monster with horns and wings.

They fought. Tristan had trained for this so hard, for so long, and yet this moment was nothing like swinging sticks and rocks at Halt in the forest of their youth. This made his body hurt like never before, bleed like never before. The sound of their fighting filled the night, roused faraway wolves from their sleep. They howled until his father's knife found its way between Tristan's ribs.

His father grabbed Tristan's shoulder, retrieved his knife, then drove it in again. Twisted it.

Tristan fell backwards. The moon slipped free of the clouds, and suddenly everything was radiant: the trees, the river, the mountains beyond.

The young man staggered to his feet, his lungs as heavy as lead. He remembered that day in Halt's cave when his friend had walked on coals and told himself he felt no pain. Tristan longed to go back to that cave, to its shadows and warmth, where a body was nothing.

But here he was. He bayed like a dog under the forgetful sky. The air smelled of acid and blood. It wasn't enough. His father kicked him in the groin, then under the chin.

Tristan looked at his father's hand, then at his own, then at the ground. Who was it that said, you become what you behold? He looked away. He would stay on the ground, then.

His father approached again. Tristan noticed the man's hand was bleeding; had he cut himself on his own blade, or had Tristan wounded him, too? He couldn't remember. His father knelt next to him, his hands resting on his legs. Tristan felt his eyes roll into his head, and he saw such things there: his mother's face, her hands. The wind, the wheat, the sand. He had imagined this scene before, hadn't he? The clearing in the forest, the wolf, the moon, the murder in their eyes. It was all as he'd pictured it, except the way it ended. He wished his mother were here, now, to witness. He would open his hands, show her his palms and say: Here, Mother. I finally have a story for you.

Eunice falters. She cannot continue, so I pick up where she leaves off, speak for her instead. I tell myself this is a kindness.

Tristan opened his eyes again, aware that he was dying. It was hard to breathe. His father watched in astonishment, as if the whole thing were a surprise to him, the scene plucked from a story that belonged to someone else.

The mare neighed, not two feet away. It was a happy sound, and her flesh was so good and so warm. Tristan could almost touch her if he reached out. Almost. The world so good and so warm.

Pain shot through his body. He climbed to his knees and threw up blood and bile. He was shaking; his teeth clattered. Doubled over, he held his stomach, trying to keep something in, something else from running out. He fell to the ground again, his eyes and mouth wide open, his limbs twisted into knots, and he thought, What things make a man kill another! What things!

But he was too tired to make a sound. His lungs too worn out to be filled with air. He thought, I never did learn how to swim, after all, did I? Only how to drown.

His father stood before him, the bloodied knife still in his hand – is that blood mine, Tristan thought wearily. And what if it is?

The man patted the mare's flank tenderly. The moonlight fell on his face in such a way it made his beard look blue.

'Your horse is beautiful,' the man said, and it occurred to Tristan that, for all the forests he'd come to know so well, he never knew his father's heart.

The mare snorted and stomped. She was ready to leave this place.

So was Tristan.

The man took his knife and buried it in Tristan's chest.

(BLACKOUT.)

You shift where you sit by the sofa. You look betrayed. Here, like this, you resemble your father the most: The angle of your jaw, the curve of your lip. The colour of your hair.

I'm sorry. I know this is not the story you wanted.

Eunice's ghost is on the floor under the window, her back against the wall, her head in her hands, not weeping.

For a moment there is no light, no shadows. I would stop here, if I could.

But I need you to hear the rest now, before your path is set. Before you too become a photograph of a boy in a shoebox, against the background of a castle's ruins.

Eunice, the first wife

When they brought her Tristan's body, Eunice didn't recognise it. She thought it a belated changeling, her son's body replaced by a wax effigy or a piece of wood that everyone worked hard to convince her had once been her baby.

The men laid him on the kitchen table and her mind couldn't make sense of it, this strange banquet, what was she supposed to do with it? His skin was cold. There was a roaring in her ears, and she thought she could hear the sea. Surely, somewhere, a river was flowing backwards.

Eunice put her hands on her son. She touched him the way you touch something you are used to seeing every day, but one day something changes imperceptibly and you see it again for the very first time. You wonder at it, touch it to make sure it's real, to make sure that it still belongs to you, that it still belongs in the world.

I pause briefly to search your face. I think, don't look at the bedroom door. I breathe, or at least I try. The ghosts won't meet my eyes. They know this story; all women know it. How it started, how it ends. I tell them, don't. There's still time. Tristan is not you. I won't let them mourn for you.

Eunice's husband was at the kitchen door, holding the frame. When he moved his hand, it left behind a smear of blood. He said a word she couldn't understand. Said it again. Her name. He said, 'I killed Tristan. I killed our son, who tried to kill me.'

The words were strange, but she had always known she'd hear them, one day.

The men who'd brought back the body lingered silent behind her husband. Some held hats scrunched in front of their chests, solemn. She recognised none of them. Where had they found her son? How had they come upon him? They looked away when she sought their eyes. They had not taken the knife out of her son's chest. She knew that knife, her husband's – she'd used it herself to cut open rabbits before, and once, on a night of ill sleep when she'd felt as if she were standing at the edge of a precipice, high up on a cliff, looking down, to cut her own hair. It had been sharp, then. Was it still as sharp now?

And her husband at the door, what was he called? He cradled his hand, bled through his short-nailed fingers onto the floor. Good. He was so changed, she thought, so very changed. Had she loved this man, once, did she love him still? She stood up and approached him, took his hand to inspect the wound – a deep, ugly gash across his palm. What line was this? Was it the fate line or the heart line? She couldn't remember.

She fetched a clean cloth and alcohol for the wound. Her husband sent away the men. They went silently, the way they had come, the way they had stood.

Eunice tended to her husband, and he let her.

Had she really always known? Was it better if she had, or worse?

'This is the last time I touch you,' she said.

She remembered herself a bride, how strange it had felt. Would she get used to the idea of it, she had wondered back then, of this man, her husband, this man who had touched her, to whom she had said yes? And then, when she was pregnant with Tristan, she kept dreaming of horses. Mares running wild in a field of black poppies, stallions drawing chariots across the sun, foals falling from their mothers to the ground, covered in mucus and blood, their thin limbs trembling in the bright air. When the child was born, she eyed his full head of hair with suspicion. She couldn't help but check his body for soft fur, count the fingers on his hands and the toes on his feet, inspect his teeth.

'You will have no more children,' she told her husband, and the words are not easy for me to speak. 'Not by me, and not by any other woman. Never,' she said. 'Never ever.'

He nodded but didn't say anything, so she jutted her chin at him. She would have touched him if she hadn't said she wouldn't. 'Do you promise?' she asked.

He lowered his eyes. His voice, when he spoke, was little more than a whisper. 'I promise,' he said. 'Never.'

Eunice wished she had given birth to a young stallion instead of a human child. Something that would not have listened to her stories of castles and blood-letting and knives. Something that could have bolted when there was still time.

At night, Tristan's body was still on the kitchen table, cold and grey. Eunice sat in a chair next to it. She could no longer bring herself to touch it, so she kept her hands in the air in front of her, she didn't know what to do with them.

Her husband dared to come near. He put his hand on Eunice's shoulder, on her belly, sought her lips, and suddenly she was sick with rage. So filled with it nothing else fit, her organs pushed aside. She felt as if she were shedding her skin, as if she were becoming a strange thing herself, a changed thing, a natural disaster, like him.

He felt it, too, because he recoiled. Took a step back, then another.

'You killed our son,' she said.

'He tried to kill me first.'

'You should have let him.'

But she knew it as she said it: this man could not be killed. He was larger than life, and so were his crimes. Who could possibly destroy destruction?

When he spoke again, his voice was hoarse, gravel-full. 'Sometimes I think my father cursed me,' he said without conviction. His eyes streamed, his hand welled up with blood despite her care. 'This is why I'm like this.'

'It's not what you are,' Eunice said. 'It's what you choose to do.'

'And the fields?' he asked. 'The animals? I can't help it.'

'Perhaps,' she said, avoiding a glance in the body's direction. 'But this? You could help this.' Her breath felt shallow. She was running out of air. In that moment, she thought of her stories. She wanted to recount them all and wonder, was this her fault? Had she tried to use her son to kill her husband, to be free of him and everything he was? She wouldn't know where to start. With which stories? Her mind was upturned soil.

'Your father didn't curse you,' she said. 'You are not cursed.'

Some time passed during which neither of them spoke, and all they could hear was the steady dripping of rain against stone outside. When had this rain started?

'No, he didn't,' he said finally. 'No, I'm not.'

She thought of the knife in her son's chest, how it would stay there for ever, how the earth would rust it until the blade was useless, and, she told herself, I've had enough of this place. She imagined Tristan and his father outside under the moonlight, embracing and blood-letting, and herself here, alone, here, here.

Why did she stay?

'I need to go home,' she said, and for a moment he didn't seem to understand what she meant. Weren't they home already? So she added: 'I need to bury my son in the land where I was born.'

In the land that birthed you, too, she didn't say. Where it all began.

You stand up, your fists balled, indignant. You're angry, I know. At me. At her.

I'm sorry. I'm so sorry. I wish—

'But how could she stay with him?' you ask. 'Why didn't she just leave?' A sound draws your attention to the window, and a hint of fear crosses your brow, though the anger is not gone. Your face is red. Your lips a shade of blue.

I reach for you, almost touch your hair. I would take your anger over your fear any time, given the choice.

There's no one there, I tell you.

I can see you want to ask again: Why didn't she leave? Why didn't she just leave?

The ghosts turn their backs to us. They will not hear of this. Not again. Not ever.

I resume my tale.

Before they left, I say, Eunice washed the sheets, bleached the floor, cleared the fireplace of ash, which she stored in buckets she then buried in the ground outside, as if anything that had come in contact with them could contaminate whoever inhabited this place after them, and she needed to eliminate all traces of their life here. Then she cleaned her hands and her fingernails, her neck and her lips, her breasts and her belly. She had been doing this all day yet there was no end to it, as if she were trying to wash herself back into a maiden, a girl, a child. A childless child – a strange concept, yet she remembered it, so she must have at one point been so.

Her husband was in the other room. He grunted as he applied alcohol to the wound on his hand. She made her way to the other room and watched him. The gushing still hadn't stopped, but he seemed unable to run out of blood, as if he contained entire wells of it. Oceans of it.

Bleeding, he emptied his cabinet and put away his precious things, his strange possessions. Tenderly, she thought. He could still be tender, if he wanted.

Then they were off.

The carriage wobbled on the long road home, weighed down by its expensive load. This was the first time they'd left a place without being chased away.

They didn't speak. The man sank into his seat, buried in his furs, and Eunice looked out the window at the barren land. She hadn't wanted to touch her son's body any more, but now she longed to touch anything else, everything else, to plant her fingers deep in that lifeless land. Tristan was in a wooden box tied to the roof, her mind told her, over and over, a box next to the chest that held her dresses. Tristan. In a box. On the roof. The barren soil didn't care. Tristan. In a box. On the roof. Lucky soil.

Somehow along the way she closed her eyes, and when she opened them again the horses were struggling up the road to the manor house. Soon it came into view, like a distant stone mirage in a sea of leaves, the roof upholstered in lichen. The garden seemed wilder, greener in places and yellower in others, vernal shoots breaking through the soil.

The carriage pulled to a stop in front of the house. Eunice climbed down, and the magnitude of the decline hit her. The once-impressive front entrance with the large oak doors had sagged on its hinges, the grey stone covered in tendrils, the wood peeling, eaten slowly by worms. Some of the balconies that overlooked the grounds had collapsed, and most of the stained-glass windows had shattered. Still, the house remained as imposing as ever – more, perhaps. It had been in her husband's family for generations, and she had always felt a bit out of place in it. It was too cold and formal, and she much preferred the little cottage she had lived in as a child.

Eunice pushed open the oak doors. It was easier than she had expected.

The house was lightless and musty, and it took her eyes a few moments to adjust after stepping in from the sun-drenched day outside. The interior hadn't changed at all, except for the thick layer of dust that covered everything.

She walked through the house, the sound of her footsteps muffled somehow, and it seemed to her the house itself wished its silence to remain undisturbed. Eunice's fingers brushed the furniture, leaving behind long trails in the dust, as if something much larger than herself had ambled through these rooms. Outside, dusk was thickening as her husband wrangled the horses, unloaded the carriage.

The box, her mind screamed, the box.

Eunice wiped her forehead; her skin was clammy against the chill in the air. She walked down the corridor to the kitchen, following a crackling sound. Someone had set a fire in the hearth; had her husband sent word of their arrival? Had someone come here to light the fire for them, to keep the cold from getting into their bones?

The kitchen was in the same state as the rest of the house: the shining copper pots now blue-green and dull with dust, the wood countertops cracked dry. Eunice walked further in, running her hands over it all, as if touch were the only way to see now, her fingers her only connection to the world.

Her breath caught. Someone was sitting at the table, huddled, unmoving. A corpse, she thought, old and desiccated.

Then the corpse moved, like something out of a nightmare; it turned towards her, its eyes shining in the flames.

Agnes. Eunice hadn't given her the merest of thoughts, sure the woman would have left the house long ago. But she was still here, thin and small, her cheeks hollow, her face gaunt.

'Did I scare you?' the woman asked.

'You didn't leave,' Eunice gasped.

Agnes unfolded her arms. 'Where would I have gone?'

Something climbed Eunice's throat.

Her husband used to say every person was a house, and that there were hidden rooms in both of them, as in everyone. For a time, he had been right. In hers, there had been Anne, nights spent outside under the wide sky, and secret desires held close to the skin. Not anymore. He had raided those rooms. Ransacked them. Her house was empty. Not even Eunice lived there.

'Anywhere else,' she told Agnes. 'Living your life.' Agnes could not have been much more than sixty by then.

'I knew you'd be back. I said I'd keep the place for you.' The woman paused. Her face changed: something pleading in the eyes, a softness around the corners of her lips. 'How's my little lord?' she asked. 'Is he here?'

Her little lord. The one with the knife in his chest, Eunice wondered, or the one who had wielded it? But no, this woman had never met Tristan.

'Come see for yourself,' Eunice said.

Together, they walked down the hall, Eunice in front, Agnes following a small step behind. 'He's here,' Eunice called ahead, quickening her step. 'Just outside.'

The woman struggled to keep up. Her breath came in short, laboured bursts that almost made Eunice feel sorry for her, for this unwarranted cruelty. What had Agnes ever done to her? All she had done was care for her charge. Love him. So had Eunice, hadn't she? So she still did. Didn't she?

When they got to the front door, Eunice stepped aside, cowering from the sight of the box. Two men from the village were helping her husband take it down. They deposited it on the ground like luggage, like any other burden. She couldn't stand to see it there, on the grass and the cobblestones.

Agnes supported herself on the door, looking out, her eyes half-closed, as if unaccustomed even to the light. The man's back was turned, so Agnes stayed like that for a while, staring at those broad shoulders, as if trying to divine in them the form of the child he had once been. Then, she stumbled down the stairs and fell at his feet, sobbing, her hands reaching for the fabric of his trousers. 'You're back,' she gasped, again and again, 'you're back.'

The man turned, a little surprised, a little annoyed. How long did it take him to recognise the woman who had fed him her milk, who had raised him as her own? Not long, for he grasped her by the shoulders and stood her up in front of him and, a fleeting moment of disgust later, he folded her into his embrace and let her sob there for a long time.

Then, as if to show her something he had brought back from his long travels, he lifted the lid off Tristan's casket: 'This is our son,' he told her. 'Our son, whom I've killed.'

At her son's funeral, Eunice felt nothing. Her chest was empty, her bowels, her veins, empty. No part of her was warm. Would ever be warm again.

The land around them had recovered in their absence. Most of the townspeople seemed to have forgotten, too, and those who remembered appeared to have grown beyond caring or come to doubt their own memories. A few of them made their way to the cemetery to see off the young lord who had come and ceased to be in one long-winded sentence. A middle-aged man even walked up to Eunice and put his hand on her arm, overly familiar.

She stared at him for a moment, his stranger's features, his wandering eyes, this face that meant nothing to her.

'I told you not to spend time with that boy,' the man said, and it was the voice that transformed him from a stranger into a brother. Her only brother, whom her husband had hurt all those years ago. 'But you insisted. It was your choice.'

The voice, and the scars.

'Brother,' was all she said, because that wasn't how she remembered it. The way she remembered it, it was her mother who'd forced her to go up to that house in her brother's stead, as if she were a replacement, as if the two of them were no different at all but entirely interchangeable in their function.

It was her mother who'd forced her to grit her teeth and look kindly on that strange and violent boy. Before she'd glimpsed the good in him. She remembered how long it had taken her to find it, how long before she'd grown to love him. She wondered, Which story was true?

Did it matter?

Her son was in a box.

Her brother was crying, and she had to support him from the elbow to keep him from collapsing. 'I just wish I could have met my nephew,' he said brokenly. Eunice felt nothing.

Her friend came, too. Anne. How had she known to come? Eunice remembered their long conversations in the garden she'd shared with Tristan when he was so young—and now, in his box, wasn't he still too young? Her friend's visit had felt like power; she remembered that too. They'd talked about Eunice leaving, then. Anne had urged her to. 'There's a life for you away from him,' Anne had said. 'For you both.' But Eunice had decided to stay. For Tristan's sake, she'd said. This Tristan, in the box.

Anne approached Eunice, her face pale, her eyes red. She took Eunice's hand and squeezed it in her own gloved one.

'Had you seen it?' Eunice asked. 'In the lines of his hands, or mine? Why didn't you tell me?'

The woman didn't let go of her hand. 'What would you have done if I had?' she asked.

She mouthed the answer without thinking. 'I'd have left,' she said. 'Taken him far, far away, kept him safe.'

Anne shook her head. 'No, you wouldn't have.'

No, she wouldn't have. 'How do you know?'

'Because you knew already. You didn't need to read the lines on a hand to know.' It was said plainly, with no blame.

Eunice leaned her head on her friend's shoulder as the casket was covered for the last time, and her son's eyes were lost to her.

When the box was lowered into the hole, she recalled other mothers who'd shrieked at that moment, who'd wished to follow their children into the ground. Eunice wanted to be filled with soil. Not to be covered by dirt but to be abundant with it, pregnant with it, to consume it, the entire earth if she could, so that none would be left to claim her son.

She thought: I'll never see him again. I will never see him again.

They shovelled dirt onto the wood. Women she didn't know cried over her son's grave. Why are they crying? she wondered. None of them knew her son. Someone snuck her a handful of dirt and she closed her fingers around it. Threw it into the hole.

And then he was buried, in the same way his grandfather had been buried, under the same trees, the same sky. She remembered she wore black for that man for a long time. Why had she done that?

There are so few ways to mourn, she thought. Her mind conjured up stories like the ones on which she'd raised Tristan. The prince was dead, eaten by the moon. The king ordered all the wolves in the kingdom slaughtered in his grief. The queen was kept captive in a box, in the dark.

They didn't speak on the ride home. Eunice thought of leaving, then – of jumping out of the carriage and throwing herself on the ground, then picking herself up and walking away from all of this. Let her legs take her as far away as they would carry her.

Her legs, motionless, kept the peace. Tristan would remain here, and so would Eunice.

Her husband was silent in the driver's seat, his face set, his eyes focused on the road ahead. He seemed to be waging a war within himself, a battle against his grief and his loss. From the corner of her eye, she saw his hand shake when he reached for the reins.

Back at the house, she wanted to feel the wind on her skin, but there was nothing. She looked at her hand. There was dirt in the lines of her palm. She no longer needed her friend's help to read them. She was fluent now: a past of soil, a present of soil, a future of soil.

Agnes hadn't come to the funeral. She stood now at the threshold, watching them return without Tristan, without a box. Anne had left as soon as the last words were spoken. They were on their own again, the three of them.

She remembered a story Agnes had told her once, about curiosity, a set of keys, wives disobeying their husband one after another, bearing witness to his awful deeds. 'But what about the first one?' she had wanted to ask Agnes then. 'What was in the husband's secret room when the first wife discovered it?'

She asked her now, when her husband left them alone by the door. She wondered if Agnes had told this story to her husband as well, when he was but a little boy.

Agnes smiled. She remembered the story, too. 'That's the thing,' the older woman said. 'That's what I always liked best about this story, and the thing I found the most fearsome. It was nothing, you see? The room had been empty. It wasn't his fault.' She glanced at the unburdened carriage, then reached for Eunice's shoulder but stopped short of touching her.

*   *   *

Eunice found herself grateful for the darkness of the house. She spent hours curled up on her bed, staring mutely at the naked walls. Agnes came to sit with her sometimes, though neither of them spoke. There was no friendship between them, no animosity.

Her husband spent his time struggling against the decay that had consumed the house over the years of their absence. He tore down the wallpaper and polished the floors. He replaced the broken windows, made sure the fire in the big hearth was always lit to drive out the mildew and the cold. He repaired the roof and had new balconies built to overlook the grounds. Finally, he brought in gardeners to prune and replant, he tilled the land and hired workers to bring it back to life with crops. He planted a cherry orchard in the back.

And then, he went to town and ordered the most expensive furniture he could find to replace the creaky beds, the gutted armchairs, the tables gnawed by rats. He hung new art on the walls, found more strange things to fill his cabinet.

It all left Eunice unmoved. The opal, the gilded mirrors, the rugs the colour of arterial blood.

(BEAT. DIM LIGHTS.)

I wonder about this constant decay.

Was that your doing? I ask the ghosts, but no, of course it wasn't; these women are not the women of my fairy tale, and there were not yet ghosts.

Their hair is longer now, grown hastily over the course of this telling. It trails on the floor, gets tangled around their shuffling feet.

They don't respond. They contemplate a flaw on the wall instead, an indentation in the blue, the white plaster exposed underneath.

Their fingers trace the flaw, and I remember: it's where my head hit it, once.

I fall silent for a while, until you reach for my hand. Stop short of touching.

Summer begins again

Summer came, and with it, the garden's bounty. Eunice walked through it often, even ventured into the forest, remembering the places where she'd gotten to know the boy her husband had once been. This rock, this tree, this spring, now dry and wreathed with rotten leaves. She wondered: was he always like this? Was I?

And then, Eunice thought – he had been tender, once, before he changed. Maybe he could change again.

She started going out more and more often, until, without knowing it, she spent an entire morning gathering the early strawberries, plucking their little green heads and popping them into her mouth.

When she realised what she was doing, how sweet the fruits were, she spat out the last mouthful. She forgot to breathe. Scooped up a handful of soil and stuffed her mouth with it.

Her husband's hand still bled sometimes. It was one of the few things that pleased her, these days.

They no longer shared a bed. They found each other in the same space now and then but exchanged few words. Occasionally, he brought her dresses, which she wore once and then abandoned, folded, in the wooden chest at the foot of her bed. It kept getting heavier, until it was impossible for her to move. When she asked Agnes for help, the older woman joked, panting, about the corpses that must be hidden inside.

Then the summer was ended and winter came and the house grew cold once more, its draughts fierce, its foundations creaking its true age, despite all her husband's efforts to disguise it. The rooms reeked of mould, and Agnes kept plucking mint from the garden and scattering it over the bedsheets to mask the smell. She built fires in every room, lit all the stoves, but nothing could drive away this chill.

Eunice started dreaming of warm limbs entwined with her own, soft lips against her skin and hair. She woke in a cold sweat, on those nights, left her bed and walked barefoot down the hall until she found Agnes's room, her door ajar. She watched the woman stir in her sleep, her lips parted.

She felt guilty for none of it, neither the dreams nor the coveting of someone else's peace. Guilt went away, along with everything else: the grief, the rage, the urge to slay or leave or both. It was too much to hold in her body, or she was too small for it. So she shut it all away, locked it in the chest that held her dresses, swallowed the key.

She allowed herself to feel so little, now.

On a cold winter day, Eunice put on her nicest dress, slathered perfume on her skin to mask the smell of the house, and adorned her neck with a sapphire pendant, blue as the deepest sea. Then, she paid a driver to take her to a town a few hours east.

She found her first lover at an artists' café, the walls decorated with paintings of actors from long ago dressed as princes and kings. The man was young – perhaps too young, but who's to say? – with light hair and watery eyes that never seemed able to focus on anything for long. She was charmed by the way he held his cup, the way he drank, daintily, like a bird. He had a sketchbook in front of him, a piece of charcoal in his hand, his fingers black with it. She approached and inspected the sketch – a lady on a horse. 'You're good,' she told him, though he was mediocre at best.

He smiled, encouraged. 'I'm trying to make a living out of this,' he said. 'I prefer landscapes, but I do portraits like these because they pay the landlady.' Later, when they were together in his small bed, and her body felt emptier than it ever had before, he asked if she wanted her portrait made.

She said no.

The next lover was a woman she found at a run-down pub, drinking alone. She had short red hair, green eyes, and a face too wrinkled for her age. She smelled of honey and lavender. Eunice paid her handsomely, and the woman gave herself over gladly and easily, her lips nothing like Anne's. In her small room above the pub, the woman pulled Eunice's hair and bit her shoulder, and, when they were done, she told Eunice she much preferred women to men.

'Why?' Eunice asked.

The woman came closer. She took Eunice's hand and placed it on her cheek. 'Because when you do this,' she said, 'I don't flinch.'

The third lover was another young artist with a big Adam's apple and bright eyes. This time, Eunice said yes. He drew her naked, and she loved it, the pointlessness of it and the artistry.

There was a passivity to her body the way he drew it. Her gaze was vacant, as if she were already dead.

On her way back to the waiting carriage, Eunice tossed the drawing in the river. She came home with the taste of that man still on her tongue. She found her husband in Agnes's bedroom, his head in her lap, her fingers in his hair. Agnes whispered soothing words to him, as if he were a baby.

Her husband took lovers, too, she knew, men and women. He had the good sense to seek them in other towns, as she did. Some of his lovers were found dead later, one cold in a well, the water poisoned and rich with putrefaction, the body preserved perfectly except for the eyes, which were gone. Another, left in the woods, the man's body picked over by the wolves and the crows, his mouth full of soil. Most were never found at all.

When the first person from their village went missing – a young woman, Agnes's distant relative, in fact, which was to be expected; everyone in the village was related to everyone else – Eunice waited for the people to come with their pitchforks and torches. She woke up sweating in the night, sure she heard footsteps outside her bedroom door. She locked herself in her room with the big wooden chest that held her dresses, sat there breathing in their powdery smell.

But the people never came. Nobody shunned them, either; the villagers were still willing to till their land, feed them their fruit and vegetables, butcher their animals for the Sunday table.

The next villager to go missing was a young man, then a girl no more than twenty. And still, the people didn't come. 'These things happen,' they said. 'This is the way of the world.'

(BLUE LIGHT, OTHERWORLDLY.)

The ghosts crowd me, their dresses fluttering, moved by a long-ago breeze. I smell dust and soil, the musty insides of enclosed spaces, lids shut tight.

My head hurts. I bring finger to forehead, touch my papery skin. Oh, my mind says, oh, but I stop it, hold it together. A little more. A little further.

The ghosts kneel around me, like children eager to listen to the rest of the story, like you. An audience not for the cavernous vastness of a big theatre but for the intimate, soft-spoken trag-edies of a *Kammerspiel,* or the miniature flatness of a shadow play. I try to close my eyes, but I can still see their faces. This must be what it's like to be a ghost, I think for the first time: a wide-eyed existence, when you can no longer look away.

I say to you, remember that toy train set he gave you once? You were so little. He laid down the tracks in a circle for you, built the whole town around it, the post office, the church with its red, pointy bell tower, the train station. And then he set the train in motion. Round and round it went. Every time the train passed by the church, the little bell rang. It delighted you. You wanted to watch it again and again, waited for it with bated breath. I wondered at it. How weren't you bored? You knew what was coming, yet you received each ringing of the bell like a gift. You clapped your hands and said, 'Again! Again!' Then, I understood: you watched that train go, not despite knowing the bell would ring again but *because* you knew it would. The cycle was the draw. The pleasure was in the repetition.

Your face is dark. I think, perhaps, you don't remember.

'Where is that train now?' you ask, and I say, Lost in a move between homes.

Eunice catches my eye. There is guilt there, I can see, there's shame. For what comes next.

I don't want to speak.

But you need to tell it, her ghost whispers.

I slip away and pace around the dining table the way we once paced a garden.

Tell it now.

The girls

Eunice was the one who brought the first girls to the house. 'It's for a feast,' she told them, and nobody questioned this or asked what they were celebrating. All that mattered was the invitation, the coming, the bathing in the marvels of the house: the butter-smooth sheets, the delicious food, the abundance of everything. Eunice didn't feel guilty, because her intentions, she believed, had been good. She had thought that maybe this was the way to spare them all – herself, too. That, perhaps, if her husband's effect were divided among as many of them as possible, it would be diminished. Perhaps, that way, no one else would have to die.

Much later, she would come to think of this choice of hers as a form of self-destruction. A way of punishing herself by becoming finally and undeniably complicit.

But at the time she didn't think of any of that. She didn't let herself see the girls as witnesses, or as mirrors to her own pain. Neither did she think of these invitations as a form of self-preservation, another exchange, a sacrifice. But even if that's what it was – even if all she wanted, deep down, was to save herself – wouldn't that be natural? Of course she didn't want to be next. Can you blame her for that?

Can I?

So she escorted the girls to the house herself, through the woods and the fog. On the way, she told them about the castle and the people who lived in it, how nice they were, how kind. She told them about her husband, so young, so handsome, so kind. The girls giggled, their eyes lit with promise. She made sure they walked through the lush-again garden, under the branches of the cherry trees. She showed them around the house, let them wonder at the tapestries and paintings, at the bedposts and marble floors. And then, she fed them cherries herself. The girls were so absorbed by the experience, they hardly noticed her husband when he joined them. They accepted him as if he'd always been there in their midst, as natural as the blackness of late-harvested fruit. The girls smelled like vinegar and sugar. The cherries painted their mouths red. Wine flowed in rivers, and bottles were emptied and broken. Still, the house remained cold.

Eunice worried he would send them away, but her husband went along with it all. She wondered if this was a favour to her. He didn't do anything to the girls. He sat casually in their company, not speaking, observing them until they were too tired to stand. The girls went back to their homes at the end of the day, heads buzzing and eyes unfocused, a sweet exhaustion weighing down their limbs, something deeper, older, coiled in their bellies. Some of them got sick later, their faces ashen and funereal, their bodies impossible to warm.

When the first girl died, Eunice understood she had been mistaken. There are some things that can be neither measured nor divvied up. Some things take up as much space as they can, all the space there is, and if you keep feeding them, they will keep growing. She could have blamed herself then, asked herself: What have I done?

But she didn't. She imagined, instead, how much simpler it would be if she could just bring the girls to her husband's room one by one and watch him devour them, their fingers and toes, their hair and tongues.

When the girls were gone, Eunice and her husband sat side by side in the fire's pale light, between them only silence and the sour smell of cherry pulp. 'You're bleeding,' she told him sometimes, and he held his hand out, expecting her to tend to his wound, tie a cloth around it, or kiss it better, perhaps.

She didn't move.

Eunice never went to the cemetery. She roamed the area around the house, on foot or on her horse. The road, when she took it, was choked with roots and the skeletal remains of the trees that once stood there. The fog was so thick she could hardly see the horse she was riding, could hardly hear its breathing; so thick it absorbed even sound. But she could feel the mare's shivers against her thighs, its hesitations and exhaustion, as if it too were decaying, like the world.

When her long walks took her near the cemetery, she caught herself at the last minute and swerved, head bowed and fists clenched, steered herself in a new direction, circled the village and arrived at the house hours later, her legs aching, her feet blistered in her shoes. It didn't matter, as long as she avoided that place. She didn't want to step on its dead-full ground again, didn't want to lay eyes on the marble and soil of her son, his name inscribed on stone.

Every so often, she woke to the sound of footfalls in her room, wooden floorboards creaking familiarly under beloved feet. 'Tristan,' her lips spoke into the night, but when she opened her eyes there was nothing but the moonlight lancing through the curtains.

The girls kept coming, cherry-scented and red-lipped. They sickened, more and more. Around them, the walls were black with mould; her husband kept scraping it off and repainting them, only for them to return to black a few days later. The garden faded and died, the crops withered, the animals turned to ashes in their pens, their young coming out of the womb deformed, pregnant with maggots. Only the cherry trees blossomed wildly, their scent sickening-thick. It rose up the staircases and filled the house. New garments disintegrated in their wardrobes and chests, and they ended up wearing their old clothes, even those they'd donned on their wedding day. She, a white dress, yellowed at the collar and sleeves; he, a black coat that had started fraying at the shoulders. The clothes were turning to dust, leaving only whispers of fabric behind, like the wings of a moth.

Eunice spent most of her time in her room, now, a seasonal confinement of her own. She sat by the window and gazed at the faded world outside, the empty, silent world. She could feel it out there, the chill and the death, sprouting, infecting the air. The sickness was spreading out from them in circles, with the house at their centre. Eventually, the people who hadn't noticed, would, and those who had already noticed would stop denying what was plain. It was only a matter of time.

She passed her finger over the window and watched the fog gather around it in the shape of a white, silent bird. It was a while before she noticed that her husband was standing next to her, his hand on her shoulder, his mouth at her neck, as if this were one of her fantasies, as if he would devour her like one of her cherry girls.

She wondered if – how – she had ever loved him.

It was a slow process, this noticing. At first, it was one of the girls' fathers, who escorted his daughter to the house. He lingered near the door and inspected the decomposing garden with disgust. The cherry trees still prospered, their branches heavy with a last shower of petals before the coming extravagance of fruit. Eunice tried to distract the man with food, with wine, with small talk about the strange weather, the dead birds. He shook his head at the feast she laid before him, the wine in his cup. 'It's unnatural,' he muttered, yet he drank the wine, ate the food. He appraised the mouldering house, the vines suffocating the windows like the veins of some great black heart. 'You're right,' Eunice said, and she filled his cup again, and she watched him drink as his daughter's laughter reached them from inside. They always drank, she'd noticed, they always ate. She made her offerings. No one ever said no.

He was wrong, of course, about what is natural. In her years with her husband, Eunice had come to understand a thing about nature, the one that surrounds us and the one inside. It is what distorts, what rots and infects, what festers. Is anything man can do or be unnatural? Are all the horrors and all the monsters that nature births not of nature itself? Still, people make their choices.

The garden, yes. It was foul, nothing like the sunny meadows of her childhood, and nothing to be done. But she took her guests to the cherry trees all the same, not just the girls, but the men, the fathers, the brothers and husbands, and with them the mothers, the wet nurses and sisters and wives. As they came, she imagined them tainted by the house and his presence within it, marred by the rotting walls and the shuddering floors, infected by the air heavy with the smell of the trees and the mould that permeated all the curtains and sheets her guests slept on. They entered, they drank, they ate, they smiled at her and at one another, until the flesh beneath their skin started to turn ashen, until their eyes darkened, until all the wounds they carried inside them opened up and dripped.

It had been a long time since they'd last slept together, Eunice and her husband, but she let him watch her at night, naked, her skin like parchment under her own fingers, her bones marrow-thin beneath her skin. He said nothing, but his gaze moved over her, eloquent and slow. Eunice listened, her eyes shut tight, her lips bitten raw. His breath smelled of spoiled cherries. She couldn't tell if she was listening to him or the wind, the trees, the soft thump of the dead birds in the garden below. Still, she didn't move.

The taste of cherries lingered on her own tongue, too, numbing. She had swallowed the pit of the last one she'd eaten, and she could feel it now, growing in her belly, making of her a slowly ripening fruit. She wondered when she'd bloom.

The girls kept coming.

They were soft and young, their eyes glassy, the palest hazel or green. Her husband held them, whispered to them, and they giggled, flushed delirious, cherry-stained. They went with him to his room, or to the garden, where she found their dresses the next day, sometimes torn, sometimes intact, but always, always red.

In the end, the villagers arrived with their pitchforks, their fire and scythes, their anger old and true, its roots deep. She spotted her brother among them, and some of the cherry girls, too. They surrounded the house, put their torches to the garden. The dry grass caught immediately, the dead trees like burning men, their arms outstretched, their flaming heads thrown back, mouths open to devour the sky. The smoke drifted into the house as if the building itself had inhaled. It choked them and brought tears to their eyes, and, somehow, the smell of roasting flesh. They were all sick now, inside, outside. The cherry trees' petals littered the floor, otherworldly and bloodless. The rooms smelled like bile, like rot, like the sour milk of dead women.

They fled quickly, their belongings already in boxes and chests as if never unpacked at all, the carriage already horsed and waiting. Agnes followed them this time. The horses were fast, the streets empty. Eunice thought they passed her child-hood home as they raced through the village. It was smaller than she'd remembered, the roof sagging, the door hanging open to the wind.

They picked a new village a few days away. When Eunice and her husband asked if the villagers had heard what happened at this place in the north, people faced them blankly. They insisted: 'Have you heard of the lord who brings death and pestilence wherever he goes? Have you heard of the man who killed his own son? Have you heard of the son cursed by his father and mother before he was born?' The villagers shook their heads and squeezed the newcomers' hands and shoulders. 'No,' they said, 'no such stories here, we're a happy lot, an untroubled lot. We don't believe in stories.'

She barely registered what the new house was like. All Eunice cared about was which way the old land lay, the one that held her son. She went out at dawn and pondered the distance. She'd have liked to say she could feel her child's bones calling to her, that this direction felt different from every other, that the earth was landmarked by her grief. She felt nothing.

The house her husband chose had cherry trees growing in the garden, but Eunice no longer invited anyone to the house.

Her husband found company in the village, befriended the men who joined him hunting with their rifles and their dogs. They brought back bloodied game that Agnes cooked over the large hearth. Once, while the men were away, one of their wives gave birth to a stillborn child. Eunice held the woman's hand the entire time, and, when the child was swathed, flower-blue in its white swaddle, Eunice begged the woman to let her hold the baby. She clung to it until her husband came home from the hunt and took the child away.

'Forgive her,' her husband said. 'She is not well.'

One day, Eunice felt pregnant again. She knew this the moment she woke up, the moment she had a cup of tea and felt her body shrink into itself, felt the end of her girlhood all over again, the beginning of something else entirely. She thought this might be her blooming, that cherry pit in her belly, that latent seed about to transform her. She was not afraid. The most terrible thing had already come to pass – Tristan, the box. She had lost her husband too, to the house, to the forest; or, no, she had never had him at all. His heart had always been the forest, the stones, the rot in the walls.

*   *   *

She decided she needed to kill him. She spent hours pondering the different ways a body can break, even one like his, one so like a castle. She imagined taking a knife to the tender flesh between his ribs as he slept, or slitting his throat and listening to the gurgling breath of his new mouth, a halting narrative she could almost understand. She imagined pressing her thumbs against the cherries of his eyes, peeling the skin from his body like a fruit. She planned to go down to the cellar, crush the bottled wines; and call for help – when he rushed down the steps, she would take a shard to his heart, watch him spill, the thin membranes of his body torn open, blood slick on the stone floor.

Instead, Eunice held his hand as he slept. She ran her fingers over his knuckles, the long nails that he now neglected to file down, his thick skin. She imagined all his future wives lying exactly where she was now – plotting and regretting, scheming and planning, while her body dried down in the cellar.

Eunice shut herself in one last time. No more gardens, no more forests for her. Through her window, she glimpsed the men and women from the village, visiting the house. She desired them at first, their warmth, their liveness, the pulse beneath their skin. After a while, she desired nothing at all. The seed grew into a tree in her belly, spread its branches through her chest, pressed against her skin. She walked to the mirror sometimes, opened her mouth, and there it was, the shuddering beauty of a petal behind her tongue, the hint of a cherry.

'Why don't you leave?' the woman in the mirror asked. 'Isn't it time?'

Her hair was white, her skin perfect, her lips red.

*   *   *

'I'll leave you,' Eunice told her husband, in the end. She reached out to caress his beard. He closed his eyes and nuzzled her palm like an animal.

'You promised you'd never leave,' he said, and then, with a softness that would have broken her heart if that tree hadn't sprouted fruits in its place, he added: 'Everybody leaves.'

'I know,' she said, and, before she could say anything else, said it again: 'I'm leaving you now.'

'There will be others after you.'

'I know,' she said.

'Don't you care what will happen to them?'

'Are you blaming me for what you haven't yet done?'

He sobbed quietly, her hand still on his cheek, and Eunice let him, though her palm was barely wet when he was done.

'Can I keep your dresses?' he asked.

(BACKLIGHT, COLD.)

'She was gone,' you echo. 'But she didn't leave, did she?'

And is it me, or do you glance at the pacing ghosts, then focus back on my face quickly, your expression guilty, as if I caught you doing something you shouldn't have?

I think of the door, the closed door. Hope we have enough time.

Eunice runs her fingers through my hair, her ghostly touch cold but caring. No, she didn't leave, did she?

Nor I, not yet.

Should I be telling you these things at all? Is it right to paint for you a world of monsters and then hold up a hand and tell you to be different? I could have picked some other tale, or made one up from scratch. Perhaps I should have told you the stories of good men, of a Shopkeeper and a driver and a boy with a weak chin.

The ghosts can't stand still anymore. I recognise faces among them, match them to stories gleaned from broken sentences and fragments kept in boxes: This one was a ballet dancer, a singer, a spoken-word poet – her body was never found. That one was an usher. She wanted to keep the child.

The women run in circles around the living room, climb the walls, hold hands, an ineloquent chorus. There are roles for them to play here, the youngest one, the haunted one, the moonlight one. *Now tell mine*, they demand. *Now mine, and mine, and mine.*

The second wife

After Eunice was gone, the man was bereft for a while, with his bleeding hand, the walls of the house slowly spoiling from within. Black patches cropped up on the stone, and red veins spider-webbed across the floor. For the first time in his life, he wrote letters. To Eunice, to his mother, to his dead son. 'Who will love me now?' he asked them. 'Who will love me again?'

He didn't intend to send any of them, so he went out into the garden. He uprooted a white flower and, after moments of thought, buried the letters in the wet soil.

A few months later, he took a new wife. She was small and young, her mouth red, her eyes an ashy grey. He thought she barely looked human, and this endeared her to him. The wedding took place quickly, and all the village came to celebrate the new couple.

Their marital life went by sweetly. He had told his wife she was free to roam the house, to go into any room she liked and rearrange the furniture as she pleased, to sell his old things and buy new ones – but she was not to disturb his cabinet of curiosities. The little bride was content with this arrangement, though she had no interest in roaming, or buying, or redecorating. It was not an easy house to love, but with time she learned to ignore the mould that stained the walls, the fetid smell that oozed from the floorboards. The couple had Cook to look after them – what was her name? She never asked – but his young bride liked to take over the kitchen sometimes, then come up to his bedroom with a tray of food that she set on his bed and urged him to eat. When he complained that it was the middle of the night, she laughed with her hand in front of her small mouth and said she'd lost track of time.

She expected to be with child immediately. She was ready for her body to swell and bloom, her organs taken hostage by a new beast. She lay with him eagerly, her body opening up like a flower, and all the while she thought, irrationally, of cherry trees.

She liked to listen to his heart beat inside his chest. He turned her away sometimes, taken by one of his dark moods that made his hair look blue. But she still found her way to his room at night, crawled into his arms and coaxed him until he kissed her mouth deeply, until there was nothing in the world but the warmth of him, the fullness of her. In the mornings she thought of the children she would bear, the shapes of their bodies, the colour of their hair, the smell of their skin.

Yet her blood kept coming every month. It stained her white nightdress and left her with a hollow feeling, as if this child were something she used to have that was taken away. Her skin paled, her hair thinned, and she fell ill with a sadness too vast for words. Her husband filled her room with pretty gifts, flowers and jewels and dresses, but she only ever asked for one thing. A child, a child, a child. One day he grew angry, met her requests with a fury she hadn't seen in him before.

'Never a child,' he told her, his eye cold and sharp.

She tightened her grip on the bed covers – she so rarely left her bed these days – and held her breath. Something melted in him then, and his face softened. 'I'm sorry,' he said. 'Aren't we happy, my love? A child will bring you nothing but grief.'

Was he right? She imagined tiny fingers and little feet, something that loves without question, beyond words. The thought of not being a mother was madness. Her body was transforming day by day in all the wrong ways: her legs were like water, her arms like glass, her skin like sand, her hair like thread. How could he be right?

Slowly, the new wife became obsessed with the mould and the house's smells, the ruinous exhalations of the earth. 'It's this house,' she told him. 'The house makes me ill. It won't let me have a child.'

He looked at her darkly, something working behind his eyes. She could leave this place, he told her, if she wanted to. For her health. There was a cottage nearby she could inhabit instead. It wasn't far; she could live there. His eyes were sad when he said this, and she cupped his rough cheek. 'But, husband, how could I live without you?'

Nobody could say he didn't try.

The wife took to exploring the house, looking for the source of the noxious vapours that made her body inhospitable to young life. She thought it might be something in the walls. She opened any door she could find, walked sniffing through room after room, made herself sick with dust.

The walls groaned, the floorboards creaked, the windows shuddered, as if the house had finally entered into a dialogue with her, a strange architectural duet. When she closed her eyes, she saw the house's insides like a map, a labyrinth of rooms, corridors that didn't connect to anything, blind windows that opened into hallways without doors.

She was peeling away the wallpaper, ready to tear down the walls, when he took her small hands in his and forced her to sit on the floor, where he joined her to explain why there could never be any more children.

After he told her the story, the whole story, from the first plague to his son's death to his first wife's departure and the dresses he'd kept, she didn't go looking any longer. She thought, perhaps, dresses were not all he kept.

She tried to leave, but the house was too vast, its rooms too complicated for her to find her way out.

After his second wife passed, he could not bear to go near the room in which she'd died. He bricked up the doorway, then built another room for himself, a new room with a brand-new bed, never touched by his ill-fated bride.

And then, he asked: 'Who will love me next?'

The third wife

didn't even go looking, her death either plain misfortune or plain violence, devoid of excuses. But the next one did.

She noticed the strange smells of the house early on, the food that rotted too quickly, the walls that, when palmed, left behind a wet, black residue on her fingers. But it was after she saw her husband in the garden one night, on his knees, his back curved, digging, that she knew he had secrets. Her husband was searching for something. When he reached into the hole, she thought he pulled out the pale carcass of a flower – but it was only paper, pages upon pages with ink scribbled all over them. He bundled them under his arm and hastily covered the hole. The sky was starless, the air heavy with the promise of a storm.

She went into his study, later, where he'd left the papers. He hadn't hidden them well or meticulously – almost as if he wished she would find them. They were letters, black soil still clinging to them in clods. She read them, the words of her husband, who always smelled of earth.

So of course she went looking. And, of course, she found.

At first she thought they were clothes hanging on the walls, things left out to dry, but as her eyes adjusted to the dark, she saw them for what they were: bride-shaped things, their hair tapestries and their skin crumbling, versions of herself, women just as innocent and just as guilty, each one a story she could have inhabited, victims neither less intelligent nor more gullible than her. Forgotten things, unspoken things, covered in the dust of her husband's heart.

She joined them before long.

The fifth, the sixth

went looking too. All of them searched for traces of their predecessors, tried to piece them back together into a garment, a story, a cautionary tale. They wondered if he was born this way, or if he grew into it, this plague-ridden existence.

So they surveyed the furthest reaches of the house, the attic, the basements, the cellars. They broke through walls and dug out the floors.

When they brought back the things they found, he didn't touch any of it. He simply sat there staring, fighting to put names to faces, match dresses to bodies to plagues.

The seventh wife

'We'll travel together,' she said over a breakfast of soft eggs and expensive cheese. 'I want to visit the sea. I want to walk through foreign forests with you holding my hand and carrying my purse. I want to visit faraway countries and dine on quails and caviar out of the most exquisite spoons.' She showed him her small, perfectly spaced teeth. 'I'm sure you haven't done these things with any of your other wives.' Her neck pulsed in tiny little flutters. 'Have there been many?'

He told her she was the seventh.

For a moment, she marvelled at this. Seven wives before her, and not one of them had thought to take him to a beach! So much to be remedied, so much to make up for.

She leapt out of her chair and kissed his beard. 'What a wonderful life,' she said, arms twined around his neck. Sitting on his lap made her feel small and precious, like a doll. 'You'll see.'

Another wife, I don't know which

The storm came and the house creaked. The walls dripped.
With her palms flat against them, she felt the size of it, the
magnitude of its anger. It breathed and it waited.

When this wife found the dress, she held it against her body
and walked around the house, until she came to the place that
smelled of earth. She knew that she was following in the footsteps of others, that they were all abiding by a set of rules, the
plot of a story told many times before. And so, she found a hole
in the wall. She knew what awaited on the other side. Still, she
walked through it.

And he?

He saw the corpses pile up, the limbs, the red mouths. He
saw the hand he had in their fates. Something seized his heart
then – because yes, he did have a heart – the terror that no one
would ever truly love him because he simply wasn't worthy of
love.

And yet he thought, maybe the next one.

Maybe the next one would love him enough.

(SUNDOWN.)

I'm straining your suspension of disbelief, aren't I? It couldn't all have been so awful.

The ghosts shift behind you, out of sight, their heads bowed, avoiding my eyes as if in shame, which sends a little shock through me.

Because you're right to doubt. Sometimes he was nice. It could be nice, this life with him. No, not nice; it could be lovely. Wonderful, even. And doesn't that make everything worse?

The eighth wife, perhaps

When he was married to her, life seemed easy, and that summer lasted much longer than usual. He spent it wandering the flowered fields careless and shirtless, as if he'd never hurt anybody.

He brought his wife a flower every afternoon. One day he brought her a dress that looked like the sky. He thought she'd like it, relish the way it flowed around her, how it caught the light of the sun. The dress didn't fit her – the waist was too wide, the collar too tight on her neck. 'I prefer the flowers,' she told him, 'but thank you, nonetheless.'

He made her wear it, helped her into it despite her protests. The wound in his hand opened and smeared the new dress with blood.

The eighth wife clasped his hand and worried over his unknitted flesh.

'Does it hurt?' she asked, pushing down a mild malaise at the sight of blood. She kissed the wound, painting her mouth red.

'I don't know how to love gently,' he replied.

This wife didn't bother asking for a child. She understood he'd never wanted one, and didn't question his reasons. What she did, instead, was pray to the forest and, when she finally found herself pregnant, told him nothing until she showed.

He brooded over the possibility of offspring, spent days locked in his room and weeks away with his horses. When it was time for the wife to give birth, what came out of her after a night of screaming and blood, was a round, white stone.

She insisted on holding a funeral, and, when he refused, decided she would do so on her own. She made her way north, to the cemetery where she knew her husband's family lay buried, and found his father's grave, and Tristan's next to it. Clutching the stone to her chest, the eighth wife ran her fingers over this half-brother's gravestone, traced that boy's name. Her own child didn't have one.

All night, she grieved for it, her first child. Her first stone.

The ninth wife

She was poorly often and had a love for books, so he built her
a bedroom with wall-to-wall shelves. He made sure there was
a regular supply of volumes to satisfy his bride's needs. He
afforded her some privacy, nursed her through fevers, offered
her the most beautiful gifts: paintings of pomegranates and
bowls made of nephrite, seashells, pearls. Every meal he brought
to her room was a feast: fine bread with butter squeezed from
gardenias, soft quail and plates of jelly made from its bones,
honeyed wine and pastries steeped in rosewater. Foods she'd
never seen or eaten before: iced plums, figs pressed into jam,
coffee flavoured with cloves and cardamom.

And sometimes the food he brought her was no food at all
but a bouquet of flowers with intricate petals and unusual
colours, black and maroon and a deep, vibrant blue. She told
him, 'I can't eat those,' and he stared at the flowers for some
time before he laughed and scratched his head. 'I'm sorry,' he
said then, 'I forgot.' He looked to her like a boy then, someone
too young to know how to be in the world. In those moments,
she loved him more.

It didn't last, of course. The longer he spent in her company,
the more her health declined. He allowed himself only a few
hours each day by her side, but still she grew weaker and

sicker. This did not surprise her. As a child she used to have this anxiety, this knot in the middle of her chest, about the future and what kind of life she would have. Now, the future was no longer a thing that existed. She felt she had somehow avoided it.

At night, she longed for his body; they'd lain together only once, and the thing she recalled the most vividly was how rich with hair his body was, covered almost entirely by a thin layer of fur, like an animal of the forest, a bear or a buck.

When he wasn't with her, or perhaps to stay away from her, he built another room in the house. He spent days measuring and planning, poring over sketches, his hands tracing imagined walls. He consulted architects and engineers, carpenters and masons. He ordered materials from all over the continent: marble from Italy, wood from Norway, tiles from Spain.

It took months to complete, but, when it was done, he came into her bedroom in the smallest hours of the night. He knew she hadn't been sleeping – she'd been restless, her breathing harsh and irregular for days.

She was reading, pages yellow and brittle in her lap. He asked what it was and she refused to tell him, so he walked closer, laughing at his wife's sudden reticence. But then he saw them: the letters he'd written and buried, so long ago, exhumed from his garden in a bout of despair for another wife to find.

'Where is she now,' the young bride asked him, 'that other wife?'

He said, 'Come, I'll show you.'

She wavered, uncertain, but then she pulled away the covers

and swung her legs onto the floor. They looked transparent in the moonlight.

'Where are we going?' she asked, her voice as insubstantial as her body.

He held the candle higher to illuminate her way. 'Around the back of the house,' he told her softly.

He went first, and she followed.

She walked out into the garden in her nightgown, her feet bare and uncertain, the soft grass beneath them wet. She followed him deeper into the garden first and then into the forest, the smell of him growing stronger with each step. She couldn't tell them apart, the smell of him and the smell of the forest, and for a moment she stopped and put her head in her hands because she should be able to tell. Because a husband is not a forest.

Before long, his candle went out, snuffed by an ill-timed breath of wind. But he said, 'Keep going,' so she followed the sound of his footsteps and his smell until she stood at the edge of a hole as wide as the span of her arms. Somehow, he lit his candle again, and there, at the bottom of the hole, among the roots and the soil and the leaves, she saw the pale claws of a skeleton. That former wife, almost intact, her bones a secret alphabet.

'Now you know,' he told her, his voice inflected with joy or even triumph, as if he were proud of her for coming this far, this steadily.

The air was so thick with the smell of him she could hardly think, so she opened her mouth – she didn't know why; to speak or to scream? – and found it filled with leaves.

*   *   *

And then, later, there she was in his bed again. She said, 'I want to live,' and so he took her by the hand and led her to the woods once more. She was a bird in his palm. He let her go.

The tenth wife

thought she was with child when she found something in the garden, something beautiful and terrible and pale, that looked like a shell but moved. It opened slowly, and she saw a pulsing mass of black and red inside. She nudged it with her shoe, hoping to make it stop, but it started moving again, sluggishly, so she thrashed it with a stick until its flesh was broken and its insides spilled out of its body.

She vowed never to tell anybody. She kept her vow until the day she died, which was not very long at all.

The youngest wife

She was the only one Cook liked.

'Why did you marry so young?' Cook asked, and the young wife laughed, because it was funny to suggest she'd had a choice. Still, it gave her no grief.

'Wouldn't your father marry you to a rich and handsome lord, if he had the chance?' the youngest wife asked.

She liked to walk without slippers on the wooden floorboards of her bedroom. Once, she got a splinter in her pretty foot. She called for help – it was Cook who responded. She held the girl's foot with care, picked out the piece of wood with a needle hot from the flame of a candle.

'You should leave him,' Cook said, her face a dark twist in the candlelight. She looked like the paintings on the walls.

The young thing laughed at the absurdity. 'But he's my husband,' she said, 'and I love him.'

'So do I,' Cook said. 'Yet you should leave.'

The young wife looked at Cook. There was something in the old woman's eye that she didn't have a name for. 'Are you jealous, is that it?' she asked, though she knew that was not it. And then: 'But where would I go?'

She didn't go. I wish she had, her more than anyone else, even though she was no more or less deserving than any of us.

Still, I think of her often, see her pacing these long corridors, these lonely rooms.

I fall silent for a while, until you prompt me to continue:
'And what about the villagers?' you ask.

What about the villagers

While the wives perished, nature didn't, the land's occasional reluctance attributed to a kind of natural capriciousness, the animals' nervousness a thing that happens sometimes. Yes, people admitted to each other when they dared speak of such things, always late in the night; yes, maybe their children had stopped growing as fast, and the dogs tended to sleep a little longer, and the rooms of their houses had grown colder and the sky a bit dimmer. But, the villagers told themselves, so what? These things happen. The world has seasons of its own, larger than the seasons of the year, and some things just die in their own time.

And so the villagers and townspeople didn't drive them out, but only came to them with servile friendship and honest work.

Of the man, they said, he's a rich lord, with a big forest at his back and fertile lands at his feet – of course he's going to be a little eccentric, his wives a little unfortunate, a little unhappy. This man is a rich lord with a big house and plenty of servants – of course some will be lost within that maze of rooms and cellars and doorways. They said, this is a rich lord and rich lords' wives are so bored, sometimes they bury themselves in the garden.

For a long while, his plagues remained domestic, of an intimate kind: fabric disintegrating in a box, some sallow skin, a stone child.

(FOOTLIGHTS.)

The ghosts proliferate. New faces join us. They stand around us, clothed in garments that suggest different eras, foreign lands. These are not your father's victims, I know. Can't be. There are more women here than any one man could hurt in a lifetime – even someone like him, who can get away with so much.

Who invited you? I ask them. A foolish question; in the end, we're all haunted by what happened to the ones who came before.

We heard you speaking of us, the ghosts say. *We came.*

But these are not your stories, I tell them, before they even have a chance to make their demands. I don't know yours.

Don't you? they ask.

The next wives, in pieces

Few of them lasted more than one winter, and summer found him trying again, throwing feasts at his house, inviting the girls, feeding them sour cherries that stained their lips red. His weddings became the talk of the town, and so did his wives' disappearing acts: one, they said, was spirited away in the night together with a chest stuffed full of rare stones, rubies and sapphires nestled in gold. Another was too sickly, went back to her mother; a third found a lover her own age and eloped. Maybe the villagers did believe in stories after all.

One wife liked to spend her time admiring the portrait of the one that came before. Willowy neck, a clutch of pearls. Small red lips. Dead eyes.

Another liked to go for long walks in the forest. Once, she brought back an old, cracked mirror with a frame of twisted roots. She picked the dirt from the mirror's corners and hung it in the library. She looked at her reflection and didn't recognise her face.

Another still gave birth to a creature with a full mouth of teeth. She was visiting her mother's grave when the baby-thing slipped out of her and screeched for an hour. She wondered at the black dot of its eye, the skin that quickly turned slack and blue. She buried it right there among the graves. She spoke not a word of it to her husband.

And then there was the one who couldn't take her eyes off the crystal chandelier in the big entranceway of the house, where the wide staircase began to rise towards the second floor. When alone, she lit the chandelier and lay on the carpet below, marvelling at the luminous crystals as if they held the light of a thousand stars.

One day, her husband gifted her a pair of earrings made from the crystals that used to hang at the very centre of that chandelier.

It was his last gift to her.

The next one was so infatuated with the house and its structure, the way it seemed always to escape her perception, its totality impossible to contain, that she hired a craftsman to create a miniature of it.

It took him an entire year. The craftsman came to the house and studied it, scribbling down his copious notes. For months he worked on the miniature, but the result justified his efforts, and, almost, the work's price. The miniature was perfect. It contained each room, each wall complete with its tapestries and paintings, every cellar and hidden cavity, the garden with its cherries and brambles and thorns. The house was so completely and perfectly recreated that the miniature contained even the miniature itself, set on a tiny table in the bedroom of the tiny wife. She stood by that table, the tiny wife, contemplating the miniature, and so did the real wife, matching her double precisely. And the longer she contemplated herself contemplating the miniature, the more certain she was that she could see within the tiny house another one, even smaller, and within that an even smaller miniature, and another one inside it, and so on and so on, a *mise en abyme*.

The time she didn't spend in her bedroom, she spent pacing the house and its gardens. But everything seemed blunted, diminished somehow, like an imitation of what it once had been. She thought of her husband and waited for him to come back from his business trips. She chatted to Cook, who only responded peevishly and slipped away as soon as she could. The wife thought of planting new flowers in the garden but decided against it; it would make the miniature diluted and incoherent, she thought. She would need to have the craftsman update it, and would her husband accept the burden of that cost? So she didn't plant the flowers, never changed anything in the house at all.

Sometimes, as she paced the cardboard corridors and ran her fingers across the vague walls, she wondered if she'd stepped into the miniature at one point and simply hadn't noticed; why else would everything in her life suddenly seem so small?

The haunted one

Every wife, at one point or another, entertained the thought she may be haunted by the ones that came before. But for one of them – the eleventh? the twelfth? – it was true.

She could sense them in the house, ghostly fingers reaching through her hair, green ribbons tied around their necks. She was the spirited sort, though, and she would have none of their nonsense. Wrong fairy story, she told the ribboned girls. Go bother someone else. The ghost wives laughed, untied their ribbons, their wounds gaping like mouths caught mid-tale. They sat at her table, played with her food, laughed at the gap between her front teeth. *Simple Mary*, they sing-songed, just like the girls who used to torment her at school, their tragic fates making no difference at all to their cruelty. *So simple, she speaks with the dead.*

Still, they crowded around her, and it was not always to taunt or scare her. There was a grief to their teasing, and their mouths were full of demands; because the dead are needful things, unstoried things. They spoke as urgently as their unfeeling tongues allowed. They didn't know, yet, what they were asking. One said: *I was the first to bleed but not the first to die.* Another: *I was the first to rise again.* And yet another: *I was the one who longed for the comfort of dirt.*

*　　*　　*

In the end, Mary threw herself into the well.

When her body was retrieved, off-blue like a duck's egg, eyes open white to the unseeing sky, her husband cradled her head and wept into her hair. 'Gone too soon,' he said, and the people around him took the words for those of a grieving husband robbed of a beloved bride. He didn't correct them.

One way or another, they all left.

But not entirely. You see, there was the one still searching in the attic, pawing through the storeroom above the servants' quarters on her hands and knees. And the one who had lost the taste for eating anything but earth. And the one who had gone mad and still sat in the parlour, talking about wives in cabinets and waiting for her story to end.

These lingering wives spoke. They still speak, because the present is present and the past is past, but the ghosts are always. They are shapeless things, static, a desperate pleadful *I am, I am, I am.* I pass no judgement, only witness – though there will be no trial, and witnessing can only do so much. These wives say, *We are fragile,* and I see it, their bones like glass. They snap at the slightest pressure. Their features are defined by the empty spaces between them: the red head, the green eye, the blue one. The one with a forest heart and the one with a forest head. I can't always tell their voices apart, so I hear them often in the plural, full of stops and starts, in words like these, borrowed from dreams and fevers that burned and were gone:

We are all tall like trees, lost in our own forests. It is always night here. The wind is always blowing, and branches creak like bones. The trees gather together to form a great house. We stand in the centre of this house-forest, waiting.

There are one hundred of us.

Each of us wears a veil, red, black, white. Only our feet are bare.
We stand in a crescent, the curve of our bodies like petals on the floor,
the line of our heads a single stem. It's hard not to repeat ourselves.

The house behind us is silent. After all, it was never the house
that was haunted.

(AMBIENT LIGHT, WANING.)

And now, here, they flicker in their costumes, in this unhaunted place. A couple stand guard outside the bedroom door; others drape themselves over the back of the sofa behind you and bleed on the tasteful velour. They have wounds, those openings to the body. Doors for things to go in and out of. Some are even self-inflicted. The mouth, too, a wound.

The ghosts reach for my arms, slip searching fingers under my sleeves, treacherous.

What other doors are there?

And yet, the fifth, the sixth

did not blame him. They knew what his wives were like. Boiling a body takes a long time; it makes the air taste of bone and skin, smell bitter like burnt hair.

The bodies piled up. The house groaned with the weight of them.

'There are many bedrooms here,' he always told the next ones when they hesitated at the thresholds, and it was true enough. So many bedrooms, so little space.

The one who didn't speak

She could – she remembered speaking as a child – but decided early on that she wouldn't. She didn't like the way words felt in her mouth: too furtive to be trusted, like birds escaping her lips. Her family thought nobody would ever love this strange daughter, so when he married her, her parents were relieved. He claimed no dowry, either. Said her silence was enough.

She surprised herself with how much she liked being a wife. What she enjoyed the most was watching her husband: how he worked in the garden even though he didn't have to, how his muscles moved under his shirt, how he wiped sweat from his brow and sometimes smeared his forehead with soil, how he tended to his horse with a soft hand on its flank and his head pressed against the powerful jaw. It made him seem so human to her, this large man whom everyone feared and called lord.

Soon, a pattern emerged between the lord and his silent wife. He was gentle with her all winter: he lavished gifts on her, combed her hair, wrapped her in furs to keep her warm. In spring, he grew needy and cruel, demanded of her things she didn't have the heart to give: a wifely sentence, a loving word. Then, a tooth plucked fresh from her mouth, a tuft of hair, a patch of skin. He took it all anyway, by summer's end.

(I IMAGINE A FIRE.)

Another joins us, one I've never seen before. She's older, her body ripe with the scent of soil. *Are you the third wife?* the ghost women ask her. *Are you the eighth?* But she refuses to answer. Instead, she asks, *Do you know my name?*

And the ghosts say *No, he never said it to us, no.*

She looks at this place, the state of it, the state of us. She looks at you. Then she asks, *What is it you do here?*

The ghosts show her. They have a number of keys they know not what to do with. They roam the apartment, looking for things, a make-believe forensics. They collect all sorts: a doll, a knife, the clipping of a nail. An eyelash. The ghost women put everything in a pile in front of the door we must never walk through.

Should we burn them? I ask, but no one is ever brave enough to let go.

Maybe the next one

He caught glimpses of them, sometimes, his collection of dead wives. Once, he woke and saw a figure in white standing at the foot of his bed. He thought he recognised her – she'd been one of his first. The woman took something black and gnawed out of her mouth. She looked asleep, her eyes closed. He followed her down the hallway and into the great room. There were others there, too, upside down, swinging from the rafters like bats. The woman turned, acknowledging him for the first time. She said of the other wives, *Look, they're like books.* She didn't read them, didn't unfold them, yet he already knew what was inside: Pictures of women with gone bodies, bloody smiles. Dropped threads. Words that make a village ill.

They spent a long time there, the hanging women and the living man, and he couldn't leave because these were his own rules and this was his own game, one of whispers and warnings and locked doors, the women stepping through each other's stories and timelines in a house alive with their longings.

And he?

He was a white bird, he thought, with a black, swollen eye.

Still, he didn't stop.

He looked for the next wife, and the next, and the next. He

let his wives throw parties and invite others to join them. In the end, he told himself he hardly participated. Gone were the imagined wastelands of his youth, the hands on soil, seeking to take it all back. It was the women who chose. They held power over him and over themselves. They were in control of their own disappearances. It was always them.

Stories of his wives spread across the land. He heard them whispered when he passed through the streets of towns and villages, had them repeated to him by friends who laughed at their absurdity. And, sometimes, they reached him through some merchant or other, recounted as something that had happened to someone else, at some other time, in some other land. The stories always contained a measure of the fantastic or the fanciful, and not even he could always put the correct name to the given version of woe and misfortune suffered by the people in these tales. But he could always identify the kernel of truth in them, grasp it in his palm, keep it close to his chest. Reminisce, even. Cherish it. Not without some fondness, as he looked for the next one, the one who wouldn't even think of leaving.

(BEYOND THE WINDOW, A GLIMPSE OF OVERCAST SKY.) The ghosts avoid the window. They cover their eyes or turn away, don't wish to break character, to see the world outside as it is. They imagine, instead, the one where my story began, back when the forest was near and the sky encroached, back when dirt roads, when crops, when birds, when wolves.

But I look. You sit on the floor, hugging your knees, and I make my way to the window, pull back the gauzy curtain, touch the cold glass. Barely, my breath still mists.

The long shadows cast by the trees and shrubs on the concrete-strangled slope across the street make me want to cry.

You know, the trick – the one I used, the one we all used, at one point or another – is this: you have to believe it doesn't hurt as much as it does. Like Tristan's coal-walkers, remember them? That's how you survive. The body is negligible. It is not real and so cannot be hurt. You walk on fire but convince yourself you can't feel it. You watch the shadows dance on the wall but can't see the light behind you, so you tell yourself – and everyone agrees: the plays, the fairy tales, your mother and father, the television, the myths – that there's no way to escape and nothing to escape to. The cave is all there is.

And yet, here: a window. A city, a street.

I, too, have imagined a different time, a different place.
The phone rings again.
I ignore it, speak quickly to drown out the sound.

The Baroness

He even married a baroness, once. It was a risky thing to do, and perhaps *that*, a brief, ill-thought flirtation with self-destruction, was the reason he chose her. Peasant girls were one thing, but high-born women with powerful fathers and ambitious brothers were another thing entirely. If someone like that suffered at his hands, everyone would notice, even the villagers who depended on him for their livelihoods. Everyone would care.

The baroness was young, beautiful, and yes, she had a temper, but she was also kind and giving and not afraid to tell him when she found him wanting. He liked her so much he thought he might love her.

When she reigned over his mansion and commanded his household with an almost natural, innate ease, the ghost wives fell quiet around her. They turned away, feigning distraction by a flaw in the gilded mirror or the strange shapes made by the passing clouds. They drooped sullenly to the floor to recount their own shortcomings, their litany of beheadings, wasting-aways, ill-chosen doors.

The baroness did notice them, though. She asked her husband about them, the other women who had lived in this house before her, but he could only shrug, pretend ignorance or incomprehension without much art. So, like many before her, the baroness went looking too.

When she fell ill, her baron of a father arrived at the house on horseback and proclaimed her husband a wicked murderer, a gold-digger, a crook.

'My daughter has never been bedridden for a day in her life,' the baron's reasoning was, 'so this sudden affliction must be of your own making. Whether it is by neglect or by design, I care not a bit.'

The baron gave the man two options: annulment or execution.

The baroness rode away with her father, sweat clinging to her brow, her skin like ashes.

She thought of the ghosts often, especially when news of the lord and his new wife reached her. But, even after she recovered, it never crossed her mind that, with her power, money and influence, she might have been the only one who could help.

She lived a life of luxury and chose never to marry again. For years, she was free of him.

And yet, here she is now, in the chorus.

The Baroness in the chorus

She is not like the rest of us, dropped like a pearl in a bowl of
humble beads. Her only haunting is her escape. She finds no
solidarity with us here, and offers little in return.

The last wife

She didn't know she would be the last, but she knew she wasn't the first. Still, she didn't go looking until the house shook and white dust coated the furniture. She saw it for what it was: the bones of all her predecessors, his dead wives. When she found it on her own skin, sticking to the damp of her nightgown, she asked herself: 'What am I doing here? Why don't I leave?'

The villagers were telling the truth when they said they didn't believe in stories. Perhaps that's the reason it took them so dreadfully long to accept what was happening. Eventually, they came with their pitchforks, as always. But the house was a fortress and the people were much too tired from working stubborn fields, much too worn from hunger and sickness and pain.

But before any of that, the last wife started inviting girls to the house, giving them cherries and jams, echoing those early soirées, in another house, another time. The man was certain he'd never told her about those, not even when she'd begged him to recount the whole tale of his life to her one night in bed and he'd obliged, mostly.

Maybe it was one of the ghostly wives who had planted the idea in her head, with a whisper in the dark or a bite mark, a cherry pit left under her pillow, licked clean of flesh. It doesn't really matter.

All that matters is this: one day, in a room full of girls, one of them caught his eye in a way that made even the ghosts pause and listen. That girl made him want to speak a word of caution to her, turn her away from this house, this life, tell her to leave while she still could. But she didn't, did she?

I didn't, did I?

(DUSK, SLOWLY.)

And now, finally, here we are, almost at the end. This Cherry Girl. I pick her the way the ghosts picked the wives.

She becomes me, doesn't she? We weren't always so alike. But now, I wear her like a costume, let her whisper the story I couldn't bring myself to speak otherwise. Easier this way; that's what I tell myself when I doubt, when I falter, when I pause. Easier to tell you of a man who was a myth, a natural disaster, a fairy-tale thing, than to say your father is a wife-beater, a rapist, a murderer.

And me? What does that make me?

You lean in. You have forgotten all about the closed bedroom door.

My throat is dry, but I don't reach for water, and you don't offer me any. You are eager for my story to begin, as if it's not the one I've been telling all along.

Cherry Girl

In the beginning, I liked to pace the house on bare feet, to feel the polished wood under my soles. I ran my hands over the door handles, the windowsills, the banisters. I had never seen a house like it before. I counted the steps as I went up the grand staircase, and then I stood at the top and counted them again. The number changed every time, no matter how often or how diligently I counted.

I walked the garden, too, barefoot always like another wife, my toes sinking into the soft earth wet with dew. Although my man employed a number of gardeners, the grounds always looked unkempt, the grass too tall, the roses too thorny, the ivy growing wild enough to suffocate the trees. The estate was traversed by cobblestone paths that led nowhere. I walked them anyway, counting.

In the back of the garden, I discovered a thick patch of weeds, and in it, the bones of lambs, or dogs, or wolves. Death never upset me. I saw a lot of it growing up; my sisters made sure of it. They liked to torment me when we were children, to leave dead things in my bed for me to find. Once, they put a dead rabbit on my pillow; its murky eyes were the first thing I saw when I opened mine in the morning. I was too terrified to move, my breath trapped in my lungs. So I simply closed my eyes again and went back to sleep. I learned early how to look away.

In my wanderings, I did not know yet to look for the ghost wives, though I sometimes glimpsed them as I walked the halls: stooped and cloaked, dragging their feet, their heads bent. I could say I denied their presence then, my mind squirming against what my eyes told me, my heart fluttering in rising panic. That I looked away, until I couldn't look away any more.

Is that the truth, or close enough?

I've spent so long trying to narrate them. Now how do I narrate myself?

Cook feared the ghosts, though she'd never admit it. She accused me of misplacing things she couldn't find in the kitchen, of leaving the cabinet doors open, of spilling flour and sugar on the counters and the floor. She never went into the woods herself, only the gardens and the village, but never beyond. And when she entered the house, she did so walking backwards, unwilling to turn her back to the forest. She said you need to face the things that scare you, to face them always and for ever. Who knows what will happen if you take your eyes off them.

I took my food to the window in my room and watched the forest, listening for the sounds of things that didn't scare me, my back to all the things that did.

I first stepped into that house back when his last wife – the final wife – was still alive. She was a colourless creature with ashen skin. I remember thinking she wouldn't last the winter, and she didn't.

I had come with my sisters, all older than me. A servant took my hand and led us in. Everything was polished: the wood, the banisters, the marble. Paintings sat on ornate stands in the corners, portraits of men and women long dead but still smiling.

We joined his wife in the parlour, were given strong and bitter tea to drink, paired with small cherry-flavoured cakes. He entered when we were halfway through our cups, our lips tingling with the sweetness of the cakes. His frame filled the doorway, and there was such a shadow cast across him that I could barely see his face. My sisters held their breath, immediately attracted to him in the way most people are – his strange combination of rough textures and gentle eyes, strong features and a voice as soft as velvet.

The fabric he wore made a dry, rustling sound as he moved into the room. It was black, something with hair, and his beard was gathered beneath his chin, so dark it appeared blue in the evening light.

He sat in an armchair across from us, inappropriately far away from his wife, and asked us all our names. My sisters introduced themselves – Rose, Violet, Lily, Alyssa, all flower names. I told him mine, too. He repeated my name back to me, his mouth lingering over the syllables, as if he could taste each one. I sat quietly in my chair, eyes lowered, and listened to the rustling of his fabric, and to my sisters' laughter when he told them their names were lovely, even though they were not. Who wants to be named after a flower?

He told us stories from his youth, unprompted – and who would ever think to stop him? He told us of a time he went hunting, of a hunt gone awry, and of a hound so seduced by something hidden in the undergrowth it ran howling into the forest. He had no choice but to go after it – such is the way with beasts one claims as one's own. They ran for a long time, man and beast, and finally the hound led him to a village near the mountains, where everyone was dressed in black. Though none of the villagers were blind, they all had eyes that could not see him. The villagers cried, Where are you? Where are you? in voices like falling stones, and the hound was gone. The villagers told him that, if he walked into the cold river and didn't breathe for some time, then they'd be able to see him, and they would embrace him as one of their own. They would give him food and drink, make him happy in any way he wished.

He refused it all, their offers of food and drink, their promises of a long and happy stay. He preferred to live, he said, and he was not done living. But to this day he was pulled to that village always, and he could never shake the feeling that he wasn't where he was meant to be.

Is that why you moved so often before you settled down here, one of my sisters asked, my lord?

Is this what you've heard of me? he responded, forehead wrinkled with concern I thought surely false. He was not concerned at all – and I know now that my sisters had the story only half right.

It is what the people say, my sister replied, her eyes downcast. And that you used to take a new wife wherever you went.

The man's wife remained quiet.

Perhaps that is so, he said. If it's what the people say. He smiled, and the hint of concern was gone completely, because I had been right: it was never truly there at all.

He continued with his stories, told us of the time his father was ambushed by a wolf in the forest, and how mightily he fought for his life. And he told us also of a time a surgeon was called to see a man with terrible aches all over his body. He found the man's belly stuffed with dead birds. The surgeon removed them all, and the man made a full recovery, except, the lord said, the man could still hear them, sometimes, the birds and the ruckus they made inside.

But the birds were dead, I wanted to say. This story is clearly false; the dead can make no fuss.

How wrong I was.

You tell such strange tales, my lord, another of my sisters said – I forget which.

While her husband told stories, the last wife kept her eyes on her tea. Her fingers shook slightly, and her back was stiff and straight, as if she was waiting for something to happen. I still remember the way the skin around her mouth wrinkled when she brought the teacup to her lips, the way her eyes narrowed and her throat worked, as if swallowing required great effort. She dropped her cup more than once, spilling her tea, and cursed as she bent to pick it up and refill it. She wore a dress of green silk, with small yellow flowers. Her face was round, her eyebrows permanently arched.

The clarity of the memory surprises you. So much else has been lost or obscured. Why hold on to this – the yellow flowers, the wrinkled skin, the green silk – of all things?

Finally, the man turned to his wife and dismissed her, as if she were a servant. We watched her out of the corners of our eyes, too polite to stare. She did not look at my sisters, but her eyes lingered on me for a moment, the youngest sister, never meant to speak. Our tea had grown cold. She did not say goodbye.

Night fell swiftly. The moon rose like a bright orange. The

sky was clear, the air still. No breeze to move the trees, no clouds to veil us.

Emboldened by his wife's absence, my sisters fawned over the man. They asked him questions, begged for more stories, and he obliged; they were so excited they could hardly keep their voices hushed the way propriety required. I remained quietly in my corner, watching. His beard was streaked with a faint grey. He caught my eye across the room, and something as fleeting as a shadow passed between us. He continued his story, and I continued watching. He turned to me and asked me a question, but I was so fixated on his mouth and the way it spoke each word that I didn't hear what he'd said.

He asked the question again:

Do you like the woods?

I said that the forest made me feel like I was being watched.

He smiled, said I could walk it with him whenever I pleased. That way I would have nothing to fear.

And then he turned his attention back on my sisters and their playing.

How could I not be moved by his words? I'd always had so much to fear.

The evening passed quickly, and I was surprised to find myself still sitting in the parlour in the middle of the night, surrounded by the sound of my sisters' gentle snoring, the room dim and lit only by moonlight. The man was nowhere to be found.

I walked into the hallway, the wood cool beneath my feet, and called out: My lord?

I heard nothing but my own voice, loud and echoing. The house felt empty. I climbed the stairs to the second floor, then the third, the fourth. I walked down the hall past the master bedroom. I can't put a name to what I felt; a familiarity, perhaps, the kind that might develop between a person and the wild animal with which she shares a cage. An intimacy with the house and all who resided within it. Even now, I can recall every detail of that house, the first place I lived after I left my father's. That night was the first time I counted the doors, the number of windows, the paintings in their frames, the legs of every table, the chairs, the knobs on the cabinets, the handles on the doors. Of course, the steps.

If I close my eyes tight enough, I can still see everything. The house whole, ghosts and all.

(A LAMP, ALL WRONG.)

You turn on the ivory lamp, and in this light I think no, this is not how we met. Not in his wife's drawing room, but in my dressing room, after a Russian play full of cherry trees. Chekhov, yes. Isn't that right?

You stare at me, in this light, searching my face. What are you looking for?

I knew of him, of course, like everyone else at the theatre. He'd funded so many of our shows. I knew, also, of his reputation – who didn't? A powerful man, an influential man. My friend warned me to stay away. Nadya, the one who's calling, who's coming, who cares. She was always more clear-eyed than I was. She had fled her own story and country long before, you see, but never talked about it except in the most fleeting of terms. And that's just it, isn't it? We don't talk about it, the absurd, incredible details of it, the wolfy snarls, the trophy hearts, the sheer number of them. This improbable parade of wives. Who would believe us if we did?

So I didn't listen. He was the first man to show me kindness after a world of cruelty, homes lost for good, in this new country where I'll always be a stranger, no matter how long I stay put.

He called me Cherry Girl, said he liked my accent. Told me to come. And I went. That part is true.

The light, please. Turn it off.

Other parts that are true

At night, when I was about to fall asleep, the ghost wives tried to tell me things. They didn't always succeed. The air was thin, their lungs forgetful, they could rarely form words – and so they stayed like that around my bed: their hands in fists, their fists in their mouths, exhaling nothing.

Eventually, I asked him who the ghosts were, and he told me all about them, the previous wives. Or tried. He spoke of what they were like, what they'd enjoyed, how long each of them had lasted before she went looking, or wandered shoeless into the forest in the middle of the night. Of the children that kept coming, too, and didn't; of the stones, the dogs, the little lambs buried in the cold earth.

Of the middle wives he remembered so little their stories often changed. Their names shifted, faded, or became muddled: was the fourth one Sélysette or Mélisande? Was the next one Eleanor, or Angela, or Alix?

Here, my chorus leans in: here, the Ophelia, here the Medea, here the usher, here the girl who sold ice cream in the foyer.

I knew how he met most of them – I'd been one of them, in all but name and ceremony – but sometimes his narrations slipped. He claimed that he took them in, salvaged them in their time of need, or that they came of their own accord, left behind by relatives and friends, or that they just appeared to him, sprouted from the earth or climbed out of the well, if you believe in such things, which he didn't at first, though he did eventually.

He told me of the baroness, too – who are we to choose for whom we fall? – the one who got away and in doing so taught him about regret. He remembered, sometimes, how he'd held her and whispered in her ear, told her the stories of the women who came out of the wells to drag him back with them. How she'd sighed, how his hands had found her waist and her small breasts, her belly.

He told me, also, of a promise some of the wives made him sometimes, by standing motionless on rainy days near the windows, or in the garden, or by sitting on the bench next to the well, in a way that made him think they wouldn't leave.

I listened. He seemed to me a man who needed to be listened to; who was used to being obeyed but not necessarily believed. Not being believed, I knew what that was like.

He spoke carefully, in measured tones, pausing to find the right words, or to let me imagine my own. He told me about the wife who liked to bury herself in the garden. He'd found her like this often, covered in dirt, only her pale feet and face peering out of the ground. In the end, he said, he'd obliged. Then he talked about the wife who wouldn't stop dancing, and the wife who wouldn't stop crying and the one who wouldn't stop laughing, and the wife who wouldn't stop kissing – his mouth, her hands, the mirrors, the walls. He told me about the chests that got heavier every time he married. And last, he told me about the one who wouldn't stop dying, and all her transformations: a dying-wife, a dead-wife, a ghost-wife. I saw the sadness in his eyes as he told me these stories, something appalling in the way he looked at me. Something trembling, like he was afraid I might disappear, too.

They all leave, he said, they all left.

They all left you? I echoed. In the end?

Yes.

And there are only dresses in these chests?

What else?

I didn't know their stories yet – neither the real ones, if there is such a thing, nor the ones they'd tell themselves if they could, when they could – but still I sensed he couldn't tell the whole truth. So I asked to be shown where he kept them, leaving the exact object of my curiosity unnamed. He obliged eagerly. Surely, I thought, as only an innocent man would.

And yet. A couple had graves in the forest. Others lay in a well in the garden, and more still were kept in an underground cellar; dresses, yes, and more. So much more. The most recent ones were hanging in the back room, attached to the walls like heraldry. He didn't look at them.

Will you leave me, he asked, like they left me?

A glance at the walls, a pause. This was the reason he kept them, wasn't it? The dresses, the headpieces, the locks of hair.

Will you? he asked again.

I understood, then, about the ghosts. How they were made, why they lingered. Leaving meant dying. But dying? It meant staying.

Never, I said to him. Never ever.

(INTENSE LIGHT, RIGHT TO THE FACE, IMAGINED.)
Should I say I thought about leaving, then? That I was too
scared to try because I'd seen what it could mean? Besides,
where would I go – a girl like me. A girl like me, so good at
looking away. Or maybe I should say that I did try, and that he
caught me? Do you want to see the bruises, the broken bones,
the hair pulled free from my scalp – these things that are always
either too much or not enough?

But no, of course you wouldn't. You know better than to ask
for proof. You've grown up around ghosts, after all.

You nuzzle up against me, like you used to do when you
were younger. There was a time when we'd have adventures
together. Remember? Perhaps we can do that again, imagine
a magical world of our own. I could take your hand and open
the window. We could pretend to slip out, ignore the smell of
exhaust, the sound of cars. We'd have a garden just for the two
of us. I'd pull on your hand, and you'd humour me. We would
crouch on the ground. In the garden, we would say life is hard.
A thing of knives, of spite and needles. There would be solitary
flowers, and poems that don't rhyme.

You laugh when I tell you these things. You say your mum
is crazy. You wonder if a heart as big as his, as big as a house,
could ever live inside a body as small as yours.

But you'd stay by my side, in our inside garden. We'd muffle the sun with velvet curtains. Bow our heads, fill our mouths with peppercorns. We could ignore the ghosts until they were little more than smoke, a light breeze that brushed our skin and was gone. We could break the moon and swallow it like jagged silver pills.

I wish I could tell you a different story. One in which I revolted when I discovered the women in the secret room, in which I asked for help and got it, in which I burned, in which I left.

Cook, or What's in a name, again

Cook was not a kind woman, but she wasn't cruel either. She had curly, greying hair and small, strong hands. She reminded me a little of my late mother, though where Cook cursed and threw things, my mother had only wept. I understood Cook to have been a wet nurse, once, and to have known my man since he was a boy. But, in his stories, the woman who raised him was named Agnes, a name he never used to address Cook. He told me of the way Agnes smelled – sour milk mixed with soil – of the way she let him walk his fingers all over her body when he was small, how safe he felt when she was near. He blamed her, sometimes, for the way he was.

I never asked him whether Cook and Agnes were the same person, and he never volunteered that information, as if people, for him, were nothing but the roles they played in his life, and once they slipped from one to another, there was nothing left to connect them to who they were before, no continuity, no spoken memory.

One of the ghosts scoffs loudly. *Cook lost her name*, she says. *You never even told us yours. Why don't you talk about that?*

I did call Cook by that lost name, once, loudly, when she was in the garden hanging the laundry:

Agnes!

She paused, her back stiffened for a moment, but she never turned.

A policeman came once, in those early days, at the insistence of a couple whose daughter had died tragically a few months into her marriage. One of my man's most recent wives. The policeman seemed embarrassed to address the lord with such concerns, made it clear he never believed the rumours himself. My man wore his most charming face. He plied the policeman with wine and then took him to inspect our chests, our basement, our back room. It was all too dark to see, but the policeman assured us that our openness was proof enough of the lord's innocence. He left, dazed and smiling, his head hurting sweetly from that day on, until the day he died.

It never occurred to me that I could have asked that man for help.

There were still things I liked, little refuges. Of the rooms in the house, I had a favourite. It smelled of freshly cut pine. There was a modest fireplace, forever cold and unused. The room was small, with a floor made of wood and a window that looked out into the back garden with boxes piled on either side. The boxes were full of knives, tiny bottles, spoons made of mother-of-pearl, elegant figurines, and smaller boxes that were impossible to open. The village was too far away to see from the window, but sometimes I heard horses neighing in the distance, or people calling to each other, long words I couldn't make out. They could have been names, cries for help, or nonsense words, spoken carelessly into the wind.

*   *   *

We'd visit the house I grew up in sometimes. We'd arrive, and I would look around the place, which seemed so much smaller than I remembered it: the entranceway poorly lit and narrow, the kitchen dirty, its brickwork smudged with soot and years' worth of grease, the bedrooms crumbling and cramped. My sisters flaunted themselves, dressed in their best dresses, which were not very good at all, my father hovering in the back, a stern look on his face. I tolerated them for as long as I could, then took my man by the hand and led him outside, showed him the river and the row of birch trees that lined it. There, we didn't talk. He didn't like to listen to stories from my past, and I didn't like remembering them. It had been a hard life, full of long, hungry work, a friend who died young at the hands of her own father. A boy I got to know in a barn one spring, soft and anxious, then a girl, so much sweeter.

One of my sisters' favourite torments when we were small was taking me out into the woods, pretending we were to play hide and seek, and leaving me there, blindfolded. At night, they opened the window next to my bed and said they had asked the birds to fly into the room and peck out my eyes while I slept.

I never told anyone, not even my mother when she was still alive, but every night I was visited by a huge bird with a hooked beak. It came to my bed and carried me out to the fields, showed me a small patch of black soil. It had a voice like a woman's, and it spoke so close to my face I could smell its corpse-full breath. Only this belongs to you, it said, and nothing else.

My father never visited me in my new home, but my sisters did come. They acted deferential and interested in front of my man, drawn to him like we all were, but they harboured no kind feelings towards me and never pretended well enough. You're so lucky to have each other, they told us over the tea and cakes I served. I walked them through our rooms, pointed at the rich curtains, the dressers, the hand-stitched sheets. They marvelled. I wanted to show them the cellar, too, the well, the back room. Cook watched me like a hawk around them, as if I were foolish enough to give them the full tour of the house.

When I knew my sisters were coming, I'd sit on the porch and wait for the sound of the carriage rolling up to the house, then brace myself for the endless chatter about the fishpond or the garden or the blooming spring, about babies and the dazzling colour of the sky.

My sisters had five daughters among them, whom they brought and paraded, eager to impress me with the fruitfulness of their lives. The children all looked too similar to me, nauseatingly so, dressed in pleats. I could not tell them apart.

When they left, I scrubbed the floors myself, then gathered everything they'd touched – the dainty cups, the tall glasses, the gold-rimmed plates – and locked them in a box, unwashed.

Afterwards, we lay together, my man and I. He kissed my thighs and my belly, then placed his hands on either side of my head and held me down, though he didn't need to. No children, he'd told me early on, there are never to be any children, and I'd told him I never wanted any. I breathed him in, and I imagined myself drowning, sinking into the soft bed, into the folds of the sheets and the things that lay beneath, the moss and the dirt and the worms that burrowed under the earth, deep and deeper still, where no one could see. Underground, he joined me. He taught me the names of things, of roots and bones and blind beasts. When we resurfaced, he played with my hair, his face slack, an ease over his brow.

We never married, but we lived together like husband and wife. I think he took some pleasure in that, especially when others addressed me as his wife, as if he were getting away with something. We needed no god to reign over our union. When people watched, he liked to throw one arm around my shoulders, rings glistening on his fingers with their sharp nails that he no longer filed down.

Still, sometimes, I wondered: if he'd discarded the others with such ease, despite their oaths and ties of matrimony, what would it take for him to do away with me? So little tethered me to this life, to this world, and I didn't want to join them.

Often, he left for the city, or wherever his business took him. I didn't like to see him go, but I never asked what his business was. His stories left such details obscure, so to me his wealth was as mythical and unquestionable as the smell of the forest on him or the untameable growth of his nails. I knew he owned a number of houses, bequeathed to him by his father, and his father before him, and more fathers before him. He owned houses all over the country, as far north and south as I could pronounce, with plenty of sheep and cattle and horses, as well as sources of fresh water and a lake like a giant eye. As for the rest of the details, either I leave them blank or, when the telling of this story becomes too vague, which is to say too threatening to my own believability, I make things up. Investments and taxes and trade with faraway lands allowed us a comfortable existence, through plague and blight and travel. People still

called him Count or Lord, though I never learned which title,
if any, was appropriate.

While he was gone, Cook and I neatened the house, which
was difficult because that house had a tendency to fall in on
itself, the unseen wives stitching themselves into the walls and
furniture, gnawing at our belongings, causing their small damages that added up in time. In that house, no clothing stayed
new for long. I tried not to hold it against them – it was the
only hurt they could inflict any more, after all. This chipping
away, this war of attrition.

Sometimes my man returned with new dresses and soft-
coloured ribbons, or more curious things, like pickled berries,
a stuffed hare caught mid-motion as it stood on its hind legs, or
a small piece of jewellery wrapped in cloth as thin as a spider's
web. Once, he brought a caged bird for me. It had a long blue
tail and a golden band around its neck, adorned with a small
key. He didn't tell me where he found it, how he bought it, but
he knew, he said, that I would like it. I put it on the mantelpiece.
Its cage was made of twigs woven together. The bird whistled
and chirped, flapped its wings and pecked at the twigs.

Other times, he returned empty-handed, his eyes overcast,
his skin smelling of rain. I sent Cook away and cradled him
then. I ran my fingers through his long, hard hair, worked out
its knots and tangles. I kissed his hands, his claw-like fingers, held him until something in his chest loosened and his
breathing came calm, the thunder behind his forehead quiet
at last.

It was Cook who taught me how to bead. She came into the
living room where I was sitting by the tall window, the morning

light soft and intricate through the lace. She sat next to me, laid out the beads and thread and needles on the table.

What are you doing? I asked.

Teaching you something, she said. A dying art.

You're a strange woman, I told her.

She laughed. A rare sound. Maybe so, she said. You'll be one, too, soon enough.

She threaded a needle and strung a number of beads on the thread, then performed an elaborate sequence of loops and knots that resulted in a little flower made of blue and black.

She handed me the string and the needle. Now you, she said.

I don't know how, I protested.

You'll learn, she said.

But how do I begin?

Begin with me.

So I did.

I tried to follow her instructions, but my clumsy fingers kept spilling the beads onto the floor. Cook was impatient with me, though I could see the love in her eyes as she showed me the intricate stitches.

You'll need something to occupy your mind, she said. She glanced at the ghosts I hadn't known she could see. Keep it off other things.

It worked. The stitches were complicated, but I learned how to sequence them, how to create patterns and loops. Cook taught me how to make flowers, letters, small animals, people.

Time in his absence passed quietly, without incident. The beaded flowers and the letters and the small animals and the small people kept me occupied while I sat by that window. The wives peeked over my shoulder, the wind knocked out of them long ago. They never said anything, back then, or nothing I could listen to. I'd heard that, when you die, you remember everything except your own name. I wondered if that was right. Did the wives still remember their names? They never told me.

When I was feeling dangerous, I went into the forest to look for their graves. It always felt a little surprising to find them, as if they were merely artefacts waiting to be discovered, ruins encountered by archaeologists who had nothing to do with their creation. Amidst the belladonna and blackberry, the gravestones lay flat, the wives' names rubbed smooth by the years, unreadable. The forest had swallowed them; they belonged to it now, to the rain and the snow.

One time, the moon hung low in the sky, a sliver of light in the deep blue of night. There was a chill in the air. The wind whispered through the leaves, making a throat of the forest. Above, bare branches scratched against each other, like hands reaching down, searching for what lies sleeping in the undergrowth. One of the dead wives followed me, tried to show me her decaying face, the clutch of horrors in her mouth.

Little rabbit, I said, I won't look at you.

We left my hometown as soon as the crops showed the first signs of blight and the ewes started bleating mournfully in the night. He had our belongings loaded onto a carriage along with Cook, but the two of us rode ahead on his horse, threading our way through the mountains, his hair loose in the wind. We rode in silence, but every once in a while he turned to me with an unspoken question, to which I responded with a touch on his chin or my head resting against his back, breathing in his hair. I'd never seen these mountains before, and for a while I wondered if we were headed to that strange village from his stories, the one with people who can see but can't, the one that lures beasts, the one my man is still pulled to. But we left the mountains behind and went through a forest instead. We kept close to a river until we arrived in a town where neither of us had ever been before, but where he owned several houses, empty and waiting to be lived in.

How long have you owned these houses? I asked.

Years, he said. Lifetimes. I owned them well before I was born.

He let me choose, and I picked one on the outskirts of the town, a house dusty and grey, so different from the one we'd left behind. The exterior was covered in dry ivy, and the garden was overgrown with weeds. Inside, the wind moaned through the crevices and rattled the windows. The shutters sagged on their hinges. Everything smelled of old wood and rain and plants gone to seed, and when we walked into the kitchen, a tang of blood clung to the backs of our throats.

This will do, Cook said. And then, looking at me: What a pair the two of you make. What a pair.

Before we moved, I had set the gift-bird free. I'd brought it out to the garden and opened the door of its cage, waited until it took a few tentative steps out of its prison. It walked on the grass for a while and then stayed there, staring longingly at the thick foliage above.

It was born in captivity, he told me. It will not survive freedom.

I expected it to be vacant, but from the very first night the new house declared itself full to the brim with the things we'd brought with us, so many more than a carriage could hold. I imagined them, the women hanging off the carriage like grapes off a vine, bruised and juicy, or stuck to the roof like barnacles, their faces turned up, their mouths open to the sky. If you sat in the living room of this new house in the night and kept very quiet, you could hear the roar of the ocean, far away, and other things, too. I held my breath, put a finger to my lips, hushed the new tenants until they obliged. Listen.

The scuttling of insects and mice, the falling of birds, the bruising of flesh, the slow decay of flowers.

I had Cook spread salt and flour on the floor, but the wives were somehow still able to move across the house without disturbing the white at all, to inflict their little damages without leaving behind a single trace.

The first day of our new life, we walked to the market, my arm looped through my man's. The streets were lined with stalls overflowing with produce, the air thick with the smell of spices and sweating bodies. This was a prosperous town. My ears dinged with the noise of people bargaining and haggling. When we passed, people watched us with bare-faced curiosity, and only a few of them turned away, averted their eyes the way one does when one has seen something obscene. The boldest among them held my man's gaze briefly, nodded a greeting.

At night, I took stock of myself in front of the mirror. And though I could see my own face, though I could feel the warmth of my own hands and the stretch of my own skin, there was another sensation behind it all, something else underneath, a putrescent layer that was not entirely mine. Another woman was trapped beneath myself, and my body was a house with no windows and no doors that I was doomed to wander endlessly. One where light never broke, where nobody entered or left.

The curtains in the new house were already faded when we moved in. He had them replaced immediately with rich brocade threaded with gold, but that, too, faded quickly. The floorboards creaked when I walked across them. He had these replaced, too. Still they creaked, and, eventually, I found out why: I caught one of the wives waiting for me to step on a particular floorboard, and when I did she mimicked that creaking sound with her mouth. The little fool, I thought – she gave up her voice just so she could see me squirm.

Others picked up this trick too, and soon the house was filled with wife-shaped ghosts that sounded like bells, and spoons, and crows and nightingales and even birds so rare they may not exist at all. When, in time, they tried to speak again, they got the sounds wrong and ended up laughing at themselves, a rattling sound that made my skin crawl.

I pause.

Do you believe this story? Do I? I've told it to myself so many times by now, and each time I'm less sure it fits. That it says what I need it to say, what I need you to hear.

Did the wives really give up their voices then? Perhaps it's simply easier for me to think so: it was they who chose not to speak, not I who wasn't ready to listen.

My sisters wrote to me in the beginning, but I threw their letters away unread. I wanted nothing from my old life. In the mountains, fleeing my hometown, we had rushed; here, we took our time, as if we'd done nothing wrong, and we were only fighting the house's eagerness to decay: mending the fraying fabrics, nailing the floorboards back in place, propping up the crumbling walls. We opened the windows to let in fresh air, as if that has ever done anything for the ghosts. They followed me into the cellar when I needed to fetch a jar of pickled cucumber or plum preserve. I could hear them sloshing around in the dark, sighing and chattering, creaking to one another incoherently. Sometimes it sounded as if they were dancing. I caught the smell of bad meat.

We created new habits. My man and I started the day with breakfast in the kitchen, Cook hovering over the stove, her sleeves rolled up and her hair tied back, the kitchen warmer than any other room in the house. We ate porridge drowned in butter and honey, spiced with cinnamon and nutmeg. I sat by the window, my feet tapping against the chair, and watched the trees sway in the wind. After breakfast, he inspected his cabinet of curios, straightened a box or dusted a porcelain figurine. He went to the cellar to check on his wine, to run his fingers over the labels, and then he came back up with a glass in his hand, and we drank it by the fire, which was always burning, the weak glow of flames lapping at the logs.

The garden thinned inescapably, the trees stooped and withered, the ivy spread over the windows, trying to lock us in. But the house leaked; an entire building gushing, full of pores and holes, permeable like our bodies. I marvelled at it all, and Cook looked at me with contempt, as if saying, Haven't you learned yet? Don't you know? Nothing can be contained for very long.

Then the harvest moon came, so we walked down to the village for the feast and let the people gawk at us, the lady and her gentle man.

The men who'd helped move us into the house a few months ago greeted him like old friends. They had carried his furniture and his paintings and the many boxes full of the dresses he'd had made for me and for the ones before, amassed over the years, hundreds of them. Last, the men had carried the long wooden chests into the little back room where my man hung his secrets out to dry. What do you have in there, corpses? the men had joked and laughed, gasping under all that weight.

I had picked a dress from our boxes, for the feast. One of the oldest ones, a deep wine colour. It was too long for me; its hem trailed on the ground. I knew not which wife it had belonged to, only that the lady had worn it on her wedding night.

He spent his days with those men sometimes, him sweating in his finery, them pretending he was one of them and failing, falling back on that distant deference that wealth wedges between people. But, that night, we were all friends. My man and I danced together, and then he danced with the town women and I danced with the town men, and then we danced together again. When the lutist tired and the music ran out he defied social norms and leaned so close to me I could smell the wine on his breath. He smiled and hugged me in front of everyone, the way a bear embraces his victim – if you don't look closely, you might mistake it for love.

Later, when we got home, his eyes were full of clouds. You flinched, he said. You embarrassed me. His lip quivered. Are you sick of me, then?

It was a dangerous question, I knew. The wives pooled around us, as if drawn by his gravity. Their voices sounded like the snap of bones, the crack of head against wall. Don't listen to the ghosts, I told myself, don't, don't.

I touched his knee and reached for his beard in placation, and I wondered how long it would take this time, how long before dead crops, before human mouths on foals, eggs filled with ashes, lambs cut open to reveal hearts made of stone. It could be months, years perhaps, and when people came to our door with torches or crosses or long, slender muskets, they'd find only empty rooms, curtains rotting on the windows like shrouds.

Never, I said. Never ever.

And then, his fury thwarted, my gentle man bled. His blood welled up from the skin of his palm, unprompted, smelling of soil. I held his hand and wiped the blood away with a clean white towel that I would later throw into the trash.

My love, I said, and kissed.

Then the harvest was done and the evenings were only just starting to turn cold. I sat by the window, stringing bead after bead after bead, my eyes straining against the failing light, the tips of my fingers raw. Cook finished her chores and joined me. She sorted my beads by colour into tiny cups. She said nothing of the bruise that had bloomed around my lips.

Time passed slowly in that house, like something pulled taut, spread thin and imperceptible across an empty surface.

Long hours later, after the sun had set, we spotted him riding his horse up to the house, his shoulders wide as a mountain range, his long beard gathered in a braid beneath his chin. My man, I thought, my handsome man. Cook disappeared into the kitchen, mumbling something about meat that needed to be cured.

I left my beadwork and met him by the door, like a wife,

like this was my house, though it wasn't, though I'm not. He'd brought me cherries, he said, a whole basket of them, firm and shockingly red.

I took two, put them both in my mouth and chewed, without a word.

I fell ill.

It was a fever but also a weight in my middle that made me think of stones. Pain folded me in half, and I could do little but curl up in bed and moan. I thought, maybe, it was my turn to die. Cherry Girl, blue in the mouth. I clawed at my throat. I want to live, I tried to say, though my voice wouldn't come out. I want to live.

I imagined he might withdraw from me, recoil from this display of rot.

Instead, he seemed even more drawn to me than before. He sat on the bed next to me and felt my forehead with his wide palm. He brought me tea with honey and lemon, looped his fingers through the tendrils of my hair until I fell asleep.

It was Cook who didn't dare come inside my room, but only hesitated at the threshold, peering in, her face unreadable.

I slept fitfully, my mind filled with the garden, with white stone birds and a stone woman staking a claim to a patch of earth that could never become her grave.

I surprised everyone by getting better a few weeks later. The fever went down, and the fist in my belly that had pulled my organs aside dissipated, leaving behind only a trace of discomfort. Colour returned to my cheeks and, when I looked at myself in the mirror, for once, I saw my face alone.

When I finally left my bed for good, my man gave me gifts of feather and silk. You're not like the others, he said, his voice almost admiring, his face perplexed. He lowered himself before me, embraced my waist, touched me like something precious and rare.

Why are you sad? I asked him.

He said: I didn't think you would survive.

My miraculous recovery was followed by a different sort of dying. The wells dried up, the leaves of the trees curled and fell to the ground, and even a number of town youths perished after a long withering strange enough to make the townsfolk suspect us. They came up to the house at night and tried to peer through our windows, the eternally threadbare curtains allies to their cause. If we betrayed that we noticed them, they crossed themselves and muttered prayers under their breath.

I felt some guilt over this, as my survival seemed to mean others' suffering and death, but – is there any use denying it? – a certain amount of pride, too. The survivor's glee, the smug vainglory of the trapped animal that eats its own foot.

Soon, it was the year of dead cows, of snows that came too early and blight that came and came. I was alive. I was unmarried. I was the lady of another house we had to leave behind.

In the carriage that took us to the next town, he held my hand for a long time, until I freed myself to rummage through a basket Cook had packed for us. I gazed at the passing fields, the rivers, the trees, then bit into a shrivelled apple that had been fresh just that morning.

In the new house, the wives left me alone for the most part, except I always found eyelashes in my food. Sometimes I picked them from between my teeth; others I swallowed, washed them down with sour wine. My man fell into a cycle too: settling, building, destroying, fleeing. He went away, he came back. I beaded, I waited. Bruises bloomed and faded and bloomed again, the seasons of his doubt.

Why do you stay? Cook asked, loud enough for the ghosts to hear.

Why do you stay? I asked back.

We moved often, but I was not unhappy. I know now that part of what drew me to him was his roots: how long they were, how firm, and how unlike my own. That old country, hastily abandoned, so long ago, so far gone. In another story. But here, I could claim his roots as mine. No matter how often we moved, no matter the house or the place, everywhere in this country he was at home. Everything, everywhere, was his.

The houses that received us started out so different from one another: some were large and sprawling, others austere, and others still were small, barely enough room for the three of us. Yet by the time we moved out again I could see in them a certain resemblance in the way they smelled, the way they stood, the pregnant quiet of their nights. Maybe this is what happens when you love a man like him. You think you're moving from place to place, but the houses move with you, until you're clinging to their walls, to the windows and doors, to the floors and ceilings, like a layer of dust.

Once, as we sat in our house, surrounded by the ghosts of his wives, I asked him: Don't you think it's wrong, to keep doing this?

He looked at me, his head cocked to the side. Doing what? he asked, eyebrows arched, as if he didn't understand.

Day after day I watched the plants for the moment that they became tarnished, that their petals turned brown, their leaves curled inwards. I imagined I was one of the dead wives, toiling in the ground, the dirt cool and soft. I was a bone, a set of teeth.

A few months passed quietly.

He enjoyed this new place; he gave himself over to the task of resurrecting the grounds of the new house, filling them with fruiting trees and rosebushes. We even organised fêtes and entertained guests. He introduced me to newfound friends, people from the city.

At his happiest, he grasped my hands.

Tonight I'll conjure flowers for you, he told me, and he did, filled every room in the house with them, until the hallways and bedrooms and staircases were full of bright red and purple and yellow, petals covering every inch of the floor, lying thick under my feet, until we were both suffocated and there was nowhere left to go.

It didn't last. The plagues came faster each time we moved, as if it were my own lingering that caused the rapid wasting of the land.

We made do through the fallow years, taking advantage of his wealth, the rich imports, the hoarded goods. Cook smuggled as much as she could to the starving villagers when she thought we wouldn't notice. Once, I overheard a man tell her: The rich are the blight of this land. They take and take until our backs are broken and the soil is dead. It's in their nature. They can't help themselves.

And so we moved again. I touched his shoulder lightly, coaxed him like I'd seen him coax his young horse. You should go to the woods more, I told him. Roam free, like the old days.

What old days? he asked.

The days when you were a boy. The days when you were happy.

There were no such days, he said.

We left our new land unfarmed, to summon a future without blights. A few months in, a rich old lady from one of the neighbouring estates visited our house. She gazed at our barren fields in surprise and shook her head. Look at all this land, she said sadly. Something must be able to grow there. Why don't you put it to use?

And yes, I wanted to say, yes, everything here grows eventually, grows blacker and worse than when we arrived, bursts with mould and decay.

I touched her hand. You're right, I told her. We don't want to waste this land.

After a while he stopped trying to make me comfortable, each house smaller and less hospitable than the last, the walls growing unbearable around us, as if trying to drive me away. I would catch him contemplating the broken earth outside, or on his knees pushing his hands into the soil as if believing he could somehow revive it, reverse the effect of our presence on the land. He even tried planting things again, trees and seeds and bulbs, though we both knew it would all die in the end.

When he sensed me looking, he got mad. He raged against the air, the soil, the sun, until, drained, he fell on the ground and wept for himself.

I filed down his nails, combed his hair, braided his beard under his chin.

Sometimes I come back and I'm sure you won't be here, he told me.

Do you wish this? I asked, his head resting on my knees. Do you wish me gone? I whispered as I kissed his forehead. The wives peeled themselves from the walls, as if to listen in.

He stared at the destruction outside. Said nothing.

One winter day he came back hunched, walked a few steps up the path and collapsed. I saw him through the window at which I sat, my beading work on my knees, my beads arranged neatly before me.

I thought he was dead. There were no thoughts in my head, or none that I would admit today. I ran outside, the snow biting at my legs. Cook yelled something from inside the house, but I was already closing the distance between myself and his body, his body. My mind couldn't make sense of it, his body on the ground, in the snow. I reached for him in the drowned grass. His arms lay trapped beneath him at an awkward angle. His chest was barely moving.

Not dead, he was not dead.

I tried to pull him upright, but all I managed was to turn him over, taking myself down with his weight, his head on my lap. I cried for Cook and she finally came running, carrying coats for us both.

We loaded him onto a blanket and pulled him back to the

house. We laid him in the middle of the drawing room, dripping onto the carpet, and lit a big fire to drive the cold from his bones.

He came to hours later, his eyes bleary. I was still next to him, my back stiff from sitting motionless for so long. He reached for me, squeezed my hand. He looked like a boy.

What happened? I asked him, but he wouldn't say. He stared into the flames for a long time.

When he spoke, his voice was hoarse. You should have let me be, was all he said.

When he managed to pick his body up off the floor, he got himself to bed and slept for an entire day. I stood at his bedside and watched him. The wives were still and quiet, numb since the moment they'd seen him collapsed on the floor. I left him to the ghosts and their cold attentions. Somehow, we had come to a kind of peace.

While he slept, I listened to their voices, their dry laughter, the rustling of their clothes. Outside, the world was getting darker, the days unnaturally short even for this season, the frozen grass cracking as I walked.

I knew we would leave again soon.

Of course we did leave.

We went to another village, and then another, and another. We took less and less of the wives with us, yet the ghosts persisted, clung to as little as a scrap of dress, a comb, a lock of hair, all that was left of them reduced to a single chest. It almost felt wrong; our escapes shouldn't be that effortless, that regular. We should be more burdened by the past, our disasters less easily overcome.

I think perhaps he felt the same because, after a time, I real-ised he had started to spread the rumours himself, when he was restless and despairing. But then, so was I. So were all of us.

It was a cold morning, the sun hardly up in the sky, and he'd already gone out, wading through the decaying earth. I helped Cook with the dusting. I was the only one who dusted his curio cabinet in those days. It took the utmost care; these things were so fragile, more and more fragile, it seemed to me, with every season that came and went. I palmed the skin-thin glass of each figurine and passed the softest cloth over it, holding my breath as if even the lightest breeze could shatter it. The wives looked over my shoulder at the tiny glass man with his hand on his hip. They breathed as hard as they could, asking too much of their ghost lungs. Outside the land withered always, and I thought of how odd it was, and how mundane: while his wives perished, his plagues were thwarted, the crops spared. And I was reminded of old stories about virgin sacrifices, girls thrown over cliffs, throats slit over funeral pyres, ending wars and beginning new ones, lives cleaved – isn't that how it's always been?

In some ways, I thought, he's not remarkable at all. His vio-lence has always been the violence of the world.

A wife shifted behind me, eyeing the figurine in my hand, and I thought, maybe the wives never died, maybe they're just sleeping, their bodies buried in snow, their blood frozen in the earth, deep below, and one day they can be warmed again, walk the earth once more. But the ghost wife shuffled – are you the first one? I wanted to ask her. The second, the fourth? – and her feet hardly made a sound, her weight as negligible as an eyelash, or a knuckle scraping across flesh.

I looked at her again – she looked back. Was that a nod?

I held the figurine high above my head and then with one swing smashed it against the wall.

Then I collected each shard carefully as the wife watched, eyes sharp and mouth stretched with glee. We buried them all in the garden, in the cold earth of that house we were bound to leave soon.

I could tell right away the last village we moved to was different from the ones that came before. The people seemed more suspicious, and they'd heard rumours about him before. They didn't say it to our faces, but I felt it: we were not welcome.

The houses were made from stone and the streets were cobbled and the people looked healthy and well fed. Women clutched their children when we passed, and the villagers refused to work our fields, mend our clothes, prune our hedges. The work fell to Cook and me. She grumbled, but I didn't mind. Once, when I accompanied Cook to the market to help her buy meat and fish for pickling, someone called me a whore, an unmarried urchin, a witch. I rarely went to market after that.

It took only a few weeks, a month at most, for the land around the village to go fallow, for the wells to bloom with lichen red as blood, the lambs to grow human teeth, the children to forget language and bleat.

(IN THE DARK, SOMETHING MONSTROUS.)

'I don't want to be like him,' you say, your voice barely audible.

Tristan said something like that, once, didn't he, asked his mother if he would grow up to be a monster. He wanted to know if he, too, would one day cause plagues, cause bruises to bloom around another's mouth, cause the earth to crumble where he stepped.

I turn to Eunice, but she won't meet my eyes.

I still ask myself, like you ask, like Tristan did: Is he a monster?

And still, all I can answer is: Listen.

I walk to the window and wish I could stay here, not speaking, spend hours next to it, like the woman in my story. Outside, a city I won't set foot in again, sealed up as I am in this place, one more story and then one more, as if that will keep me from the world, a reverse Scheherazade who can't be saved until all her stories are told, retold, told again.

And here, a city and its factories and the first signs of a plague that always comes.

The radio next door sputters a melody – something I recognise distantly as Bartók.

Stones

The night before the stoning, I was woken by the sound of the ghosts shuffling in the drawing room, paired up in their best dresses, dancing a sleepy pavane.

I spent the day haunted by their dead dance. I beaded, absently waiting for him, waiting for night, for what would come next. In dread and in hope.

When the sun finally set, I opened the window and leaned out, breathed in the smell of night, of the cold earth, of the fruit trees festering in the field. I looked at the sky, which was heavy with stars, the moon hidden behind a single line of cloud, and I wondered if all the horses had died, if they, too, had been pulled down into the earth.

He was late to come home. I heard him on the horse, its legs pounding the ground, hooves cutting through the grass. The horse whinnied, and Cook came to the door to take his heavy coat. She always stared at him when he returned, and in those moments I really did wonder if she was Agnes, because of the careful way she had of looking at his face, as if inspecting it for fresh bruises and cuts.

He didn't tell us where he'd been, didn't utter a single word. He ate his dinner in silence and took his leave. I had my own bedroom in that house, but that night I joined him in his. He was already on his back on the bed. His eyes were red. The wives smudged the air, naked skin translucent, barely there. I drew closer to him, my knees against his side, my hands on his chest. I leaned in to kiss him. His mouth tasted like metal, like blood.

Are you worried? I whispered to him, and he nodded that yes, he was.

Don't be, I told him. I pressed my lips to his again. I can still remember my name, you see.

They caught us in our sleep. I woke up to the sound of glass smashing. In his fright, he swiped at my skin, his nails shredding it like claws, but I felt none of it, nothing at all. I rushed to the drawing room and found the tall windows broken, glass strewn across the floor. He joined me there, held me back to keep my bare feet from being torn to ribbons by the glass.

Then the door crashed open and people barged in. I couldn't see their faces; the house was dark and my eyes still lidded with sleep. Of course they had come for both of us; this wasn't about the ghosts, after all. It was for the blight, for the inexplicable terrors, the bad dreams. In their eyes, I was just as culpable. In their eyes, I was no different. And who's to say? Perhaps they were right.

They handled me roughly, pulled at my clothes. They dragged me out into the garden where someone threw me against a stone wall. They left Cook alone.

They had a harder time with him. It took five men and a struggle to subdue him, but in the end he was on the ground next to me. I crawled over to him and let myself be held as the first stones were cast, his hands on the small of my back. I wondered what would happen if he died; would he haunt this place, merge with the land and rot it for ever so that nothing would ever grow from it again? Would the ghost wives still be here, forever peeling the wallpaper? Would I?

But then I was torn from his grip and held at a distance, made to watch as they kicked and cursed him until I felt the sky change above, getting lighter though it was not yet morning. A long time still to sunrise.

As if signalled by someone or something up above, the people stopped. They stood us both up again and drove us out with stones, without any of our possessions, with only the clothes on our backs.

By the great iron-toothed gate a rock struck him on the forehead and tore the thin skin there. He brought his fingers to that cut and then looked at his blood, astonished, as if he hadn't thought he could bleed from anywhere but that old wound in his hand.

We carried on. Cook joined us at the bend of the road, though she didn't have to.

Somewhere behind us, a stone-birthing wife cackled with glee.

(IN THE DARK, A CITY.)

You left then, one of the ghosts says, *left us for a while. Remember?*
As if she already knows the whole story. As if these are the same
ghosts, and this is not a fairy tale at all.

   Will you leave us again? the ghost asks.

   I say: There was, once, a city.

The city

Our best option after the stoning, we knew, was to go to the city, that place of money and luxurious anonymity, so different from what we'd known before. Somewhere people were unlikely to have heard of us, or, if they had, to believe, or, if they believed, to care.

We were on foot for most of the journey, as we had no other means of transportation; besides, there were places where the roads were treacherous, littered with spontaneous bogs that could swallow a carriage whole. All through the first night, I felt the ghosts behind us, empty wives seeping silently into the ground.

We walked for days. I grew so thirsty and hungry my feet hardly obeyed me. To keep myself upright, I imagined I was on a horse, a strong steed with fine brown hair. It wept, too, tears of tar that fell to the ground with a plop, fat as cherries.

I don't know how Cook survived that. She seemed so old by then. How old was she? Too old to be his mother.

In the city, it was easy to become new people. We rested in a hotel for which he paid with one of the rings still on his fingers, and, when he finally managed to use his connections to obtain a loan from the bank, we got an apartment in the centre of the city, high up on the third floor of a once-majestic building, an aristocrat's mansion turned into tenements. The wives seemed not to have followed us here, so the apartment felt unnaturally peaceful. The bed was too soft for my liking, and yet, the first time I sank into its mattress and closed my eyes against the quiet dark, I slept more soundly than I had in years.

We learned our former house had been smashed up after we were driven out: the curtains pulled from their rods, our armchairs gutted, the china cracked, my beads sown into the fields. I don't know if Cook intervened on our behalf, or if it had a knack for finding its way back to us, but here it was a few weeks later, the precious clutter of our lives: a chest full of dresses and wifely things, a crystal goblet, and my man's curios, miraculously wrapped in tissue and placed, unspoiled, in a wooden crate.

At first, we rarely went out. He sulked and waited for his head wound to heal. My body was bruised, too, but I felt rested and strangely alive. I paced the apartment, ran my hands against the peeling teal wallpaper, polished the windows and spied the teeming crowds outside, breathed in the dirty smells, not a hint of cherry tree or fern or lovely rosebush in sight.

It was dreadful. It was perfect.

The city bordered the water. It was not a sea, but the vast cold ocean that separates this country from the rest of the world. I wanted to see it. I thought, to see this vastness would be to understand how small and fragile this land is, how narrow the passage between what is and what can no longer be. What's a spoiled fruit, a fallow land, a dead horse, compared to that?

He was still healing, but the wound didn't seem to bother

him too much; whenever we asked, Cook or I, he said it was nothing. And he did seem untroubled, younger, flourishing even. With his loans, he began to infuse our lives with their former extravagance. In the evenings, he dressed in furs and jewels, his hair combed back and his beard braided, magnificent, beneath his chin.

Don't you fear you will be recognised? I asked him.

Nobody knows us here, he said.

How can they not have heard of you? I asked.

He shrugged.

It's a big country.

We began to be invited to parties, and of course we went. Some were grand affairs, given in mansions with marble staircases and silk sofas and crystal chandeliers and a band of musicians as flashy as a flock of stunning, rare birds, and others were smaller, more intimate gatherings that guests could only reach by boat. The people were beautiful, dressed up and burnished, as if they kept their faces and hands always washed of the earth. I tried to remember what the real world was like, that the earth was full of ash and the body a fragile membrane that can rupture at the merest touch. It was so easy to forget.

And then there were the gatherings in the outskirts of the city, in small, elegant houses with rose gardens and small, elegant guests dressed in black. These parties were the most lively, full of music and dancing – not the kind I'd learned back home, but different, new, a kind of moving that looked wild and free, like the ocean. They came on ships, they said, the people and their dances, from lands where the flowers, I imagined, were made of gold. I didn't dance with them at first, but sat alone, picking at the gold-leaf wallpaper that covered the walls, drinking the candle-smoke from the thick air. Little by little, I relaxed, and I learned to enjoy these gatherings and even the attention we received.

Near dawn, when we walked home, the crowds had dispersed and the city seemed empty and silent. We made our way around potholes and piles of trash, his arm supporting me, almost lifting me off the ground when a puddle was particularly large. My heels clicked. The light from the oil lamps flickered and the shadows shifted, as if parting to let us through.

For a while, he seemed so benign. It'd been months in the city and no disasters had bloomed around us; the walls of the apartment remained untainted, uncrumbling. People suffered, of course, they suffered and sickened and died, but who could blame him for that? Who could say for sure this wasn't simply the way of the world, here, in the city? So at the parties I sat on his lap, resting my head on his shoulder, watching the people dance and the sun set. He liked to put his hand on my back protectively, possessively, and the rings on his hand caught the light just so. If you tilted your head to the side and squinted, he might have seemed to you like a king of old sitting on his throne. And me? Something round and small, served on a golden plate.

Cook was bored, and she responded to boredom by giving herself more to do: wash the floors, reupholster the furniture, take down the curtains and mend them, then hang them up again, polish the bronze handles of every cabinet and every door. Her boredom turned out to be infectious, and I grew bored, too. But Cook was unwilling to share her chores, so I went out and roamed the streets, entered shops and bought things I had no use for. I quickly got tired of that as well, and I ended up sitting at the window and watching the streets below for hours. I missed the view from my windows in the countryside, the blue-black shrubs, the lush ground, the cherry trees in the distance. The air here seemed wrong, too heavy. It stifled me.

I was certain by then that the ghost wives hadn't followed us to the city; or, if they had, there was too much noise and too many people for me to notice them. I wondered if such a thing was possible, for a place to be too much, to have so much presence that it erases those of a feebler will or a subtler disposition.

I tried to take up beading again, but not even that could fill the endless hours I spent inside the apartment with its empty walls, its too-still wallpaper, its quiet floorboards.

So sometimes, I retreated into fantasy.

In my mind, I sat in my old garden and made flower crowns. I was alone for a while, but then, eventually, always, my man came and sat next to me on the ground or on a bench. He looked down on me, took my hands in his.

How is it, I asked him, that you keep finding me?

It's not as hard as you think, he replied. I'll always find you, no matter where you go.

At the parties, he left me alone often and mingled with his new business partners or entertained men and women who found him not only endlessly fascinating but also worthy of their pity, with his bear-like past, his ghastly secrets, his many dead wives. In my lonely hours, I met women who taught me the names of colourful drinks, then took me aside and showed me the secrets of their skin. I found them soft and pliable, their flesh giving under my touch more easily than I'd ever thought possible, and I wondered, why aren't I more like them? Would I be happier, if I were?

Afterwards, he took me in his arms or pushed me against a wall, his nose in my hair. I thought he caught a scent of the women on me. Did he wonder the same thing about my flesh that I did about theirs? Was my fate already inscribed on my body, etched on the inside of my skin? Wasn't it yet my time to be read?

I felt the wind in his breath, glimpsed the forest in his eyes. Don't you miss our home? I asked him, and he said, Silly girl, what home?

(IN THE DARK, NOTHING HURTS.)
I pause. You seem tired, your face older, so much like your father's. A trick of the shadows, perhaps, but I think I can almost glimpse in your face the man you might one day become.

Your mum is seeing things that are not there.

'What's wrong?' you ask.

Did I gasp?

I bring my hand to the back of my head. My fingers come away bloody.

'Does it hurt?' you ask, your voice barely audible.

Seasons without names

In the city, it was hard to know seasons, so I counted time in months. Eleven passed, and in that time I felt myself grow smaller and smaller, like a child, or a doll. I tried to remember the house I grew up in, my family, my flower sisters, but their faces seemed dull with dust, far away across a nameless sea. Once or twice, I thought of swallowing a needle, letting it stitch inside me what it may. I imagined being cut open one day and found full of embroidery, my body held together with bead and thread. I missed the ghosts.

Cook said I lived in the past, with the ones that came before. That I should let them go. But, you see, she had it backwards. Ghosts exist always in the present. They're like scars that way. In the past, they're wounds. In the future, who knows?

My man let his nails grow long again, and when I commented on them or tried to file them down for him, he laughed and told me I used to like him the way he was.

Now you want to change me, after all this time, my love?

And yet, he liked to change his name often, giving different versions of himself to different people. Sometimes he was Conomor, others Conor, Carnelian, or Cormoran—

You take in a sharp breath, making me stop. One of these

275

names is your father's. I didn't mean to let it slip, but it seems I'm unravelling steadily as time is running out, my tapestry undone before it's even done. My beads will scatter if I'm not careful, and then, who will gather them again?

It's true your father moved often before settling down here with me, but he never changed his name – powerful men rarely need to reinvent themselves, their scandals easily covered up.

I hasten my pace, push my voice to continue – I say: In the city, for the first time, he afforded himself a wealth of appellations. He became an abundance of himself. Often, he told people he was an orphan, a self-made man, until he, too, believed it. It irritated me to see him make such claims – this, of all things, was the thing that irritated me! – and on one of those occasions I asked him, as innocently as I could, a simple question about his father's taste in clothes. So convinced was he of his fiction, that he didn't understand whom I meant. I pointed at the ring on his finger that still bore his father's initials, though faintly, smoothed over by the years. He remembered, then, and sulked.

He only recovered when the next invitation arrived, the nights of self-invention stretching before him like a salve.

On one such night, he introduced himself as Lord Cee. The party was a rather dull affair, the music watery and the wine weak, so we sat apart from everyone else and waited for the appropriate time to pass until we could leave without offending the host. All around us, the walls were lined with glass and mirrors, where I could see my distorted reflection. I chatted to him about the ladies dressed in white and green, the wine making my head feel fuzzy – perhaps it was not as weak as I'd first thought, or maybe it was the mirrors – when

I noticed he was hardly listening to me. I followed his gaze and found him studying a tall young man with dark eyes and a soft chin.

Do you know him? I asked, and he shook his head.

But I want to, he added.

I looked at him, then at the young man. You'd like him? I asked.

The music swelled as he made his way towards the man. I watched them talk for a while, focusing on the young man's expression, which seemed to me to be one of genuine interest. After some time, he put out his hand, and the young man hesitated for a moment before taking it. He whispered something in Lord Cee's ear that made him smile, almost with a blush.

They parted, and we returned home.

The next day, the young man came to our apartment and asked if Lord Cee was in. I told him he was not, but he could keep me company until Lord Cee came back. He was glad to.

He introduced himself as Julian, and I had Cook serve him biscuits and too-strong tea. She wasn't pleased at this intrusion, so I sent her to the market for cherries. They're out of season, she complained, but she went anyway, thankful to be released.

We studied each other over the lips of our cups. He let his gaze roam the wallpaper – no longer peeling, thanks to Cook's efforts, but marbled by large swaths of exposed plaster.

How long have you known Lord Cee? he asked, and I noted with some pleasure that he didn't assume I was his wife.

It's been many years, I told him. I can't recall how many.

Is he a good man? he asked.

277

What a strange question, I said.

But is he?

I told him, Yes, he's a good man.

And, he added, loyal?

Loyal to what?

He shrugged. To anything. To you.

I looked at him for a long time. I thought of the wives, following us faithfully across our many homes, thought of the land, necrotic without fail under his touch.

The heart is deceitful above all things, I said quietly.

What? the young man asked.

Nothing. A Bible verse someone told me, once. I arranged my mouth into a smile.

How strange, he said.

Does loyalty matter to you? I asked, starting to glean the contents of their whispered conversation from the night before, to guess at Lord Cee's propositions.

He put his cup down. Yes, he said. Or, I suppose, sincerity. You see, all we have in life is our time; I want to know I am spending mine wisely.

I leaned closer and reached for his hand, then joined him on the sofa. His skin was soft, his fingers delicate; he could have been an artist. Maybe he was. Such a fragile thing, this young man. How long would he last?

I chose my words carefully. He's always loyal to the ones he loves, I told him. For as long as he loves them. And as long as they don't leave. I glanced at his dark eyes – hadn't I seen them before somewhere? Or heard about them? I squeezed his hand and told him: You'll see.

*   *   *

Julian moved in with us soon after that. He liked to sing in the mornings, which drove Cook mad, but I enjoyed not having to tolerate the silence any more.

He, Lord Cee, was pleased with this new arrangement. He'd had other lovers before, men and women both, ones he'd grown tired of quickly, or who'd left him feeling empty and guilty in the end. But this time, it was different; I caught him looking at Julian and the expression in his eyes was one of awe. As if he'd known this man before, known him deeply and intimately, this stranger who lived with him and touched him, like a miracle, a gift he'd never thought he would be given.

The first time the old wound in his hand bled, Julian paled at the sight. He rushed to bring bandages and soapy water, then fell to his knees next to our man and tended to his wound as if he'd done this a thousand times before, even if the smell of blood drove him near to fainting.

I liked the brave face he put on, his laughter, the way he looked at me, as if he saw me and I was a person to him, someone to know, to hold. More than just a not-yet ghost peeling herself from the wallpaper, doing her little damage, waiting for her turn.

I pause, think of obfuscating the details for you. But I've told you such terrible things already. Why should I cower from love?

This is how I remember it: At night, the three of us shared a bed, the sheets tangled around us, Julian and my man whispering to each other, their voices rising and falling through the darkness, and me, silent but pleased with them both. Julian slept between us, and I lay awake, listening to the sound of his breath, looking at the unblemished surface of his skin. His dreams shifted beneath the thin veil of his eyes.

I tell you: I forgot myself then, for a little while, forgot how this goes, how it always goes, how sorry I am.

Because of course the air in the apartment grew thick, imperceptibly, a little more every day. It spilled out of the cracks in the walls and the seams in the floorboards. It curled around the books and the chairs, filled the halls and the drawers, seeped into the spaces between our bodies when we slept. The apartment exhaled, but never once did it draw a breath. The mirrors grew dirty, despite Cook's efforts, the chandeliers tarnished, the curtains frayed. Sometimes I thought there was writing behind that ravaged wallpaper – though I couldn't read it, no matter how hard I tried.

At night I liked to watch the young man in our bed. I imagined a nightmare sitting on him as he slept, his arms spread, one slung over the side of the mattress, his mouth half-open and helpless. I wanted to tell him, shut your mouth. The monster is right there. It's sitting on your belly, it's ready to reach the organs of your fancy and drip its venom into you. For pity's sake, shut your mouth.

But I said nothing. I said nothing, and Julian seemed a little paler to me every morning, and dark circles underscored his eyes. When Lord Cee went out, we stayed in the apartment together, and Julian liked to perch on the window to look at the people on the street below. I joined him often, put my arm around his shoulders, and together we watched the people in their multitudes.

Can they see us, you think? Julian once asked me.

As if we were already ghosts.

*   *   *

When he came home, our man brought back strange objects, an echo of the days of his youth, when he first became a collector: tiny urns; bronze, severed arms; a miniature painting of a woman with a crown of thorns. He gifted them to Julian with a hopeful look on his face, kneeling before his lover with his hands cupped around his offerings. His affection for Julian had changed him somehow, made him soft and fragile, and this new version of him made me wonder whether everything had been avoidable after all, all the plagues and the decay and the loss, neither nature nor nurture but chance and choice and circumstance.

Julian acted pleased with his gifts, but I could see he found these things grotesque, and after he put them away in the cabinet with the rest, he forgot about them entirely. He was learning, slowly, to pretend.

When Julian happened to be out and we were alone, my man took my hand and kissed the lines in my palm. I think I'm saved, he said. Don't you?

In my belly, a cherry tree was growing, though I didn't know it yet.

One day, I opened the closet to hang up a coat and found Julian stuffed in the back, between the dresses and shawls, arms wrapped around his knees. The scent of mould hit me so suddenly it made me dizzy. The air was so frozen my breath clouded as it left my mouth. At first I thought he was dead, another cold body for our chests, and tears started streaming from my eyes before I could hold them in – but then I noticed Julian was shaking.

I pulled him out, wrapped my arms around him until his body settled against mine, his breath soft on my neck.

What were you doing in there? I asked him. I didn't ask: What did he do to you?

I saw something, Julian said. In the mirror. In the walls.

You dreamed it, I told him, with my cold-blue lips, with my deceitful heart.

And last night, while I slept, he continued, I felt a pressure on my chest, on my throat, and when I opened my eyes he was there on top of me and around me, his long nails against my skin. He called me by someone else's name. He talked about things I couldn't understand: a night in the woods, a boy holding a fish. His eyes were so strange. He couldn't see me. Couldn't hear me. He tried to stop my breath.

Julian wept in my arms. I caressed his soft hair, kissed his mouth, his weak chin. He doesn't know how to love gently, I said, that's all.

And then, I didn't ask: Why don't you leave?

I left the apartment so rarely in those days. I stayed inside, where it was quiet and where all the dangers were known to me the way I knew the contours of my own body, my soft places, my hard ones.

But that day there was a carnival outside and I couldn't help but go out to the balcony to watch. Julian joined me. Below, the city burst with new colour and brass music that lanced the air without mercy. Boys danced in white-and-orange costumes with bells in their hair. There was a man with a bear on a leash and women who swallowed flaming swords.

I considered begging Julian to go down with me to join them, but my breath hitched because I glimpsed the wives in the crowd – there, the woman with a load of stones on her back, the one cradling a rotten bouquet of roses, the one with the ribbon around her bloodied neck. When had they come?

Had they been there all along?

I glance at Eunice. Study the delicate curve of her lips, the tension in the corners of her eyes. I want to ask: Is this okay? To say, I'm so sorry. I wish – I wish.

But there, a nod so slight I almost miss it. I continue:

I glimpsed another figure in the crowd, too. A young man, hardly more than a boy, with a knife in his heart. He looked so much like my man I couldn't help but shudder. The young man kept walking, fading as he went – a few steps more and he'd be gone, swallowed by that sea of faces.

I'd never spoken the name Tristan out loud yet. And still I didn't.

Julian put his hand on the small of my back, as if to reassure me. He'd noticed nothing. Together, we watched the carnival pass. The smell of sulphur hung in the air long after it was gone.

With Julian to keep me company, I gave Cook the day off more and more often, gave her all the days off, weeks off, months, sent her out into the city and kept the apartment and its demands to myself. I cooked our man's dinner, stirred concoctions of broth made from bird bones and blood-red beets into large pots, served him using the fine china I found in the cabinets. I brought him drink in his crystal goblet fit for a king. I dipped my knuckles into his wine before serving him, put eyelashes in his food.

He never knew, but Julian noticed.

Why do you do that? he asked.

A rehearsal, I said.

*   *   *

The next time our man went on a long business trip, Julian and I were tasked with caring for his latest treasure: an egg carved from mother-of-pearl. So we stayed in the apartment together; we played cards and cleaned the egg; we ate food and sat by the window watching people pass by, my bare feet on Julian's lap.

It was a pleasant morning, only slightly cloudy, and with a breeze that had cleared some of the city's viscous air – so why did I suffocate? My lungs couldn't fill with air, no matter how hard I tried. And I was tired. I was so tired.

I can't breathe, Julian, I told him. It's so hard to breathe.

He looked at me, his brows knitted together with worry. He opened the window wider to let in fresh air, and then he sat back down and massaged my feet.

Let's go to the shore, I told him. I need an ocean.

We went. He hailed a carriage that took us to the edge of the city, past the seaport and the docks, all the way out where paved streets faded into fisheries and marsh. We stood on a narrow, sandy beach, watching the waves come and go, the water churning and frothy, grey with the mist coming in. I breathed in the briny air and closed my eyes against the all-encompassing sound of the waves. I pictured a land beyond the water. Somewhere I could have come from, in another life, a place where different tales were being told. Julian was sitting next to me, but we didn't touch, so I could imagine I was alone, a stone of a woman, my grooves and dents caused by nothing but water and salt and air. I told myself tales from that other land, remembered or imagined: children turned to stars, babies boiled and eaten, a mother's heart that cries out and speaks to her murderous son. In the end, they all spoke of the same thing: the world is a cruel place, and no one survives life for very long.

Back home, we lay together in bed, me on my side and Julian on his back, his hands behind his head.

Why does he like me? he asked me. Julian's tone was thoughtful, not anxious. He never doubted himself the way the wives did.

You remind him of someone he used to know, I said.

Who?

A Shopkeeper. I ran a finger down the soft skin on his chest. A young man.

And you don't mind?

I laughed. Why would I? I like you, too.

Other wives would, he said.

I'm not his wife, though, I said. Am I? Besides, the more love the better. Isn't that so? The more love and pleasure the better, in this grey, wretched world?

He looked at me curiously. He said: I know you're not happy here. You wish to leave.

Was that what I wanted? I thought of wives in wells, of wives with birds nesting in their hair, their stomachs embroidered, their chests filled with cold marble hearts. The only way to leave, and no way at all.

If you knew him like I do, I said, you'd want us to leave, too.

He pushed himself up on his elbows and turned to me. What do you mean? he asked.

I told him then. First I told Julian that Lord Cee only wanted him for fun, that he was neither the first nor the last, that he meant less to him than an egg made of seashell. He didn't believe me, and so I told him he'd killed his previous— wife, I said, not wives, because one can be an accident, but many, that many? And what would that say about me?

He still didn't believe me, and so I gave him the keys to the chest, told him, Go look if you want.

He did.

He came back, face paler than a sheet.

(ALMOST DONE.)

A knock on the door makes us both flinch. It's getting late, and you're tired, but the sudden intrusion jolts you into alertness. You worry, perhaps, that he has come back.

Another knock, and then Nadya's voice calling my name.

You stand up, relieved. You know your godmother's voice. You want to open the door but turn to me for guidance.

'Is someone here?' you ask.

Look at you, so young and already versed in the arts of indirectness, of asking the slanted questions, saying a true thing by a false name.

Why don't you leave?

Julian didn't leave immediately – I think because he didn't want to leave me there alone. That evening, we sat by the window together and ate grapes from the same bowl. We braided each other's hair – his had grown so long in the time he'd been with us. Our man liked it that way. We cooked food we didn't eat, poured wine we drank until our cheeks glowed in the dark. We put the egg on a pillow and looked at it, fantasised about dropping it, letting it shatter into a million pieces on the floor. We longed for something unmendable.

The next morning, Julian had gathered his belongings – his clothes and jewels and shoes, but not the curious gifts; they were all still in the cabinet, undusted and undisturbed – in a leather suitcase I didn't know he had. He had come here with nothing but the clothes on his back – but then, so had we.

Why did you tell me? he asked.

I didn't want you to suffer the same fate, I said. My hands suddenly felt too small for the rest of me. The hands of a doll.

This is not why, Julian said sadly.

No, I replied.

He looked at his own hands, then, and, avoiding my eyes, asked: Why don't you leave?

I said nothing, so he continued: Come with me. We'll go

somewhere far away. Another country, where he'll never find us.

He didn't understand. And why would he? I hadn't told him the whole story. Hadn't even told it to myself yet, as I do now. Of course, I could have said what I already knew, for all my lack of ghosts: If you leave, you die. If you die, you stay. He still wouldn't understand.

I shook my head. I asked: Will you tell everyone?

Yes, he said, I have to. I told you I love sincerity more than anything. Justice must be done.

(JUST BEFORE WE COME TO LIGHT.)

I wonder if Julian, our real-life Julian, has talked to the police by now and they're already out there looking for your father. Maybe he didn't say anything and never will. Perhaps he, too, thought: who would believe me? And then: what if they blame me?

How long ago was this? A day, maybe two, yet it feels so much longer – a decade ago, a century. Of course I lose faith in my own narrative – and yet here I am, telling you. Hoping you'll do better than any of us.

Do you understand?

Nadya is still here, pounding on the door, worry in her voice, because the failsafe was her idea, and she was right.

You're alarmed by the urgency, but you put on a brave face and pretend nothing's wrong.

The pounding numbs my mind. A little more time, I plead with no one in particular, a little more. The ghosts are fully in character now, so good at this you might believe there's never been a real story, only this fairy tale, this other world. They try to help with their metaphors, with their horrors, their gothic compulsions and repetitions:

One says she was born with a monster in her mouth – because, really, aren't we all? The other wives, they feed it milk and honey. *Close your mouth*, they say. *You'll get used to it.*

Another says she tried to leave, but every time she touched the door, it fell off its hinges. One found a dress in the back room. It was old but she could see its splendour: the long satin sleeves dripping with beads, the tiny sequins like the glinting eyes of insects. She knew it would fit her as if it had been made for her. Is it any wonder she put it on?

An ending

Julian was gone, and, when my man came back, he wanted to know why his lover had left us.

I told him everything, this truth that would surely be my end. There's still time, I said. We can still go freely if we hurry, if we don't take much. We'll go to a new place, find a home near a forest, near a river, near a sky, where few people live.

He came at me faster than a human could, and the back of my head struck the wall so hard I smelled blood and the world faded for a while. He clamped one hand over my mouth and nose, the other on my throat, squeezing. I thought, that's it, I've gone, finally a ghost wife like the rest – or not a wife, remember? Just a ghost.

I stop talking to you now, briefly. I remember his fingers on my neck, a pain in my throat, blood in my hair.

I no longer wonder if you can see the ghosts. You can see me, after all. You can hear me.

The crystal rabbit is still in my hand. I never put it back in the cabinet, did I? I open my fingers and drop it now, let it wedge between cushion and armrest. Will someone find it, when the people come? Will they wonder how it got there? Will they hold it up to the light, bag it, tag it, search for the ghost of fingertips?

Outside, darkness has fallen. Nadya is still at the door, calling for help. You pretend not to hear her. You've had so much practice, pretending not to hear, not to see, haven't you? And isn't that, too, my own fault?

I can see you're sleepy. Your eyes are red. It's almost over; people will be here soon. They'll throw open our doors, walk in on our world with their light and their badges and their tools, and there will be no more stories left to tell.

But there's still a moment to do this, to lay you down one last time, touch your hair. Watch you drift into a dream.

It's late, I tell you. It's better to sleep now, my love. Don't you think? Go to your room. Close your eyes. Sleep.

'But you didn't finish,' you protest.

I try to speak, but breathing doesn't come easy any more.

You think I'm angry, so you try to bargain like you did when you were small, just five more minutes, Mum, just five more, and five more. You dash to your room and bring back your duvet, pull a pillow from the sofa and nestle on the floor next to my feet, your eyes on me, expectant.

So I try again, I do.

Julian left and the man came back, and then the room filled with the smell of rain, I say, of wet earth and rotting leaves.

'But what happened to the woman in the story?'

I hesitate. Have I told you all I needed to?

I pull the cover over your chin, run my imperceptible fingers through your hair.

'You have to finish the story,' you say.

Tomorrow, I whisper. I'll tell you the rest tomorrow, when you wake up.

Finally, you relent. You close your eyes, and I wait until

your breath grows steady and calm with sleep, superhero duvet pulled over your ears.

In the apartment next door a TV comes on, and my mind slips again. I long for my tape recording of that first show of ours, mine and Nadya's, the leaf-strewn floor, the white dresses, the women laughing and crawling on the walls. *Bluebeard, Blaubart, Barbe Bleue.* Where is that tape? Left in another house, another country, years back, and who even owns a VCR any more? This story in its many iterations is spoken there, in that other place, too. Is spoken everywhere. A critic said, 'Gothic tales rely on distant pasts and faraway lands full of people unlike us,' except he was wrong, because the land of this story is everywhere. The people are us, the time is always.

It's full of lies, of course, this story like all stories, riddled with shifted timelines, details that don't add up: Julian never lived in this apartment, though the one your father rented for him isn't far from here. The woman who raised your father left our lives a long time ago. And then there's you. You, the egg, the seed, that child-shaped gap, all as close as I could get. The closest I dared come.

I think of roots again. I've been telling this story for so long, and in all this time what have I been telling you? Your father's wealth, don't inherit it. These roots, shed them. Your father's houses, tear them down.

A wailing starts, far away, the distant sound of sirens. The police, maybe an ambulance. It won't be long now.

'Mum?' you call for me in the dark.

Never any children and yet here you are.

Shhh, I tell you. Go back to sleep.

I wait until you do, because this part of the story is not for you.

I stand, reach for the bedroom door. I've been reaching for this door for so long, and now, finally, here I am. I need no keyhole, no doorknob, no key. The ghosts look on. They don't stop me. All I need to do is push through, walk in. And so finally, finally, I do.

Only street light falls yellow into the room.

My body is on the bed where he left it. Face up, neck blue. My eyes, open and staring. On the pillow, a little red.

The ghosts crowd around me, their hair in my face, their hands reaching as weightlessly as my own.

Will someone take care of my child? I ask them.

Empty eyes. Open mouths.

They don't know, and they don't try to lie. Our talents lay always in divining that which had already come to pass, after all.

They put their arms around my shoulders, lean their heads against mine.

Now what? I ask them. We died, we stay?

I pause.

I don't want it to end like this.

You can tell a different story, if you want, the ghosts whisper. *You could even leave.* A dozen smiles, a dozen broken lips. There's only so much a story can do. But perhaps the ghosts are right. Maybe I can give us all a different ending.

Will you leave? the ghost women ask, pleading, like they've asked before. *Will you leave us? Will you leave us now you will leave?*

The summer is ended, and we are not saved

I find myself back in the story, pushed against the wall, his hands on my neck and everywhere the smell of mouldering leaves. I cannot breathe. He says something that's drowned by the ocean thrashing in my ears. My vision blurs and all I can do is check: do I still remember my name? Is it done yet?

But then, the pressure leaves my throat and air rushes back into my lungs. I crumple to the floor, gasping, a great weight in my head.

For the second time in this story, I don't expect to live, and yet I do.

My man picks me up gently, dries my cheeks. He kisses my hands, wide-eyed, as surprised as I am. His hand bleeds. He says, Look what you made me do.

The new house has so many rooms, even without the attics, the basements, the cellars. Upstairs, there's a room full of paintings; people I've never seen before, their faces wan and severe. There is a room filled with toys and one where the walls are mirrors – once I'm inside, it takes me a whole afternoon to find my way out. There is a small room off the kitchen, too, which he never shows me, which I never see him enter, and which we pretend does not exist.

In that house, the ghost women return. For days, they walk quietly in and out of rooms, as if looking for something, their hair longer than ever, trailing behind them like bridal veils. When I sit still, they crowd around me and stare at the bruises on my neck.

For a while, they don't speak. Still, they sharpen what they can, blunt what they can.

A week in, I sit in the garden and watch the soft-eyed cows graze. I wonder at how alive they look, at the fact that they aren't yet dead in the fields, their carcasses burst open like mouths hungry for the sky.

He joins me there, his rage gone, though I have the bitter aftertaste of it in the back of my throat, as if I've bitten into raw, unpeeled bergamot.

He doesn't look at me.

Why did you betray me? he asks. Why would you force us to leave?

There's pain in his voice as he asks this. It pleases me.

I was drowning, I say; the truth, and not. The city was stifling me.

But I was happy there, he says.

He was, wasn't he? I could have gnawed at the furniture, unpicked the lace from the curtains, peeled the wallpaper. Instead, I did this.

Yes, I say of my little damage, a ghost wife in all but death and matrimony. Yes.

I convince him to buy a new horse. We have so little left of our old lives; only the cabinet survives, and the chest with its dead treasures. I think, perhaps, a horse might make him happy. Perhaps, if he's happy, this time, we will be saved.

I help Cook in the unending chores the house creates for us with its crumbling walls, its cracking windows, the plaster snowing from its ceilings. I want to tell her – we tried, didn't we? We tried so hard, as hard as we could.

When he notices the house falling apart around us, he blames me for the ruins.

You punish me, he says.

Do I? I ask.

I never killed anybody, he says, and I think he believes he's being truthful.

And the wives? I ask. I could motion towards the ghosts that stand witness to our scene, but I don't. I may carry some of the blame, but I'm not cruel.

He shrugs. Sickliness or nostalgia for their childhood homes, he says.

And those bodies you showed me, in the well and in the woods and in the little back rooms?

Natural causes. Or foolishness.

And your son?

He gets broody when I say that, then mad. The scent of earth fills the house. And I think, I know this story already. I've lived through it, I and so many others before and after me. I have always known how it ends, even though my man's beard is not blue at all.

I tell myself: I won't let it end.

And so the winter is here, and then the winter is gone and spring comes and then summer, and sometimes I look at him, his forest eyes, his foul moods, and I think that my turn is finally coming, maybe not this year and maybe not the next, and maybe not this house and maybe not the next, but one house with another little back room, one day. Maybe, just a little further. Maybe, just a little longer. I catch myself telling ghost stories again: the fourth, the fifth, the suspended one, the buried one. All the ones that left, and died, and stayed. For whose sake, any more?

I still don't know why you're here, I tell the ghosts. There was a time when I thought they meant to scare me. Why did you come? I ask. Why do you stay?

So that not one of us ever thinks she's alone.

I tell them my name then. I speak to them, for the first time, of the country I came from, in my strange accent, and ask them to imagine it all: the golden sunsets, the wine-dark sea, the wild mountains haunted by fauns.

And then my man grows tender once more, like a season. He takes me walking through the woods, gifts Cook with a cartful of expensive cheese and cured meats, and this valley, this new valley stays green and fruitful for another year. My stomach flutters with expectation, like a reflex – what if we get to stay here, what if he's changed? What if this house is the one I can finally call mine?

I think of Julian, too, wonder if his body will wash up on the riverbank one day, beautifully bruised, a cherry tree growing in his belly.

I wait, I dread, but Julian never joins our chorus.

At night, I dream of cycles, borrowed from elsewhere: a bound god having his liver eaten daily. A dead king pushing his boulder up a hill. The boulder rolls down the hill and the king pushes it up again. I'm there for both, to witness. I can smell the god's blood, see the dust kicked up by the king's heels. I don't help, just watch. Can I imagine them happy? I can't stop watching, not because I want to find out what will happen next, but because I know what will. In some dreams, my man is a white bird again, with a black, hungry eye. I am a table laid out, my bounty renewed daily: a dead rabbit, a loaf of bread, a basket of sour cherries. Daily, he feasts on me.

When I wake, he kneels before me and hugs my legs. I think maybe we'll live like this for ever, he says. House to house, town to town, we'll keep going. We'll never stop. We'll watch the world change around us. Miracles out of men's dreams will haunt the skies in place of birds. People will be born and die and be forgotten, but we will remain.

He stands, places a kiss on each of my cheeks. I knew you were the one for me as soon as I saw you, he says. The only one to ever match me.

In spring, he invites young village girls to the house, and they come willingly, faithfully, dazzled by the gold-plating that conceals the decaying wood of the mirror frames, the fine lace that veils the crumbling furniture. They babble about wanting to see the entire place, every room, every nook, every secret garden, their cheeks rouged and excited.

I release Cook to the village whenever they come. She's grown quiet, lately. She's always been distant, but now she's become almost illegible to me, eager to turn her back, look away. And so she goes, thankful for the chance to see people who are not us, or glad to be apart from the little back room we pretend does not exist. She affords the village girls only a single glance of pity before she walks out the door.

I do my best to make them comfortable, seat them in the drawing room, give them sweets, have them talk about the games they like to play when they're done with their chores, and then they leave, slightly sadder and having lost something they can never get back. None of them ask to see the rest of the house after all.

I remember when I was one of these village girls myself, many summers ago. The last wife gave me sour cherries that stained my lips for days. When she went away, months later, I didn't question her disappearance, and I didn't question his showing up at my father's door with an offering of sweet bread and good wine, either.

Cherry Girl, he said, my name already gone. Come.

I went.

I say my name aloud often. I still remember it, for all it's worth.

I pass the winter stringing beads by the window, my treasures stored neatly in trays and boxes arranged on the table in front of me.

The day his horse dies, he comes home storming, and I let my beadwork fall to the floor to catch him, contain him before it's too late. He allows himself to be held for a moment, but then he's too much for my embrace, my words too small and his wrath too large. He pushes me away, the room filling with the smell of wet soil, and I think that's it, this time I'm gone, this house is gone, this village is gone – but all he does is upend the table with my beads on it. They rain down and scatter on the floor, fill the cracks between the wooden boards.

He pauses for a few breaths, stares at the beads sadly, tries to say something, says nothing. He flees.

He seems so much smaller to me these days. Even his nails have stopped growing at their old rate, and I wonder, is this middle age, or has he truly changed?

I start doubting my memory. Was the growth of his nails ever unnatural at all? And, if it wasn't, did he tell that story first, or did I?

Cook shakes her head, but she still bends down to help me collect and sort the beads. We retrieve what we can from between the floorboards, abandon what cannot be salvaged, our knees bruised from pressing against the beads, our eyes stinging. The forest smell lingers.

He comes back hours later, tells us to get off our knees and stand in the corner by the curio cabinet. We obey. He takes the boxes and trays we spent all day refilling and empties them on the floor again, one by one, all our work squandered. Then, he kneels and starts collecting the beads in his giant palms, sorting them by colour with his thick fingers, carefully, holding his breath, as if handling tiny living things.

What is he doing? Cook whispers.

Saying he's sorry, I reply.

Then the crops fail, the corn growing maggot-ridden at first, then not growing at all. The horses tremble and run as if stung by some passing terror, then fall and never get up again. The girls no longer die, but only waste into a sadness, seeking each other's lips for comfort, openly now, their mourning as baffling to them as to everyone; a mysterious disease, the villagers say, passed mouth to mouth. They point at the house and cross themselves, speak hushed curses when they walk by our front gate, wishing to punish my man for everything except his crimes. Of those, they still say: These things happen, you see? This is the way of the world.

Cook is gone the day I walk into our bedroom and find it strewn with leaves, brown and crumbling to nothing. I don't look for her to ask why she left – or why now – just as I didn't ask the one who raised him, who knew everything, who saw it all. Perhaps she thought she was no longer needed, and never had been. Stopped asking herself if she loved him enough. Or maybe she finally understood that none of this was ever about love at all. There's only so much fairy tales can do – but I chose, given the chance, to be as kind in her telling as I could.

That leaves only me and the stories and the ghosts, and I know we'll soon uproot ourselves once more, find some other place where no one knows us and rumours have not yet spread.

My chorus gathers around me. I touch ghostly faces, put my fingers in ghostly mouths, pull, reach again, for more. Are we saved? I ask, and they ask their question in turn: *Will you leave us, will you leave us now, will you leave?*

Sometimes our man walks in on us telling each other stories. Survival stories and horror stories and ghost stories, and ghost stories that aren't horror stories. He pauses at the door, looks from one wife to the other. He doesn't understand.

I want to tell him, we're crowding you out. This is no longer about you, don't you see? Now we have each other.

We clutch our cherry stones and brace, expect him to rage, to barge in and push us against the wall, put his hands on our throats. But he doesn't. He simply lowers his head and leaves, as if he'd always known, one way or another, that it would come to this. And, this time, no one else will join us.

In the distance, bright lights, piercing. The safe darkness of the bedroom gone, the apartment flooded in halogen white and aseptic fluorescence, invaded by forensic scientists and crime-scene photographers.

The people came, they opened, they found.

And my son? I ask, but my audience is gone.

My eyes are still open, the white sheet not yet over my face, so I see: a uniformed woman wraps you in a shiny blanket. She speaks soft words I can't hear, her voice drowned out by the sudden scream of a siren. But something glimmers on your palm, what is it?

The crystal rabbit, retrieved from the armchair. You close your fist around it, hide your hand inside the blanket, close to the skin.

Somewhere beyond, Nadya's voice. She calls your name. The police officer guides you gently, taking you away. I can't tell whether you're crying – the woman's arm shields your face. She doesn't let you peek.

Yes, I whisper, like a breeze. Yes, good.

It all fades slowly, while I yearn for a last glimpse.

Come back, the ghosts call from the haunted houses, the gothic gardens, the peeling walls. *Come. Stay.*

The people come for us when the next summer is ended, the harvest done and the storerooms empty of grain, the sheep dead in the fields, bloated, feet stuck in the air. But we're already in the wind, moving on, moving away, our boxes stacked again, our cherry pits lodged in our throats. Someone else will take care of all we've left behind.

I beckon to the ghost women to follow me. One day, in some other place, we'll build ourselves a cherry orchard, one in which he'll never be allowed. We'll prune our trees and watch them grow and sit on the ground together and gorge ourselves on cherries. They'll be a ripe, shocking red. Eventually, people will chase us away again, and we'll leave our trees behind. But our mouths will be full of things that take root and grow afresh. In a new place, we'll rip up the floors, we'll peel the wallpaper, we'll pluck our eyelashes, plant our trees. Outside, the world will rot, like it does. Still, together, we'll go on.

But, for now, we're here, leaving.

I ride with him on his young horse, through a forest, towards a land that is like all the others, because some stories, I know, are countries one can never flee.

The ghosts trail thick behind us. I glance at them and their open mouths, then hide my face in his hair, breathe in his earthy scent, reach around his chest to touch his beard. His heart beats fast.

Cherry Girl, he says, like a question.

Never, I reply. To them. This time, only to them. Never ever.

ACKNOWLEDGMENTS

Writing this book was a process of accumulating the most heartful of debts, the kind that cannot really be repaid, only acknowledged. These are some of the debts I am grateful to owe:

To my entire Clarion West pride, for your brilliance and camaraderie, as well as your help with the story that eventually became this novel.

To Andy Cox and Sean Wallace, for being the first to open the door to that short story.

To Eugenia Triantafyllou, K Tidbeck, E.C. Barrett, Ewen Ma, Isabel Cañas, Syr Beker, Natasha Calder, Ben Pladek, and Lucy Carson, for your insight and gentleness while I worked on the various iterations of this book. Drafting writers and half-formed novels are fragile creatures, and you handled both of us with tenderness and care.

To Karen Joy Fowler, for asking about Cook. Your encouragement meant the world.

To Courttia Newland, Cathy Galvin, and everyone at the Word Factory; to Cynan Jones, Gillian Slovo, Romesh Gunesekera, and all of Moniack Mhor and The Bridge Awards; to Matt Freidson and Creative Future; to the Caledonia Novel Award; to Temim Fruchter: your mentorship and support graced and enriched my creative life.

To my incredible editors, Areen Ali and Masie Cochran, for believing in this book. For your investment, your talent, and your clarity of vision. Thank you for this adventure.

To Jill Cole, Tara O'Sullivan, Jack Butler, Vicky Lord, Alara Delfosse, Ana Carter, Ian Binnie, George Baxter, Amy Cox, and everyone at Wildfire, for your attention to detail, and for welcoming this novel to its first home.

To Susan Armstrong, my magical UK agent, and her assistant Catriona Paget, for taking such good care of me and my book.

To the entire Tin House team — Win McCormack, Becky Kraemer, Beth Steidle, Nanci McCloskey, Allison Dubinsky, Anne Horowitz, Alyssa Ogi, Elizabeth DeMeo, and Isabel Lemus Kristensen — for your dedication, creativity, and hard work.

To Danya Kukafka, my champion and miracle-working agent. I've always maintained that thinking is dialogic, and I couldn't have asked for a better interlocutor. *Sour Cherry* wouldn't exist without you. I am forever grateful.

To everyone at Trellis Literary Management, for steering the ship with passion and integrity. Special thanks to Stephanie Delman for taking a chance on me, and to Allison Malecha for all foreign orchestrations.

To Danny Hertz, for your enthusiasm and tireless dreaming.

To Morgan Talty, for your generosity and belief. You handed me the most unexpected, selfless gift, and I will never forget it.

To Sam Hirst for Romancing the Gothic.

To Eleanna, Stam, Ioanna, Tess, and Anna. Your friendship humbles and uplifts me.

To Ben, Jonathan, Natasha, Eamonn, for saving me so often

and in so many ways. To Lu, who did me the honor of sitting on me when I was down.

To Phil, Helen, and Rich, for being there.

To Eugenia, for the knives and the roses.

To Vajra Chandrasekera, who is one of the brightest minds I've ever encountered. Talking to you has made me a better thinker.

To my amigo, Constantinos. For all the pandas.

To my parents. There's so much to say, and so little that can be said.

And to Konstantinos, my reason and recipient. Γιατί κάποια θηρία δεν κοιμούνται ποτέ.

Natalia Theodoridou is a queer and transmasculine writer whose stories have appeared in publications such as *Kenyon Review, The Cincinnati Review, Ninth Letter* and *Strange Horizons*, and have been translated into Italian, French, Greek, Estonian, Spanish, Chinese and Arabic. He won the 2018 World Fantasy Award for Short Fiction and the 2022 Emerging Writer Award by Moniack Mhor and The Bridge Awards, and has been a finalist for the Nebula Award multiple times. He holds a PhD in Media and Cultural Studies from SOAS, University of London. Born in Greece, with roots in Georgia, Russia and Turkey, he currently lives in the UK.